ALL
THE
LOVELY
PIECES

ALL THE LOVELY PIECES

J.M. WINCHESTER

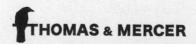 THOMAS & MERCER

Published by Thomas & Mercer, Seattle

www.apub.com

Amazon, the Amazon logo, and Thomas & Mercer are trademarks of Amazon.com, Inc., or its affiliates.

ISBN-13: 9781542041591
ISBN-10: 1542041597

Cover design by Shasti O'Leary Soudant

Printed in the United States of America

*To Marion at Audreys Books—thank you for believing
in this book before I even knew what I was writing.*

AUGUST

Drew

This doesn't feel right. But I can't remember the last time something has.

"Drew and Michael?"

"Yes," I say, forcing a smile as the principal of Northcrest Elementary appears in her office doorway, gesturing us inside.

Michael hides behind me as we enter the office, and, turning to him, I give him my best reassuring look. "It's okay."

I hand the principal the school-enrollment forms I've filled out and hold Michael's hand as I sit. He refuses the other chair, standing next to me. His dark-brown hair covers his dark-brown eyes, and I wish I'd cut his hair the day before. His slightly too-short jeans and faded T-shirt tug at my chest. We need to go shopping for new clothes.

"It's completely normal to be nervous, but there's nothing to be worried about. Mrs. Harper is so excited that you'll be joining her class this year," Principal Bradley says, taking a seat behind her desk. As she reads the forms I've filled out, I study her. She's exactly what I'd pictured. Her appearance matches her voice. Thin, well dressed, polished. She nods as she reads each and every word on the form, as if wanting to prove that she's actually reading.

The air-conditioning inside her office is doing nothing to prevent sweat from forming on my lower back beneath my sweater, and my mouth feels like I've eaten a piece of blackboard chalk.

This is a mistake.

Her gaze lifts slowly, and I know what she's going to ask.

She glances at Michael, then slides the papers toward me. "I see you've left this section incomplete."

She's pointing to the information regarding Michael's other parent.

My gaze doesn't falter. My voice wouldn't dare crack. "He passed away."

A look of sympathy flashes in her eyes. "I'm sorry to hear that." She glances at Michael, but my little boy has never known a father. He has nothing to miss.

"It was a long time ago," I say.

She nods and pushes her red-rimmed glasses higher on the bridge of her nose. "Okay. Well, we do ask to have something on record . . ."

"I understand. I'll try to find the documents once we finish unpacking." We just moved here last week. Liberty, Missouri. Kind of ironic. But at least the car didn't break down and strand us in Avila. I shiver remembering the old ghost town, famed for its sordid history and myths of shadow walkers seen roaming the deserted streets at night. Small towns are a sanctuary, but a hundred people was too small. I'm trying to slay my demons, not acquire new ones.

"No rush. Moving is a nightmare. Whenever you find it is fine. Is there anyone else authorized to pick Michael up from school—a grandparent? Aunt or uncle?" The emergency-contact section has been left blank as well.

"No."

"I don't have grandparents or any aunts or uncles." Michael speaks for the first time. "It's just me and her."

Her. Jesus. I'm his mother. I'm the only person he's ever really talked to, interacted with, had a relationship with.

I'm fine with that.

Principal Bradley smiles. "Liberty is a very welcoming place. You'll make a lot of new friends quickly."

I'm grateful for the effort to put Michael at ease, so I can't explain the twisting in my stomach and the urge to walk out of the office.

Michael will still need me, even if there are other people in his life.

"Have you purchased the required school supplies for the year?"

I nod. The one and only silver lining in my shitty-ass life is that I never have to worry about money.

"I think everything he needs is in his backpack, but if I'm missing anything, please let me know." We'd made the trip to Walmart the day before, and he'd been excited about starting school.

Six and a half hours a day away from me doesn't excite me at all. We've spent every moment together since leaving Seattle, and the fear and uncertainty I'm struggling with from leaving him in the care of strangers five days a week have me reconsidering this.

The principal studies us. She's wondering how this tiny, skinny kid is ready for fourth grade.

"Ow . . . Mom," he says, yanking his hand out of mine.

I see the shape of my nails in the palm of his hand. "Sorry, sweetheart." I clench my hands tightly on my lap. Everything will be fine. He is safe at school.

I try to focus my blurring vision on Principal Bradley. I can't afford a blackout right now. I stare at the cross-shaped pendant hanging around her neck. Gold, tarnished, most likely a cherished family heirloom. I finger the fabric of my pants—soft, silky, worn—and I breathe in the scent of the lilacs in the vase on her desk.

"Here is just an additional media-release form that we need signed," Principal Bradley is saying. "Permission to take photos, video—"

I shake my head. "No, I'm sorry . . ."

She frowns. "Okay. It's not required. But they are only used in the yearbook and some online for the school website."

Michael looks too much like his father . . .

So much so that looking at him sometimes hurts. Why couldn't he have my hair color, eye color, skin tone?

"I understand, but I'd rather not."

She takes the form back and checks the "no" box. "No problem. Unfortunately, it means Michael may not be able to participate in certain school activities, as there is usually photography of some sort, and we can't guarantee he won't be in the shot."

I swallow the guilt. No birthday parties. No playdates. No friends. Now, no school concerts or field trips. The list of things Michael has never experienced or may ever experience keeps growing.

Michael is staring at the floor, and my heart shatters. I want him to have a normal childhood. I'm doing my best, but it's not nearly enough.

Principal Bradley stands, and so do we. "Why don't I show you to your class?" she asks Michael.

His eyes are wide and tear filled as he looks at me. "Mom, can you stay?"

There's my baby . . .

"Of course she can," Principal Bradley says quickly.

This time my smile is genuine and grateful. I can stay in the classroom—be there to watch . . . keep him safe. He needs me.

I take his hand, and we follow her down the empty, echoing halls. The building smells old and musty, the new coat of paint on the walls trying and failing to hide its many years. It's only been a week since school started, and already the place feels in full swing. A trophy case boasts the school's accomplishments, and, next to it, a row of staff photos lines the gray concrete walls. I scan the faces of the people whom I am now entrusting with my son's well-being.

Tightness in my chest as Principal Bradley stops outside Mrs. Harper's classroom.

"Here we are. Ready, Michael?"

He nods, peeking around the classroom door.

Several smiling kids wave at him, and the teacher stops instructing to turn to us. "Wonderful—our new student has arrived." Mrs. Harper is shorter than I am, thin, plain looking, with kind eyes. Not exactly a worthy rival for a crazy gun-wielding madman should one enter the classroom, but then neither am I.

My grip tightens on Michael's hand once again, and he releases his hold on mine as he glances up at me.

"You know, Mom, I think I'll be okay by myself."

A look flashes in his eyes that confuses me, but, aware of Principal Bradley's intense stare, I accept his bravery for the good thing it is. "Okay. Great. You got this," I say, bending to hug him tight.

It's just six and a half hours. He's safe here.

"Let go, Mom." His voice makes the hair on my arms stand up, and I release him quickly.

"Have a good day, sweetheart."

He waves as he enters the classroom, and the teacher shows him his backpack hook on the wall.

I stand there, staring into the room. Sandpaper in my mouth, desperation strangling my breath.

Come on, Michael. Say you want to leave.

I'll gladly take him home. But he takes his seat and doesn't even glance my way.

Principal Bradley closes the classroom door and turns to me with a knowing smile. "It's always harder on the parents."

She has no idea.

I lie awake at night. Every creak of this old house threatens my peace of mind. The dampness in the muggy non-air-conditioned room is not solely responsible for the beads of sweat forming on my skin. I know he's looking for me. To make me pay for what I've done. And I know someday he'll find me. It's impossible to run forever.

Seven states in nine years. The smallest, middle-of-nowhere towns that all share one thing in common—tiny corners of the earth that aren't worth searching. Nonexciting, no claims to fame, just small dots on a map that I find by instinct, by feel.

I allow my eyes to close for a moment, knowing exhaustion will eventually win and that I'll be helpless until morning. I feel for the blade under my pillow, hoping it someday won't be used as a weapon against me. Having it there terrifies me. Being without it isn't an option.

I feel my past drawing closer. I sense our peace is short lived. I never make the mistake of letting my guard down or forgetting my sins.

I'm only desperate to remember the extent of them.

The house is quiet for an instant, and the absence of the usual creaking, the dripping faucet in the bathroom, the tree branches brushing against the bedroom window, only makes me strain to hear even more.

I hate nighttime.

The drip, drip, drip of the bathroom faucet resumes, keeping time with the old grandfather clock in the hallway, and I open my eyes. The yellowing ceiling tiles above my head suggest water damage at one point. Our new balding, pear-shaped landlord promised the ceiling won't collapse and crush me in my sleep.

Death would almost be a welcome pleasure. I long for an escape from my own mind, but there isn't one.

Drip, drip, drip. Tick, tick, tick.

I wish the nights passed more quickly.

I often try to figure out exactly when my life became a nightmare. A warped, twisted pastime. From the beginning, Adam had been a drug, one I couldn't get enough of, who became unavailable, unattainable, when I needed it most. I suspect the lies started the first time his gaze swept over me with a promise of a more exciting existence.

My life certainly hadn't been boring.

And from beyond the iron gates leading to the multimillion-dollar home, I'd once had it all. Everything money could buy.

Everything except peace.

I don't think I'll ever have it. Images of the perfect porcelain skin, silky dark hair, and dead, unseeing eyes lying on the floor of my son's nursery haunt me relentlessly. But they exist in a vacuum, with no context for closure. For certainty.

The deep-blue walls of the nursery close in around me . . . or is it the glass windows of an office?

There's blood. Lots of blood. Vibrant red and seeping into the carpet under the lifeless body.

Not mine. Whose?

I shut my eyes tight, trying to untangle the images that have haunted me for so long. It doesn't make sense. In my memory I'm not holding a weapon that night.

Night? No, it had to have been daytime. I remember sunlight streaming through the windows.

I need to get these details right.

Behind my closed lids, I envision my body moving closer to the victim . . . images of a woman change into a man. I'm desperate to see the face, to see if this person is still breathing. Michael's nanny was a woman, yet the blood oozes from a bullet hole in a man I don't know.

Two dead bodies tangle in the fractured images.

The sound of a gunshot ringing in my ears and the slash of a knife across a throat are the only clear impressions in my memory.

Somewhere, two people are dead, and I know I killed one of them.

I sit up and swing my legs over the side of the antique wooden bed. The furniture came with the house—I don't care about mismatched tables and chairs or ugly, dated curtains. My surroundings hardly matter. We don't stay in a place long enough to entertain the thought of making the walls around us a home.

I'm a shitty mother for not wanting better for my son.

I slide the knife from beneath the pillow. The shiny, sharp blade reflects the contours of my face, distorting the appearance, so only the darkness shows against the dim lighting of the room. Light from a lamp that never gets turned off.

I touch the point of the knife and clench my jaw. It could all be over so quickly . . .

Knife in hand, I go downstairs, skipping the second-to-last step at the bottom. Its particular creak is louder than the others. Several boxes of our personal items—the few that made the trip with us—sit unpacked on the kitchen floor. Even the new cheap set of dishes I bought at the Walmart outside town haven't been put away.

I haven't had a home in nine years; why should the dishes feel settled?

I open the kitchen door and scan the backyard, eyes straining in the dark, as moths circle my head, buzzing around the flickering back-door light. It's humid as hell, and the deck is slippery with condensation under my bare feet as I climb down the two steps into the yard. The overgrown grass tickles my bare ass as I pull down my underwear and squat low, freeing my bladder, the knife still clenched in one hand.

The toilet has been broken for two days, and I haven't been able to fix it. I'll call the landlord in the morning, but the idea of drawing attention to us isn't appealing. He already looks at us with suspicion, especially since I've asked to prepay three months' rent in cash, offering extra for him to register the utilities in his name.

I pull up my underwear and hurry back inside, relocking the three dead bolts on the kitchen door. I turn off the lights in the kitchen and flick on the ones in the living room; I check the three dead bolt locks on the front door and the ones I've attached to the windows.

A false sense of security. For all I know, the danger is inside this house.

I climb the staircase back to the second floor, and, passing Michael's room, I see the light on. Stopping at the open doorway, I glance inside. He has the sheet pulled high over his head; one pajama leg sticks out from beneath the quilted bedspread. His favorite stuffed animal—a bunny named Mr. Floppy—is next to him for protection. Nightmares and shadows in the dark threaten his safety.

He had a good first day at school, and I wish that made me feel better.

I go back into my room and lie on top of the covers; I slide the knife back in place as I stare at the ceiling.

A loud noise shatters the silence, and my heart races.

But it isn't the sound of footsteps or glass breaking. It's the hum of the old refrigerator kicking in. I haven't learned all the noises in this house yet. I catalog it in my mind as a nonthreatening sound.

I take a deep breath as I lie here, waiting. I know eventually I'll run out of places to hide, lies to tell. My time will be up.

Catherine

I sit and stare into this broken acrylic mirror.

A thick, white, unfading scar across my neck—a constant reminder that the world is not a safe place.

A painful reminder of the child I lost.

I touch my barely noticeable stomach, willing this new baby to move. It hasn't in days. I'm not sure I can handle another miscarriage. I hardly start to show before it's all over.

Adam wants a baby so bad. It's my fault he doesn't have a child already. The son he searches for. I don't know why he still loves me. His face has even learned to hide the disgust he must feel when he looks at me now.

My face can't hide it. Even through the distorted pieces of the broken reflection, my appearance nauseates me.

I lost him. It's my fault he's missing.

I need air, but the windows in this room are boarded up. My pearly-white skin tone has turned almost gray. Years without sunlight have my nerve endings tingling so bad that I scratch my flesh raw, but the light makes my skin burn, so I stay in here, shielded from the outside.

Adam brings me vitamins. Says I need them.

I want to do what's best for the baby, but the capsules are too big. They hurt to swallow.

Everything hurts to swallow. All my food is pureed, mashed into unrecognizable slop on a ten-karat-gold-rimmed plate. I cry trying to eat, the scar tissue on my throat making even the smallest bites torture. I want to go back to a liquid diet, but Adam says it's not healthy.

It takes me so long to eat that the food is cold and crusting on the plate by the time I'm done. Adam stays with me until the last bite.

When he is home.

When he travels, he buys me the loveliest scarves from all over the world. He says they will look beautiful. They will hide the ugly act of hate I wear across my neck.

I touch the scar, and tears burn my eyes.

My baby will never hear my voice. The moment he comes into the world, he won't hear it and know I'm his mother. He will never hear me sing him to sleep.

Never again will I perform on the opera stage.

The place where I met Adam. My first lead performance.

Adam was in the front row that night. Most men like him—rich, powerful, successful—sat in the expensive box seats. Not Adam. He brought me flowers after the performance and then came every night, sitting in the same front-row seat, his eyes never leaving me.

He'd never hear me sing again. No one would.

The bedroom door opens, and Adam enters, carrying a new mirror. "Hi, sweetheart," he says.

The baby moves at the sound of Adam's voice. Three violent kicks. The shape of the tiny foot pressing through my skin and the fabric of the expensive silk nightgown. These soft, delicate fabrics are all I wear. They don't itch my skin like everything else does, and Adam makes sure to buy the softest ones. He's so good to me. He saved me.

Continues to save me.

But he refuses to acknowledge the baby. Too many miscarriages have him doubting me . . . I can tell. He doesn't want to get his hopes up by believing this pregnancy could finally give him back a son.

He's still in his suit. It's after eight, but this is early for him. Some nights he stays at the office long past midnight. His technology company has the best minds working on a way to give me back my voice. Adam is a genius, and I trust in his ability to pull off the miracle, but it's taking so long . . .

I touch his back as he leans around me to replace the broken mirror with the new one. Scratchy wool prickles the pads of my fingertips. He smells like rain today. I can always tell the weather by the way the scent of the outside world lingers on his clothes, his hair, his skin.

"Try not to break this one so fast, okay?" he says.

The acrylic claims to be shatterproof. I'm determined to prove it wrong, but I nod.

Behind me, Adam brushes my hair away from my neck and places a gentle kiss along my collarbone.

He turns my chair to face him and takes my hands. He kisses both palms. His lips soft.

I stare at the top of his head, his dark, gelled hair showing no sign of aging. He's gorgeous. He can have any woman he wants. He wants me.

I don't understand.

Standing, he draws me to my feet and leads the way to the four-poster bed.

I'm so lucky to have this life—the beautiful mansion, the luxuries, and the future with him.

I lie on the bed and watch him undress. He unbuttons his white dress shirt, freeing it from his black, neatly pressed, impeccably lint-free pants. He removes his shirt and drapes it over the back of the vanity chair. Next, the pants . . . then socks . . . then underwear.

His body is strong, sculpted, masculine. His touch is soft, compassionate, healing. And his gaze as he lies next to me is deceptively loving. I know it can't be real, and I don't know why he continues to pretend. But I gratefully accept it and don't question him.

Yes, I'm the lucky one.

Michael

There are pictures of kids on milk cartons. Mom says it's because they're missing.

When I eat my cereal—the gross, healthy one Mom buys—I like to read about them. In the pictures, they're all smiling. They look happy. Mom says the pictures were taken before they were kidnapped. That makes sense.

I bet wherever they are, they're not smiling anymore.

I wonder if they're eating cereal somewhere, staring at their own faces.

I don't know what I'd do if I ever saw mine. Probably hide it from Mom. And I'd never tell anyone it's me.

"Don't read those," Mom says, taking the milk carton and putting it back in the fridge.

"Why not?"

"Because it's depressing," she says. "Hurry and finish eating so we aren't late for school."

She doesn't like sending me to school, but I don't know why. The teachers are nice there. They smile a lot and hug me whenever I'm nervous. They wear nice clothes, and they smell nice.

Some days Mom doesn't get dressed. She wears her pajamas all day, and sometimes she doesn't smell very good. But I don't tell her that. I try not to tell her things that might hurt her feelings.

And I never tell her things that might get me in trouble.

Like once, when I was in her room, I found a knife under her pillow. I guess she's scared of monsters too. She's scared of a lot of things. I don't tell her about the dead bird I saw in the school playground or about how some older boys poked at it with a stick. She might think I did it too. Then I'd get in trouble, and she might not let me go to school again.

I like school. I feel safe there.

Drew

The psychiatrist moved the couch. Only by a few feet, but enough that the early-morning sun makes it difficult to see as it filters in through the slits of the open blind. I move a fraction of an inch, draping my body over the arm, leaning forward slightly to find that spot where the window frame blocks the glare. Old books stacked everywhere are to blame for the stale, musty smell in the air, and the fan rotating in the corner does nothing to cool the cramped space.

Dr. Collins takes a seat across from me in a chair that looks as old as he is. What used to be brown leather is now just faded, cracked fabric that maintains the shape of his ass when he gets up. His green, itchy-looking sweater contradicts his need for comfort. He crosses one leg over the other.

Slippers. Hardly professional, but it's his office. His home. And I won't be filling out a patient survey. It's taken me years to get to this point. Desperately needing answers and seeking him out. Finding him wasn't easy.

No current website. No online presence. Almost as if he didn't want to be found.

But he'd slipped up. He'd kept a landline. And, lucky for me, there were only 172 Henry P. Collinses in the US phone directory.

"Before we start, I want to reiterate what I said last week," he says. "I'm no longer officially practicing. I see a few patients now and then, but I can't prescribe medication . . ."

"I'm not here for drugs." No more drugs. Never again. Unlike before, this time my paranoia is the only thing keeping Michael and me safe.

"Okay. Well, if you just need someone to talk to, I'm here to listen and offer some advice. Coffee?" he asks, getting up to pour himself a cup.

Can't he see I'm jittery enough? "No, thank you." I scan his office, fighting the urge to leave. I shouldn't be talking to anyone. Especially not this trained psychotherapist.

I read the title of the book on the doctor's desk. *Inside the Evil Mind.* His book. His theories. I've read it.

It gave me little comfort.

"So, last time, we talked about the accident that started your blackouts. The one that killed your husband."

A lie, backed by the fake death certificate I carry. One I try hard not to produce—adding more fraud to my list of sins is something I'm trying to avoid. "Yes."

"Have you ever heard of survivor's guilt?"

I shake my head, even though there's a chapter about it in another one of his books.

"It's completely normal for people in a near-death experience to take on a high level of guilt after the death of a loved one, and, over the years, if the grieving process is severe enough, it can manifest into unusual behavior. Like your blackouts."

The body's way of protecting itself. "The loss of time scares me. I feel responsible."

His head bobs up and down. He's thrilled that I've confirmed his theory. "For the death of your husband."

I wish. My life would be so much easier if Adam were dead. In my darkest thoughts, I'll be responsible for stealing his last breath.

"Was anyone else harmed that night?" He pushes his glasses higher on the bridge of his nose.

I nod.

"Another loved one?"

I hated her. Hated every last inch of perfection. "She was part of our family." She'd replaced me. "I didn't like her."

"The guilt can be even stronger in those cases. Our feelings about a person in life don't change because they are gone. When someone hurts us, their death doesn't provide the closure we seek for those unresolved feelings."

He thinks I'm talking about hurt feelings?

I'm talking about a slit throat.

"It's never too late to say sorry or offer forgiveness."

Isn't it?

"Saying the words out loud, even now, can help ease some of what you're suffering through from lack of closure." He's staring at me.

"I don't believe in the afterlife."

"It's not about them. It's about you. Whether you believe their spirit lingers or not, you're still here. You're the one needing the closure. Try it."

Jesus. My voice seems to have vanished, but a small sound escapes my throat. "I'm sorry and I forgive you." I'm not even sure where to look when I utter the pointless lies. I stare at my folded hands on my lap.

"Who are you talking to?"

The bitch who stole my life. "Catherine." I'm not sorry she's dead. I know killing her must have been the only choice I had. I'm not a bad person.

"Good," the doctor says. "Another way to relieve survivor's guilt is by remembering the life the person had. Thinking about the good times can actually have a positive effect on grief." He sips his coffee and winces, setting the mug aside. "Why don't you close your eyes and think about the first time you met your husband? Remember the way you felt, the little details that stick with you."

Every detail sticks with me from my life with Adam. Every last one plays on repeat in my mind, except how I escaped him.

I want to ask him if we can skip ahead, but he's staring at me expectantly again.

I hate doing things his way, but I can't remember the last time I've had any control over my life, so I close my eyes.

I met Adam standing in the rain outside the arrivals gate at Sea-Tac, praying my latest paintings were safe in the carry case. The ominous scattered raindrops collecting on the black canvas and slowly soaking through made my heart plummet. I was home on a break from my fine arts studies at Cooper Union in New York, and my plan of attack included stalking the owner of an art gallery in the Capitol Hill district. I'd sent him snapshots of my latest collection, and he'd absently agreed to view them. "Not complete shit, but no promises" had been his exact words, but I was eager to jump on any chance to have my work considered for a showing.

As long as the damn things survived the trip.

My mother was picking me up, and not seeing her at the bag carousel was a little disconcerting, though it did give me more time to adjust to being "home."

I checked my phone, but there were no messages from her, so I scanned the row of cars again.

I zipped my thin jacket higher, but it did nothing to shield my sun-kissed skin from the blasts of cool wind. Strands of wet hair threatened to whip my eyes out as I continued to scan the row of cars waiting at arrivals.

Come on, Mom! Pick any other day to be late.

"Drew?" A man to my right touched my shoulder, and my body froze.

Admittedly, I'm shorter than average at five foot two, but the towering height of the man next to me had me craning to see his face.

Seemingly oblivious to the rain, he smiled as though the weather couldn't touch him.

"Yeah. Who are you?" I asked as he picked up my small suitcase from the wet ground. I didn't care about the clothes inside getting wet; I was just desperate to keep the paintings dry. I suddenly wished I hadn't sold the expensive leather carrier my parents had sent me for my birthday to buy three of these cheaper ones for myself and two for my art school friends.

Visions of paint dripping down the canvas, destroying hours of soul-searching work, had me rethinking my values a little.

"I'm Adam. Your dad couldn't get away from the office, so he asked me to pick you up. Sorry I'm late."

My father was a corporate lawyer for C2 Technologies, and my mother said he'd been working around the clock lately, so I'd hoped to avoid him as much as possible . . . avoid the two of them together.

"Drew, you okay?"

"You work for my dad?" I knew all of his staff and colleagues. I didn't recognize Adam.

He grinned and nodded. "I work with Grant. Would you like to call him?" He extended a cell phone.

I stared at it. No, I didn't want to call him. I'd barely spoken to him in years.

"My mother was supposed to be picking me up."

"Your mom's not . . . feeling great today."

My blood ran cold. That meant one of two things, and I found myself hoping she was a big, drunken mess somewhere.

"Drew?"

"Okay, yes. I'll go with you."

"Great. I'm parked just over here."

I followed him to a black Escalade, where he opened the trunk and put the suitcase in. I reached for the passenger-side door handle the moment he did. The warmth of his large palm covering my damp, cold, paint splatter–speckled hand sent a shock of electricity coursing through my arm. His hand was rougher than I'd expected—in a good way. Most men who looked like Adam had soft, desk-job hands. His hand was different. Hard, strong, and pleasantly rough.

I shiver now thinking about those hands.

Odd how my attraction to those same qualities had quickly turned to fear.

Behind the appeal, Adam's touch was dangerous. That brief, unintentional contact had my spine tingling, setting off a fight-or-flight instinct. And, in hindsight, I might have chosen both.

I pulled my hand away, allowing him to open the door, and climbed in quickly, resisting the urge to check the paintings. I was private about my art, and most men like Adam didn't understand creative expression.

I set the carrier between my feet on the floor and tried to wipe the dampness from my cheeks and forehead. I didn't wear makeup, so at least there was no fear of running mascara or smeared lipstick. But a quick glance in the side mirror told me my hair was too far gone for saving.

"Your flight was okay?" he asked, starting the car. The engine purred to life, and another flick of a switch had his seat sliding forward just a fraction of an inch and the steering wheel rising a little higher.

He looked even taller seated, and the thick, muscular thighs straining against the expensive fabric of his charcoal dress pants stole my focus for a moment. When he adjusted the mirror to run a hand quickly through his damp hair and over his face, I forgot the question. Inside the small space, his steely, cool-scented cologne swirled around in my head, in direct contrast to the warmness radiating from his aura. I was instantly attracted to everything about this stranger, even though he personified the type of man I'd sworn I didn't want. Maybe it was because I wanted to believe that his outside appearance didn't reflect everything he was. That there were layers to him.

In one way, I'd been right.

He caught my stare in my silence, and I turned my gaze away.

Right: he'd asked about the flight. "Uneventful," I said. The plane had hit turbulence on its descent into the Seattle area, but I actually didn't mind the bumpy ride—there was something exciting about it, in a slightly morbid sort of way.

"I always hope for turbulence. Makes things more exciting," he said.

I wasn't sure how long I sat there with my mouth open.

"Home for the summer?"

"Four weeks." If my attempts to persuade the Herman Gallery to display my prints on commission failed, I'd be changing my flight for an earlier one back to New York. Being in Seattle was unsettling. As though I believed danger existed only here. That on the other side of the country I was safe.

"So, your father tells me you're an art major," Adam said, pulling out into traffic.

"Yes." The fact that my father had told this guy anything about me was somewhat surprising. Last time I was home, some of his employees had been shocked to learn he even had a daughter.

Adam glanced at my hands. "Painting, I assume?"

I nodded, rubbing at a stubborn blue spot on my thumb and trying to hide my unpainted nails. I hadn't bothered with any cosmetics in years. And the tiniest bit of debutante left in me chose that moment to raise her head and make me wish for a pale lip gloss at least. A brush . . . anything.

"What kind of art do you do?"

"Abstract expressionism, mostly . . ." He had no idea what I was talking about—I could tell, despite his nod.

"The only work I'm familiar with is *The Scream*, by Robert Munch," he said.

I couldn't tell if he was kidding or if he'd actually gotten the name of one of the most popular expressionist painters wrong. "Edvard Munch."

"Who's that?"

"Never mind." My interest in him took a nosedive, and I was relieved to find a fault in his perceived perfection.

I stared out the window but turned sharply toward him when he missed the turnoff for our house.

"Where are we going?"

"Your father asked me to bring you to his office."

"Why?"

"I don't know."

I suspected he did know, and I wondered how much this stranger knew about my family. Or how much he thought he knew . . .

But moments later, as I walked into the office building on Fourth Avenue, where my father now worked, and saw the walls covered in contemporary-expressionist pieces from Milar Constance and Bernadette Epstein, my thoughts were redirected. I spun around to look at Adam.

He walked close behind me, carrying my suitcase.

"Were you trying to be funny in the car . . . with the reference to Robert Munch?"

"I was." The sheepish grin he wore helped to ease my embarrassment slightly at having judged him. "Sorry. I couldn't resist. I actually do know a little something about art. In fact, I'd love to take you to the new Walter Bax exhibit at the Roq La Rue while you're home."

The exhibit was one of the main reasons I'd come back that summer. The chance to see the work of Walter Bax up close and to meet the reclusive artist was a once-in-a-lifetime opportunity, and this was rumored to be the last showing for this collection. Tickets for the event were by guest list only.

I wondered how Adam had secured a spot, and the temptation to say yes was overwhelming. But dating someone who worked for my father was a bad idea . . . and I was heading back to New York as soon as possible. "Um . . ."

"I know the artist. Your dad said you are a big fan. I could intro-duce you."

I blinked. "You know Walter Bax? How?"

"I went to school in Italy for a while. My flat was next door to his." He shrugged as though it wasn't the most fascinating thing he could reveal about himself. "Please. It would be my pleasure to make the introduction."

The chance to meet Walter Bax was only one of the reasons I found myself nodding. "Okay."

"Okay?" He looked surprised, as though he struggled to get dates, and the easy charm and nonarrogant air radiating from him were refreshing and totally unexpected.

I nodded again, a slight butterfly feeling in the pit of my stomach. It had been forever since a man had stirred a reaction in me.

"Okay. Tomorrow night. I'll pick you up at your parents' place at seven?"

I hesitated.

"Would you rather meet me there?"

It wasn't condescending—just oddly considerate. "No, that's okay. I'll be ready at seven."

He smiled, and I turned my gaze to the painting on the wall—the image of a bird strangled by a mess of cords connected to various elec-tronics. I'd studied the painting at school. It was part of Epstein's collec-tion of pieces that served as a commentary on capitalism. "Odd choice."

"Is it?" He didn't look at the painting.

"It symbolizes the ability of technology to strangle the purity from a community. How it can capture and kill all that is free with its invasive powers." I paused, realizing I was talking to a man who worked for one of the biggest, most successful technology firms in the United States.

But he was nodding. "Technology possesses all kinds of evil."

"Yet you work for the Crenshaws, who make their fortune from it."

"People need technology, even if it's bad for them. Progress has not always been positive." His gaze locked on mine had me holding my breath and clinging to his words. "Human beings have a history of seeking out the things that will eventually destroy them."

His stare, his words held me captive—motionless, until the earth actually shook beneath my feet. His hands were on my shoulders, and he was backing me toward an office a second later. "Stand in the doorframe," he said, holding me there, while the floor continued to rumble and shift beneath me.

My heart raced. "Earthquake?"

He nodded. "This building is built on the Seattle Fault. It's just a matter of time." And yet only excitement shone in his dark eyes as we rode out the sixteen seconds of a 4.0 earthquake. The building could have collapsed around my ankles, bricks and boards and glass scattered all around me, and I wouldn't have been able to break the hold his dark eyes had on mine. I'm not sure I even remembered to breathe. His hands on my shoulders, while I gripped the doorframe, burned into my flesh, searing through my jacket and thin T-shirt.

"Wow, did you feel that?" My father's voice.

Adam released my shoulders but not my gaze.

"Yes, wow. That's certainly a welcome home," I said, forcing my shaking hands to remain still as I walked toward my father for a quick, awkward hug, mostly for the benefit of onlookers. It was a routine we were both used to. Keeping up the pretense of a normal, happy family. He looked a lot older on this visit. Seeing his aging, tired face gave me pleasure. He couldn't live forever.

"Sorry your mother was unable to pick you up," he said, still holding my arms.

"Is she drunk, or are her eyes swollen shut?" I murmured.

His grip tightened. "You're not a child anymore. Don't test me, Drew."

His breath against my cheek made me cold, and I pulled away. I could feel Adam's gaze still burning into the back of my head, watching my interaction with my father, evaluating it, and even that early into my relationship with Adam, he'd had a hold on me. Instant. Deep. Eventually destroying.

"Well, Adam delivered me safely," I said tightly, daring a glance toward the other man. "I hope you're paying him for his chauffeur services."

My father frowned as he glanced back and forth between us. Something in his expression threw me. Something I couldn't quite discern. But something that would haunt me a year later. Something I should have trusted as a warning back then . . . the one and only warning he'd given me.

Adam continued to stand there, his hands in the pockets of his expensive, tailored suit, as though waiting for something.

"What am I missing?"

"Actually, darling, I work for him. Drew, this is Adam Crenshaw—the owner of C2 Technologies."

Even now, years later, I can't help but wonder if he'd purposely orchestrated that day to play out as it had.

Adam Crenshaw could have even ordered the ground to shake.

Catherine

I can smell the flowers in the room before I open my eyes. Adam remembered to bring them from the cemetery. The room is quiet, so I know he's not still here, but he remembered. He never forgets.

Getting up, I walk toward the assortment of fresh blooms sitting on the desk in the same plastic vase he uses every year. Roses, lilies, daisies in various colors and a big sunflower in the middle brighten the otherwise dim room.

I take a yellow rose and bring it to my nose, breathing in a familiar scent of vanilla body lotion—faint over the flower's own perfume. Vanilla. My mother. She always brings roses.

I don't even have to smell the sunflower to know it's from my brother, Tim. He would call me "Sunflower" after my performances, saying I stood out on the stage like a sunflower in a field of weeds. He was the first to believe in my talent and to convince me to pursue my passion. Disappointing him the day I walked away from the opera hurt my heart the most.

The lilies would be from my grandmother on my father's side. Nana Blair. The toughest woman I'd ever known. She'd raised fourteen kids alone after my grandfather died and worked three jobs to keep them all fed and cared for . . . my love of children comes from her. She'd make a wonderful great-nana to this child.

I hum noiselessly as I rearrange the flowers in the vase.

Then I carry the stack of letters to the bed and climb back under the covers to read them. On top is the card from Adam. I smile as I read it:

Happy Anniversary to my love

He always remembers, and so does everyone else. I feel loved and cherished as I scan the pile of letters. No one has forgotten me on the anniversary of my death.

It was nine years ago today that they all buried my empty casket.

Drew

I feel the beating of my heart increase with each attempt to restart this piece-of-shit vehicle. The end-of-day school bell is going to ring in fifty-six minutes, and Michael expects to see me standing there waiting for him. It's more for me than him. He might be okay if I'm not there, but I won't be. I can't learn to control the "what if" thoughts that drive me to the brink of insanity even once a situation is okay. Never-ending and terrifying alternate outcomes plague me until I'm reduced to tears, suffering a paralyzing anxiety as though the worst-case scenario had in fact occurred.

"Come on. Start." As if I have any kind of authority these days at all. I try one last time, then call the number for the tow truck company stuck on the dash. The previous owner had had a great sense of humor. The sticker had most certainly not been there the day I test-drove this hunk of scrap metal.

"Hello?" The gruff voice that answers won't win a medal for customer service.

"I need a tow truck right away." My debutante voice on autopilot. I almost don't recognize it. I'm not that woman anymore. I was never really that woman—one who could snap her fingers and get whatever she wanted.

It doesn't stop me from trying.

"You know, no one ever says, 'I need a tow truck next week.'"

"It's an emergency."

He snorts.

Right. "How fast can you get here?" I soften my tone despite the hairs standing up on the back of my neck, reminding me that my fate rests in this guy's hands.

School bell in fifty-four minutes.

"My guys are out . . ."

"Please."

The simple word stops him, and I hold my breath.

"Where are you?"

Who the fuck knows? Too many states, deserted middle-of-nowhere roads all meld together. I look around for a street sign. Nothing. What the hell was the name of this road? "Um . . ."

"What's around you?"

He'd be able to tell from that? So far, I haven't found any distinguishing landmarks around this part of Missouri—part of its appeal. Every road looks the same. Every house hauntingly similar. Every face just another to avoid. I scan the dirt road ahead. "There's a lot of hay-fields and a . . ." I squint in the blazing midday sun. "A boarded-up old convenience store about two blocks south . . ."

Fifty-three minutes.

"Yeah, that's not helpful."

No shit. "Look, I'm really in a hurry."

"Does your cell have GPS?"

I hope not. "Um . . . no." My pay-as-you-go flip phone could dial a number and receive calls—that's it. I'd disabled all other apps.

"What kind of car are you driving?"

"An old Ford Pinto. Green."

"Any Pinto is old."

I sigh.

"License plate?"

"Do you think there's more than one of us stranded?" The last thing I need is for these plates to be on file anywhere. If I didn't desperately need to get back to Liberty quickly, I'd have abandoned this car and walked. Dr. Collins's office being a little outside of town makes it inconvenient, but he's the only one who can help me.

"You're driving a dinosaur, so probably." He huffs. "What was the last thing you saw before hayfields?"

I think about it. "An old abandoned building was the last thing I noticed." It had creeped me out with its deteriorating exterior—broken windows and crushed bricks. Overgrown trees and grass and crumbling concrete stairs had me hitting the gas a little harder.

"Silent Meadows," he says.

"What?"

"The building you passed. It's the old insane asylum."

My blood chills, and now I'm even more desperate to get the hell off this road. Scars on my wrist glisten in the sunlight, taunting my already fragile thoughts.

"Sit tight," he says, disconnecting the call.

I blink, looking at the phone. How far away was he? An indication of how long I'd have to sit tight would have been nice. I feel my jaw clench so hard my teeth might snap off. The sweat pooling on the back of my neck tempts me to get out of the car, but outside is no cooler. The weather here in Missouri is dry, hot—the brilliant, burning sun seemingly desperate to set everything ablaze.

A glance in the rearview mirror shows a car approaching, and as it draws nearer, I see the Clay County Sheriff Department logo and the red-and-blue lights on the top of the car.

I fight to produce enough saliva to coat my sand-dry throat.

Please keep driving.

The vehicle slows to a stop on the side of the road behind me, and I reach across to the passenger side and slide my scrapbook under the seat. The news articles I printed at the library fall free from the pages, and I grab them and stuff them under me as the sheriff approaches the window.

He taps.

Please don't ask me to get out of the car.

The crank window takes effort to roll down. "Yes, Officer?"

"Sheriff Casey. Everything okay?" His shiny badge reflects the sun, blinding me, and I stare at his gun in the holster.

How quickly could I react? "Car trouble." *Act normal. Breathe.*

"Do you need assistance?" he asks, leaning to look inside the car.

"No. I've called a tow truck. They are on their way." Forty-two minutes to the end-of-day bell.

"Would you like to come sit in the car while you wait? It's hot as hell out here," Sheriff Casey says.

I'd rather die of heat exhaustion. "No, thank you." I hold up the water bottle that was left in the car overnight. "I'm hydrating, and it shouldn't be much longer."

"Okay . . ." He stares at me. Eyebrows meet in the middle over a slightly slanted nose. "Hey, have we met?"

"I don't think so." There's no way he could recognize me. My long blonde hair has been short and dark for so long that it even looks natural to me, and my glasses are nonprescription, but the dark, wide rims hide most of my face. I've gained almost ten pounds, and concealer hides any questionable scars—recognizable markings—on my face.

"I'm good with faces. Names not so much . . ." He taps the hood of the car.

"I really don't think we've met."

"Northcrest Elementary," he says, snapping his fingers.

The sharp sound makes me jump.

"You're the new single mom in town."

Oh sweet Jesus, please don't let that be the rumor. I was single. I was a mom. I was new to town, but the three were independent of one another. Interest from men would send us packing faster than the house catching fire.

"My kids go to school with your son."

Damn—we've been here a week. I nod. "That's great."

"Yeah, Ellie and Jack. Have you met them?"

"No, I don't recall."

"Great school."

"Yeah."

"You sure you don't want to wait in the squad car? I could drive you to the school in time for pickup."

Tempting. But I'm already that new single mom in town. I don't need gossip circulating, and I'd rather save my first ride in a police car for when they eventually arrest me. "It's fine. But thank you, Sheriff."

He nods. "Okay. Call the station if the truck takes longer than half an hour. You really shouldn't be out in this heat for too long."

"I will."

I watch in the side mirror as he walks back to his car, climbs inside. I wait to see if he runs my plates, radios anyone . . . if more police officers show up, sirens wailing and lights flashing . . .

It's been so long since we've been in the news. The first few years on the run had been torture. With Adam's status in Seattle, our disappearance had been broadcasted across media channels countrywide. Rewards were offered, and Adam would plead for the safe return of his wife and their child. Nowhere was safe those first few months, and it's a miracle Michael and I had managed to stay hidden.

In the rearview, I see the sheriff put on his Ray-Bans. He waves as he pulls a U-turn on the deserted street and drives away.

I take the newspaper clippings from under my ass and retrieve the scrapbook. My twisted way of remembering the past. I stuff them inside the cover and close it fast but not before catching a glimpse of Adam's face on the first page, above the headline "C2 Technologies CEO Adam Crenshaw appeals to public for any information on the whereabouts of his missing son and mentally ill wife."

I glance at the time on the dash, and by now I'm vibrating. Where the hell is the tow truck?

I close my eyes and breathe in through my nose . . . out through my mouth. They say ten deep breaths can make a world of difference. But for me, relaxing is a doorway for the enemy. I take three instead, pushing the air out of my lungs on the last one. I open my eyes, and my body lifts completely off the seat.

The tow truck is parked in front of my Pinto, and the guy is peering at me through the window. My hand to my thundering chest, I roll down the window.

"What's the problem?" the guy asks.

No apology for scaring the life out of me, and his curtness borders on rude, but I actually welcome it. "Radiator, I think."

"This thing is a million years old. Radiator might just be the start of your problems. Climb out."

His pessimistic attitude might bother someone else, but our shared disdain for this piece of garbage helps me relax. He isn't trying to reassure me. He isn't chatty. He is blunt, straightforward, and gets right to work as I climb out.

I stare at the vehicle, blaming it for so much more than breaking down. This car had become a measure of my worth. I hate being reduced to the single mom who, on outside appearances, couldn't take care of a vehicle, let alone a child. This big green lump of shit is nowhere near the vehicle Michael deserves. This life doesn't even come close.

I want to kick the tire until my toes bleed, but I check my temper because I have an audience.

An audience who is staring at me.

Immediately, I think he recognizes me, and my pulse does a lightning-fast kick start. But it's not recognition in his eyes; it's annoyance at having to repeat himself. "I said, can you pop the hood?"

Reaching back inside, I struggle with the latch and feel the guy's eyes glued to me. He sighs loudly. My breakdown is obviously causing him his own issues.

My hand finally finds the release, and the hood snaps up, nearly decapitating him. He mutters a swear word and dives beneath it.

The midafternoon sun scorches the top of my head, and I climb back in for shade at least. I can see the top of the guy's head through the slit between the windshield and the hood, and I will his dirty hands to perform their magic.

Thirty-two minutes until the bell.

He shuts the hood and shakes his head as he approaches the driver's side door. "Nope. This battery is dead. I'll tow it to my shop. Grab your stuff and climb into the truck."

I clutch the scrapbook to my chest and carry my thin wallet to the truck, using the step to hoist myself inside. Air-conditioning blasts my hair away from my face, and the icy chill goes straight to my bones. It's a relief from the heat, but I shiver as goose bumps surface on my damp skin. Thick, cool sweat drips down my back slowly.

I check my phone. Should I call the school and let them know I might be late? What mother can't pick up her kid from school on time?

The guy climbs inside the cab of the truck a minute later, and, seeing my white-knuckled grip on the phone, his face changes into something not quite a smile, but gone is the preoccupied coldness.

Damn. I'd felt safe with the preoccupied coldness.

"Is everything you own from the eighties?"

I don't answer. I hope he feels bad enough having essentially insulted me that he will shut up. Silence is my friend.

"Sorry—that was rude."

Only that? I shrug, my gaze out the window. My eyes see nothing yet perceive everything. I can notice a dark shadow a mile in the distance, but I barely see the horses in the field several feet away.

"Look, this isn't professional of me, but can I drop you somewhere before bringing this into the shop? I have somewhere to be as well."

I nod. "Northcrest Elementary School." Michael and I can walk home.

"You have a kid?" His tone is now decidedly friendly, and I'm uncomfortable. It hasn't escaped my notice that his gaze flew to my hands. Checking for a ring? He won't find one. Not even the faded circle where it used to be. The weight of the two-karat solitaire once as heavy on my size-four finger as the pressure of the lifelong commitment I'd mistakenly made to a monster.

"Do you paint?" he asks next, as though I haven't ignored the first question.

"No." I thought I'd scrubbed my hands free of any sign of creativity, but several tiny dots of brown paint remain on the back of my right hand where it connects to my wrist. At a glance, it could be freckles. Unfortunately, this stranger's gaze lingers, taking in too much. I yank the sleeve of my shirt down farther.

"Okay." He pulls the truck out into traffic, and my brain is going a million miles an hour. Keeping to myself, never sharing too much, has been the way to survive, but being mysterious, secretive, hasn't worked well in the past. Raising suspicion by being an outcast was just as dangerous as announcing our presence in the small towns we'd continued to pass through.

"Sorry. It's been a stressful day. I do have a kid—a son," I say.

"What grade?"

"Fourth."

"My niece is in the fifth grade, so it looks like we are heading to the same place." He smiles, and it completely transforms his face. The stern look gone. This new relaxed expression is friendly, warningly charming.

I look away.

Twenty-seven minutes later, I hurry inside the school as the bell rings. I push the nagging "what if" thoughts away. I'm here.

Michael smiles when he sees me, and the tension eases slightly from my shoulders. "Hey, Mom."

He's had a good day. Suddenly, I don't feel like such a failure for my beaten-down car and antique cell phone. His smile wouldn't be as wide or as sweet if we were still living a life of luxury. Money couldn't mask pain.

"Hi. Good day?"

"The best."

My reluctant heart soars. "The best? Wow."

"I have a new friend."

Heart sinks a little. "That's great."

"He invited me to his house to play. Can I?" He pushes his arm into the sleeve of his jacket, but it gets stuck at the end.

I kneel to help free his arm from the fabric. "Um . . . I'm sure I can arrange something someday . . ." Never.

"No, today." He picks up his backpack from the floor, tossing it over a shoulder.

"Oh, no . . ."

"There he is. That's my friend." Michael points across the hall, where a tall, thin blonde woman and her son wave.

"It's totally fine with me," she calls out.

Of course it is. She's the perfect suburban housewife. The darkest secret this woman hides is probably a vibrator in the top drawer of her Victorian-style dresser in an impeccably decorated bedroom.

I'm not judging. I'm jealous.

No one's skeletons are as fucked up as mine.

"Sorry, not today." I'm not sure who I'm speaking to. My gaze is somewhere noncommittal. I'm avoiding her questioning look and Michael's disappointed one.

"Why not?" he asks, the look in his dark eyes going from happy and excited to almost menacing. So fucking familiar.

"We should get going." I see tow truck guy coming down the hall with a little girl who looks like she could be his daughter. His niece.

The avoidance that worked well for us when Michael was younger won't be an option anymore. My little boy doesn't know the dangers of having friends.

Michael

I'm behind the bush in the far end of the yard. Mom's calling me for dinner, but I don't move.

Her voice changes when she calls out for the third time. I peek through the bush to watch her looking for me.

"Michael!"

She thinks I left the yard.

I never leave the yard. It's the only place I'm allowed to play. And the gates are locked. She won't let me go to Jack's house to play. She says someday, but I know she's lying.

"Michael!" Louder. Getting angry. Her voice hurts my ears sometimes.

I cover them with my hands and stare at my collection of dead bugs on the ground.

"Michael!"

She's getting closer. I pick a flower off the bush. "Sorry, I was getting this for you," I say.

She still looks angry, but she takes the small, purple flower. "Thank you. But please answer when I call."

"Did you think I ran away?"

She frowns as she looks at me. "What?"

"Nothing. Never mind."

She stops me on the bottom step. "Why would you say that?"

"I don't know. I just want to play with Jack, but you keep saying no."

She sighs. "I don't feel comfortable with you going to a stranger's house. But, tomorrow after school, we will go to the playground, okay? Maybe the other kids—and Jack—will be there."

I smile. Jack always goes to the playground after school. "Thanks, Mom."

Giving her the flower must have made her happy.

Catherine

Without a voice, I keep a journal. I write letters to Adam. Long, detailed accounts of my mundane, eventless days. A bug crawling across the floor can be turned into pages of the tiny insect's adventures—over the hardwood, up the wall, trying to escape through the boarded window and eventually disappearing under the gap in the door, leaving me alone again. I write letters to my parents. I tell them about the three babies I had and lost. I tell them not to worry about me. Adam is taking care of me.

And I write letters to the first child. Not to the others. Just him.

Pages of apologies pour out of me until the marker dries up and the notebook fills up and I have to wait until Adam comes again with new ones.

He won't let me have pens anymore. Too dangerous, he says. He's probably right. I can't be trusted with sharp things.

He's traveling, and the house is quiet and empty. Without him here, I lose myself in my own fantasies—envisioning life once the baby is born. As soon as I reach twenty-three weeks, we will redo the nursery, paint the walls a bright, joyful color, and buy new furniture . . . a crib that hasn't been slept in before.

I know Adam will love this baby once it's here. Right now he doesn't believe it will happen. We're going to be a family. A real one. Finally.

I turn the last page in my newest journal and hesitate before beginning. It could be the last time I'll be able to write for who knows how long. I need to use the space wisely. These thick-headed markers don't help—the way the ink seeps onto the page, taking up unnecessary space.

As tiny as I can, I start to write:

One day, I'm going to get you. I'm going to do to you what you did to me. I'm going to take away your ability to breathe, to talk, to sing, to eat, to live. I will make you pay, Drew. So, keep running. Far and fast. While you can.

I stare at the words; then I quickly cover them all with the red ink. Layer over layer until the words disappear. I'd never do that. I'd never hurt anyone.

Unlike her.

And now I'm out of paper. Silenced once more.

I stand, and, crossing the room, I place it on the bookshelf next to the others. All different shapes and sizes. Pretty patterns. I run a finger along the spine of the rows of them. So many unvoiced thoughts. Crushed between the pages are the flowers from my gravesite.

I sigh, turning to the mirror, but I don't see my reflection. Instead, my gaze is on the wall behind me. White. Empty. Unlimited space.

I stand and pick up my marker.

Drew

I'm running through empty hallways. Footsteps echo behind me, but no one is there. Michael is a baby in my arms, but his face changes whenever I look at him—Adam's face, the nanny's face, my face . . .

I trip over a body on the floor and slip on a river of blood. My feet slide in all directions as I struggle to find my balance. The baby starts to wail in my arms, a high-pitched, piercing, deafening sound.

I keep running until there's no more hallway. Just walls closing in around us.

Big white walls. Smeared with blood letters. Big and bold.

Keep running.

By now, I'm used to the nightmares—the senseless, confusing mind-horrors that hold no answers. Still, I'm covered in sweat, and my heart is pounding when my eyes open.

I get out of bed, grab the clothes I wore yesterday, and get dressed. Downstairs in the kitchen, Michael has eaten his cereal already. His dirty bowl is in the sink, and he's standing on a chair at the counter making his lunch when I enter.

I'm failing as a parent. It's been over a week since school started. I need to get better at this.

"Here, sweetheart. I'll finish making your lunch. Sorry I slept so late." I hug him, but he wiggles free and leaves the kitchen.

I rest against the counter, staring at the strawberry jam seeping over the edge of the bread.

Keep running.

A warning or a threat?

Was there even a difference anymore?

After I walk Michael to school, I take the bus out of town and walk the ten blocks to Dr. Collins's home.

The couch is back where it was originally. Another patient must have complained about the sun. But now open boxes occupy the space near the bookshelf. Inside, I see an old collection of salt and pepper shakers—at least fifty different sets—and several antique porcelain dolls. Their blank stares make me shiver.

Dr. Collins hands me a mug that reads, "I can help you find your marbles."

I'm not so sure. Even if the doctor can provide clarity, even if he can help me detangle the uncertain threads of my past, will it give me peace?

"Decaf," he says.

"Thank you." The warm cup gives me something to do with my hands at least.

"Sorry for the mess. I'm getting rid of some of my mother's things. This house was hers."

That explained the decor. "How long have you lived here?"

"About ten years."

"When did your mother die?"

"Six months ago." He takes his phone from his pocket, glances at it quickly, and then sets it facedown on the end table. "Last week, you were worried about Michael at school. How did he do?" he asks, his butt comfortably back in the chair. Today, his sweater is multicolored and striped but still scratchy looking and too short in the arms. It's the same one he's wearing in his author photo from the eighties, the one on the jacket cover of his books.

"Good. He has a new friend." All week, I've been making new excuses to avoid a playdate. Michael's not happy to just spend time with me anymore.

"That will make things easier for him," Dr. Collins says.

For him, maybe. It complicates the shit out of *my* life. "Seems like a nice kid."

"Friends play a big role in their developing personalities at this age, so consider it a good sign that he has good taste in playmates."

What about the years Michael spent interacting only with me? Had those negatively affected his development?

I should have tried harder. Classical music CDs, Baby Einstein videos . . . talked to him more.

Sang to him.

The sound of the nanny's voice—warm, gentle, perfectly pitched, coming from the nursery as she'd rocked Michael to sleep—used to make my head pound.

"All the lovely pieces fall to the floor . . ."

I'd wanted *her* in pieces on the floor.

"Drew?"

"Sorry, what?" I'm gripping the handle of the mug so tightly it might snap off in my hand.

"I asked if *you* were making friends in town." He checks his phone, then sets it back on the table next to his mug that reads, "Not Without My Notepad."

"You don't use a notepad." It's something I'd noticed from the first session. He didn't take notes or use a tape recorder. There's no record of me being here at all.

He looks confused, since I've ignored his question about friends; then, following my stare, he glances at his cup. "Oh. I used to, but I found it makes people uncomfortable when they think I'm recording what they say. Now, I just listen."

Today, I'm reluctant to talk. About myself anyway. I look around the office and settle on a picture on his desk. A graduation photo of a boy who looks nothing like him. "Your son?"

"Yes. Before you know it, Michael will be that age," he says.

"How old is he?"

"In that picture, David was twenty-three—just graduated from MIT." He pauses. "He would have been forty next week, but he died."

I stare at the eyes in the photo, drawn to a familiarity I can't possibly have. Or maybe it's the youthful optimism that holds my attention. The way his gaze seems to be looking past the photographer, past the glass frame, straight at me. "What happened to him?"

The doctor's face reveals no emotion. "Suicide."

Life's cruel irony spared no one. "I'm sorry."

His phone vibrates on the table. "Excuse me," he says, picking it up. "I need to take this." Getting up, he leaves the room, pulling the door behind him. It's open a fraction, and I can hear his muffled voice getting lower as he walks farther down the hall.

I get up and approach his desk. This place is such a mess, and I can't decide who was the hoarder: him or his mother. I tug the drawers in the desk, but they are all locked. File cabinets line the wall near the window, but his voice is drawing nearer.

Shortest phone call in history.

I'm back on the couch again, mug in hand, when he reenters.

"Sorry about that."

"Everything okay?"

"Yes . . . actually no. I'm going to need to cut the session short. My father's in a hospital in Springfield. Stage-four colon cancer. I have to head out there." He checks his watch.

I stand. "That's okay . . ." I'm not in the mood to talk anyway. "How much for today's session?"

"Two hundred."

I glance at the clock. Ten minutes or an hour, his rate is the same. I hand him the money and grab my sweater. "Same time, next week?" I can't stop coming here until I find what I'm looking for.

He nods. "Yes. And I'm going to give you a homework assignment." Obviously he feels he owes me something for $200.

He touches my shoulder, and there's no time to process how I feel about the contact before he yanks the hand away, as though I've burned him. "Isolation can make it feel like the only thing you have is the past. Your goal is to make a friend before we meet again," he says.

"Do *you* count?" Friendships are not possible when I can't be honest with the people here in Liberty. Our safety relies on lies and not making connections. Any day, we could be packing up to move on, and it's easier to sever ties that are only loosely bound.

"I'm afraid not." He smiles. "Take a cue from Michael. Be brave and put yourself out there."

I already know I'll fail this assignment.

"Hey, helicopter mom, come have a seat. He can't go anywhere."

The voice belongs to the mom I spoke to at pickup three days ago. Josie? Jolene? I hesitate, glancing at Michael at the top of the worn metal slide that looks like it could cause tetanus, with its rusted sides, then go join her on the bench. The sand in my shoes scratches my feet, and the intense heat that day has my entire body feeling damp.

Make a friend.

Josie/Jolene is the picture of perfection. Tall, blonde, gorgeous, with just enough makeup to know she cares about how she looks, even at a playground, but her hair is pulled back in a messy bun, and she's dressed in workout clothes. Her smile is warm and reveals perfect white teeth. In the best-case scenario, it would be hard to be friends with someone like her.

"How was his first week?" she asks.

"Good. I think." Michael seems happy. I watch him play on the monkey bars with several other boys close to his age, and he's clearly oblivious to me being there. The bars are way too high for kids this age, and the sand below has been kicked away to very little padding. I see his grip giving out on the third rung, and I stand up . . . but he readjusts his little hands and continues to the end.

"He's okay. He's got this," she says.

I sit back down. I watch him follow the other boys to a seesaw, which looks safe enough, but the others climb on one together, leaving him standing there without a partner.

"Do you want me to get on with you?" I call out.

He ignores me.

"Boys, take turns, okay?" Josie/Jolene calls out.

Obviously the normal parenting solution.

"So, where did he go to school before this?" she asks, turning on the bench to face me.

"He was homeschooled." And still would be if I didn't need time to see Dr. Collins and search for answers without him around.

"Clearly he's your only child. I have three, and I could never have them all home every day like that. I love them more when I get a chance to miss them."

I squirm on the seat, checking my watch. We've been here only five minutes. We can't leave yet. Why haven't the boys switched yet? Michael still hasn't had a turn . . .

"Where are you both from?"

"The West Coast."

"Like California West Coast?"

Close enough. I nod.

"Whatever made you move out here?"

A search for answers that I pray isn't a dead end. "A change of scenery, I guess."

"I get that. I'd always had plans of moving to Florida after graduation, and if you'd told me at eighteen that I'd be staying in this little hicksville of a small town because I fell in love, I'd never have believed you." She eyes me for a moment. "I heard Principal Bradley say that it's just you and Mike?"

Michael, I want to say, but being rude to one of the only people I've spoken to so far in town might not be the best idea, and whatever I say or don't say will no doubt circulate the mommy gossip chain. "Yes."

Are the other boys purposely excluding Michael?

She must sense my unease because she calls out to her son. "Jack, why don't you play a game you can all play?"

Her little boy nods and climbs off the seesaw, and the three kids run off toward the field.

"Thank you," I mumble.

"No problem . . . so are you divorced then?"

"Widowed." Two minutes. This woman has managed to drag more personal info—however inaccurate—out of me in two minutes than anyone has in nine years. I need to shut up . . . or deflect. "How . . . how old are your other kids?"

"Eleven and five." She points across the playground. "Ellie is the oldest, and Lila is the youngest—the handful . . . excuse me," she says and then crosses the playground, where the little girl has her dress pulled up around her waist, exposing her pale-pink underwear to the boys.

I watch Josie/Jolene talk to her for a minute, fixing her dress; then she returns to me. "See—handful. Our family can cause a bit of a stir in this place."

"How so?" If this woman and her normal life were raising flags, I'm doomed.

"I'm a sex therapist, and let's just say business is kinda slow." She moves closer and lowers her voice. "Not that there isn't potential business here. I know at least six couples that could use a little push in the bedroom . . . but this town is so small, everyone's afraid that everyone will know their business."

Not sure how to respond, I nod.

"My husband is a sheriff in Liberty, so I don't have to work, but I'd lose my mind as a housewife." Her phone vibrates on the seat between us, and I jump.

"Sorry, just my phone." She checks her message, then stashes the phone away in an oversize purse. "What do you do?"

"I'm a stay-at-home mom." I've never told anyone about my passion for painting, and I'm not about to tell her. These days, it's just a way to pass the slow-moving minutes of my life anyway.

"That's great," she says, though a minute ago she'd admitted it was the last thing she'd want to be.

I glance back toward the soccer field, but I don't see Michael. I scan the playground. Where did he go?

I stand and look around the slide, but he's nowhere. "Michael!" I yell, hurrying across the sand to the swing set. He's not there.

"Michael!"

I turn in a circle, my pulse thundering in my veins. Why did I take my eyes off him? Why did I sit and talk? Why did he run off? I told him to stay where I could see him.

A few other moms glance toward me, and Josie/Jolene calls out as I'm about to tour the edge of the grounds near the soccer field. "Drew! He's over here," she says, pointing to the woodsy area near the bench.

I hurry over, fighting to calm the rage as I see him peeking around the tree. "Hey, didn't you hear me calling you?"

"Mom! You just gave away my hiding place. Thanks a lot," he mumbles.

Aware of Josie/Jolene's gaze on me, I force a breath. "We have to go . . ."

"But we just started a game of hide-and-seek."

"I have to pick up the car from the shop." They haven't actually called me yet, but I'm tired of waiting. Without the car, I feel trapped. A sitting duck with no means to escape.

"I can drop him off. We will be leaving in about twenty minutes ourselves," Josie/Jolene offers, and I wish she'd mind her own business.

"Yeah, Mom, can Jolie drop me off?"

Jolie, right. "That's Missus . . ." I turn to her for her last name.

"Casey," she says. "And Jolie is cool. And it's really no trouble."

"Thank you, but we have to go."

Michael looks about to argue, so I shoot him a look that I hate using.

"Fine," he says, waving to his friends as he heads toward the sidewalk.

"Bye . . ." I say awkwardly, expecting to see judgment on the other woman's face, but instead a warm understanding reflects in her eyes.

Which is so much worse, because now I'm left to wonder what it is she thinks she understands.

"I can fix it, but it would almost be cheaper to buy a new vehicle."

I shake my head. "If you can fix it, that would be great." Tow truck driver's name is Parker, according to the name tag on his coveralls, and I'd been hoping to deal with someone else that day.

Repetitive contact with people here only makes me more recognizable, more memorable.

"I sourced parts this afternoon, and the new battery will be a few hundred, but an engine is running closer to five thousand . . ." He shakes his head, nodding toward the car. "I'm really not sure it's worth it. I took a look at a few other things, and the brakes might last another few months at most. The tires needed to be replaced months ago . . ."

I hold up a hand. "It's a piece of junk—yeah, I know. Can you just order the new battery and engine for now . . . and maybe a quote on tires?" I glance outside. Michael is playing with Parker's niece. He's still annoyed at me for leaving the playground.

Parker nods. "The engine I can do. Tires aren't my thing, but Al at Tires R Us three blocks from here can hook you up."

"Great. Thank you."

"I'll need a deposit to order the engine."

"I'll just pay the full amount now." I open my purse.

"That's not necessary."

"I'd prefer it."

"Okay." He punches a few things into a computer and prints off the order and then an invoice. He places it on the counter and explains a bunch of stuff I couldn't care less about.

"I sign here?" I pick up a pen and point to the signature line.

"Yep."

I do the spirally, unreadable signature and drop the pen.

"Okay . . . so, four thousand six hundred and ninety-eight dollars," he says. "Credit or debit?"

"Cash."

Naturally, that's met with a surprised look.

Which I do my best to ignore. I quietly count out the money I'm crazy to carry around with me and hand it to him.

He takes it and doesn't recount, just slides it into a bank-deposit bag and puts it into the safe behind him. "So, it will be a while . . ."

That's the toughest part, but luckily my next appointment with Dr. Collins isn't until next week. We can walk everywhere else. "That's fine. Thank you."

"Hey, Drew . . ."

I turn back.

The questioning look in his eyes immediately has me mentally packing.

"I'll rush order the part."

I relax. A little. "I'd appreciate that."

"Hey, Drew . . ."

Oh Jesus. "Yeah?"

"A good set of all-seasons should get you through the winter here . . . though if you're not used to winter driving . . ."

I frown.

He glances at the paperwork in his hand. "Jolie said you were from California."

I left the park fifteen minutes ago and already my lie has spread.

"She's my cousin. She texted to make sure I gave you a discount."

Fantastic. Tow truck guy has a direct tie to the sheriff. "Oh, okay . . . um, thank you."

He nods. There's more. I can tell by the way he's folding the edge of the paper in his dirty, stained hands, so I wait.

"Jolie also thought I should ask you to dinner."

Liberty is definitely not the place for us. I need to get answers from Dr. Collins and get the hell out of here. "Thank you, but no."

He laughs, looking slightly embarrassed. "Not even an excuse. Just no."

"An excuse would just leave it open for you to ask again."

SEPTEMBER

Drew

Years without a sign of Adam, yet I expect him any moment. He's the thing I fear most. I feel him getting closer. It's almost a twisted longing that grows stronger in the pit of my stomach as the days and years go on.

Showers are the worst—the dangers lurking beneath what should be a relaxing, refreshing stream of water. My skin crawls with a sense of foreboding the minute I turn on the taps.

But I've been painting all day and I haven't showered in . . . three days, so it's out of necessity that I undress as fast as I can and step into the steam fogging up the glass doors. Always glass doors, never curtains. Seeing what's coming is always better than a surprise. And the sight of his shadow behind the fabric would instantly stop my heart. Awareness gives a victim a chance to make peace with their fate, at least.

Did the nanny get that peace? Or did I sneak up on her in the dark? I can't remember hearing a scream or seeing a look of terror on her face.

Just the body lying there lifeless. The knife beside her on the floor.

I wish I could find a way around the noise of the blasting spray coming from the pipes and the loud tinkling sound of the waterdrops hitting the porcelain. They block out the sounds my ears have been trained to listen for. The opening of doors. The breaking of glass. Heavy footsteps drawing closer.

I close my eyes. A useless attempt to block out the thoughts creeping in, threatening to take hold of my ability to breathe. All it does is prevent me from seeing what's around me.

Footsteps on the stairs.

I'm certain of it.

My eyes open, and, pushing the glass door, I peer out into the bathroom . . . beyond, into the bedroom across the hall.

There's no one there. The hollow sound just my pounding heart echoing off the cavity of my chest.

I grab the soap and wash quickly. Damn paint takes forever to remove. I lather the soap on the facecloth and scrub it together; then I violently attack the skin, watching the blues, greens, and yellows mix into a rainbow on the suds cascading down my body.

I hate getting paint on myself.

Once, it had been an erotic experience. Once, the blues, greens, yellows, and reds had been carefully, purposely applied to every inch of my body. Every. Inch. Tenderly, lovingly, seductively, the colors had decorated my skin. The brush had tickled, cascading over my breasts. Soft bristles had teased my inner thighs. Just the idea of bringing my artistic passion into our lovemaking had excited the hell out of me. Adam excited the hell out of me. I always craved him. I was prepared to do anything for him.

The big, white, inviting canvas on the floor had been a sensual awakening as I lay on it, masturbating, while Adam watched, the paint covering the white in the shape of my movements. I rolled and rocked, my legs spreading and then clenching tight as my orgasm rose.

I hadn't thought I was capable of such a display. The sexual power he released in me shocked me.

Me—once so prim and proper. Beige. Now, a million shades of fire and ice combining to create a masterpiece for his eyes only. It was all for him. Only for him.

Then the painting hung on the living room wall.

A form of punishment for something I hadn't done yet.

I hate that remembering that day has me aroused. I hate that the memory of the most sickeningly horrible human being still has an intoxicatingly sensual hold on me.

I hear something.

I pause. I wait.

A door opening, glass breaking, footsteps? Maybe . . . I'm not sure . . .

No one comes.

Maybe no one is ever coming. But I'm reluctant to give myself any sort of peaceful hope.

I scrub the paint from my hands and let the remaining colors swirl together as they disappear down the drain.

I shut off the water, then step out and wrap a rough, threadbare towel around my body. Avoiding my reflection in the mirror, I reach for a brush and run it through my wet hair. Mirrors see too much. They are cruel and unforgiving. I can't look, for fear I won't recognize the person staring back at me.

Slowly, the colors of the person I used to be are washing away. Back to beige.

❖ ❖ ❖

Beige. Everything in my closet is beige. If I'm lucky, there may be a dark-brown sweater tucked in the back.

Beige is safe. No one notices beige. It doesn't stand out. It blends with walls and furniture.

"Don't you have anything pink?" Michael asks, staring into my closet with disgust.

When did he start caring about what I wore? I barely recognize him these days. A couple of weeks in school, and he has a million opinions on too many things. His little world has opened so much, and it makes me claustrophobic. "No."

"Blue?" He rifles through several shirts.

I shake my head. I reach into the closet for a long-sleeve tan blouse with a tiny blue stripe. "This is as close as it gets." I must not have noticed the blue stripe when I bought it. Which was probably three or four years ago. I don't see any point in owning a lot of clothes and certainly not nice things. It's bad enough that Michael is now noticing name brands and asking for clothes like his friends wear. We can certainly afford them, but I'm reluctant to give in to indulgences. My money won't last forever. I hold up the blouse. "Yes or no?"

"It's fine." He's moved on to hunt for shoes that aren't brown flats. He won't find any.

"What does it matter what I'm wearing? This is your friend's party." I go into the bathroom, and, removing the sweatshirt I'd been hoping to stay in all day, I put on the uncomfortable blouse.

"I want the other moms to like you," he says, tossing shoes out of the closet.

It really wasn't high on my priority list at all. Though I had two days left to make a friend, per Dr. Collins's assignment. I'd had a conversation with Jolie. I'd been hoping to embellish on that. Friends aren't something I think I'll ever have again. Not real ones.

Like the ones who abandoned me years before, choosing to believe I was crazy?

Okay, so, maybe I'd never had real friends.

"I want to go to my friend's house to play, so you need to be friends with his mom."

He sighs, giving up the search for nice shoes.

"How's this?" I ask, reappearing in the shirt.

"Fine, I guess." He grabs the wrapped present from the bed and leads the way out of the room.

I stop him as we reach the front door. "Now, remember . . . let's not talk too much about where we've lived before . . ."

"I know, Mom! But it feels like lying." His forehead wrinkles in a frown as a moral struggle rages in his little mind.

As he gets older, this hiding, this running is becoming more of a challenge. He has questions, but for now, he's not asking them. I selfishly accept the reprieve for as long as I can. He must wonder why he doesn't have a father, grandparents, aunts or uncles or cousins, like his friends, but he never questions me. Someday, I hope I can be honest with him. Someday, I hope he will forgive me. "We're not lying. We are just keeping our lives private. There's nothing wrong with that."

He nods, but I know he's not buying it. "Okay."

We leave the house and follow Jolie's directions to a cul-de-sac three blocks from the school. The Casey home is by far the nicest on the street. Its redbrick exterior extends three stories, and the white wraparound front porch is straight out of a feel-good family movie. A light breeze blows a wooden double-wide swing, and the red door displays a fall-colored wreath. Potted flowers still bloom in an impeccably maintained yard.

I've never had the luxury of believing in picture-perfect homes and picture-perfect families.

Jolie has spared no expense on her son's tenth birthday party. A superhero at the end of the driveway awaits us as we walk up the sidewalk.

"Wow! A spider guy!" Michael's excited expression makes my chest hurt.

The costumed hero corrects him. "Spider-Man."

"Same thing," I say, annoyed at my inability to give my son a normal childhood. I've never allowed him to watch anything other than cartoons, but now I make a mental note to rent every superhero movie appropriate for his age. Maybe he should watch movies in which good conquers evil.

When he eventually someday learns the truth about me, about what I did to save him, will I be a superhero in his eyes? A vigilante of sorts, or simply the villain?

"Around the house to the back, your adventure awaits." Spider-Man points the way.

Balloons visible from the street and the sound of kids laughing and squealing make this guy redundant. I'm tempted to tell him that.

Michael leaves me the second he spots his friend, and I look around the beautiful, big backyard. Late-September sun flickers across the pool's surface, reminding me of my childhood pool in the backyard in Seattle. So many summer days had been spent learning to swim and watching my mom cut through the water with ease. She was a former Olympic athlete; her gold medals for swimming had been displayed in our dining room, and, as a small child, I'd secretly believed she was a mermaid. I thought she was magical. Invincible.

I knew so little back then. How quickly my perception had shattered.

I also remember the pool at Adam's house. I can't bring myself to think of the house as ever being my home. Who is lying beside that pool now? Is she yet a prisoner or still happily oblivious to the reality of the life she's entering? The nanny used to enjoy that pool. Her flawless body, stretched out on the chair, her bikini top discarded next to her as she tanned her young, soft skin. The memory of it feels so real as I stare at the shimmering surface of the water that I almost reach out to touch her.

"Hi."

I jump and turn to see Parker behind me.

"Sorry, didn't mean to make you pee yourself," he says.

A smile would be appropriate, but my lips give up after a second of trying. "Where are they putting the gifts?" I ask, avoiding his penetrating gaze. Since turning down his offer of dinner, I hadn't seen him around. Though I should have expected to see him here.

"The table next to the pony."

I start to walk in the direction he is pointing; then, registering his words, I stop and turn. "Wait, what?"

He laughs. "Kidding. Though the day's not over yet," he mumbles. "The gifts are inside. I'll show you."

I nod and fall into step beside him, seeing his point about the pony. Every superhero imaginable is in attendance. A different piñata hangs from every tree branch large enough to support its weight. Not one but *three* inflatable jumpy castles are set up in the large yard, and a candy cannon is shooting out a new diabetic coma every thirty seconds to a mosh pit of children. "I take it you think this is overkill?" I'm not sure why I'm asking, but maybe I need the reassurance that kids don't need all this to be happy.

"Little bit. Don't you?"

"Why would you assume that? Because I don't drive a fancy new car and have the latest iPhone?"

He shakes his head and leans closer. "Because you're not a sucker."

"Jolie's a sucker because she wants to give her son a party he'll remember?"

He opens the back patio doors, and the sound of women laughing inside makes me hesitate before entering. No wonder he was outside with the kids. A quick glance reveals there isn't another penis-yielding human inside.

"You think Jack will remember this?" He shakes his head. "All he will remember is that he had a great day with his friends. This is all for Jolie. For show."

I immediately feel better. Which makes me squirm. I set the gift down on the table and turn to see her walking toward us.

"You made it!"

I force a smile. "Yes. Thank you again for inviting Michael. He was very excited." Until I told him he couldn't go, and he threw an epic temper tantrum, resulting in me giving in.

Bad parenting maybe, but I'm not in the running for any awards anyway.

Jolie links her arm through mine. "Come on into the kitchen. There are some moms I'd like you to meet."

Shit. I'd been hoping to go for a walk around the block, stay close but not engage in conversation with the other parents. I send a desperate look at Parker, but he grins and waves, heading back outside with the kids.

Lucky bastard.

"So, you made one friend in town already," Jolie says.

I blink. "No. He just towed my car a couple of weeks ago."

"He also asked you to dinner. Which you turned down. Which all the single women in town think you're crazy for doing," she says as we enter the kitchen and all judgment flies my way.

I feel my nails biting into the palms of my hands. Stale air surrounds me, and my pits start to sweat, threatening to reveal my discomfort to the roomful of women. I want to escape, but Jolie's hand on my arm keeps my feet firmly planted.

"She's just kidding. Some of us couldn't be happier that you aren't interested in the hottest single man to live in this area code," a woman wearing a pink sundress and silver strappy sandals says.

All eyes leave me and are redirected through the window.

Mine follow and settle on Parker. He's using his watch to time the kids through the obstacle course bouncy house. The kids are all laughing, and he's encouraging them to go faster. His "Funcle" shirt suits him. The tagline—"Like a dad, but cooler"—is spot on. He is good looking. Not in the typical way. He isn't tall, dark, and handsome, but his muscular build and slightly off-center nose make him look rugged, real. His messy hair looks like he attempted to comb it once, then said the hell with it.

I see how the other women could be attracted to him.

Watching Michael reappear at the end of the obstacle course and receiving a high five from Parker makes my mouth go dry. I hate that Michael doesn't have a father. I've done my best to fill that void, teaching him to play ball and fish and ride a bike—all the things dads do—but I know it's not the same. These thoughts, these feelings of inadequacy as a family, are so much easier to ignore when we are alone—just Michael and me.

The women start to laugh. I've missed a joke.

"You okay?" Jolie asks.

"Yeah, fine . . ." I clear my throat. "Could I get a water?"

"I have wine . . ."

Wine at a kid's birthday party. Parker's right—this is about Jolie. But I'd rather be her than me any day, so I refuse to judge. "Water is great. Thank you."

She opens the fridge and hands me a bottle of Perrier. "So? What do you all think of the new kitchen?" She gestures around her, and the other women make the appropriate comments.

I nod along to the compliments, but I couldn't care less about the aged, antique-white finishing on the cupboards or the new stainless steel appliances.

Expensive things and fine luxuries often mask a domestic house of horrors.

"This countertop is real marble. It was triple the cost of the quartz, but I couldn't resist." She runs a hand along the smooth, glossy finish, and my vision blurs as I stare at the swirling dark shades of brown and tan.

"Have you christened it yet?" a dark-haired woman asks, refilling her wineglass.

"It's Jolie we're talking about," pink sundress chimes in. "John had her bent over this the second the installers left."

The water does nothing to coat my dry throat. Laughter and Jolie's protests seem far away as my eyes continue to stare at the countertop . . .

After our first date, Adam and I barely spent a moment apart on my trip home that summer, and my decision not to return to school hadn't been difficult. In three weeks, I'd fallen for him, and my goals hadn't changed, but how I wanted to achieve them had. Adam's influence and power within the city was already opening doors, and my first painting was on display at the Herman Gallery.

Two short months later, our fall wedding was the dream I never thought I'd wanted. Hundreds of people, and a white lace dress that cost enough to make me feel guilty but not enough to prevent me from needing it. My desire to please Adam surprised me and continued to grow in our first months of marriage.

But then slowly things started to change. He seemed preoccupied with problems at the office, and he was often distracted or distant when he'd arrive home late.

One night, I heard him on the phone in his office. Muffled yelling drifted down the stairs to the kitchen, where I was making dinner, and I strained to hear what had him so angry.

I heard my father's name, and I stopped chopping vegetables and moved closer to the bottom of the staircase to listen.

"Well, someone has to pay for this mistake, Grant," he said before the office door slammed closed behind him and he appeared at the top of the stairs.

He saw me standing there, and his expression had me hurrying back to the kitchen.

Someone had to pay for the mistake.

That night it was me.

The vegetables on the cutting board blurred as he walked toward me and took the knife from my hand. Anger radiated from him, and a thick tension made it difficult to breathe. Turning me around, he bent me over the island in the middle of the kitchen. The cold marble a shock as he lowered my cheek to the surface of the counter.

Adam's hands gripped the edge of my dress, lifting it up over my thighs, my hips, my ass, the thin, stretchy fabric gathering around my waist.

"Adam, what are you doing?"

"Shhhh . . ." The sound of his zipper had my heart pounding.

"No, Adam. Stop."

He'd ignored me.

Panic mixed with confusion as I'd cried out in pain. Why hadn't he stopped?

I couldn't move. Pinned with one arm against my upper back and shoulders, I was forced motionless against the countertop. "Please stop." I'd tried to lift my body away from him, but he was too strong.

Why wasn't he stopping?

"Adam, please. You're hurting me. Please . . ." Tears gathered in my eyes as I'd pleaded. "Stop!"

He didn't.

I'd swallowed the lump in my throat as tears streamed down my face. I didn't protest anymore, knowing it was futile. I went limp against the counter, paralyzed with a foreboding sense that this was just the beginning of a different life than the one I thought I was living.

"That's a good wife. Very good wife . . ."

For a second I believed maybe that was what a good wife did.

Michael

My mom ruins everything.

She's making it all about her on my friend's special day, and I want to shake her. Yell at her to wake up. I don't know what's wrong with her, and I don't care. I just wish she could be normal.

She's passed out on the Caseys' kitchen floor, and everyone is fussing over her. I won't get to come over here again.

"Grab a cold towel," Amelia's uncle tells his mom, lifting Mom's head and placing it on his lap.

I won't get to play on the bouncy castles or in the pool. I won't get cake or sing "Happy Birthday." Jack hasn't even opened the awesome Nerf gun we bought him. My pockets are full of candies from the cannon, but that's all I'll get.

When Mom wakes up, she's going to make me leave. Then Jack will have fun with all his other friends and not me.

She ruins everything.

"Is your mom sick?" Jack's mom asks.

"No." I'm not lying for her anymore. I'm always telling lies, and I don't want to lie to my friends.

A large bump is turning purple on her forehead, and Amelia's uncle puts an ice pack on it. "Has this happened before?" he asks.

I stare at my shoes. I'm always protecting her: being good so that she doesn't have to get upset and hiding things from her so that she doesn't have to worry so much.

And she can't let me have fun for one day.

Catherine

Adam painted over my words. My demands for my voice. Words begging him to work faster, work harder, are now no longer visible beneath a dark-blue paint. The same paint in the nursery down the hall.

One that remains unoccupied.

Where my blood still stains the floor.

No one ever goes in there. Adam has locked the door and left everything the way it was, as though preserving the scene of the crime can help freeze the ticking clock, make the days, hours, minutes pass slower . . .

I stare at him as he begs me for more time. "Darling, we're getting closer. I was at the lab last week. The scientists at the Vocal Reconstruction Center are so close." He takes my hands in his and squeezes tight. "The injections are in the testing phase."

Injections of a highly elastic gel that promise to give me back my ability to speak, to someday perform on stage again. He says a voice box will make me sound like a robot. He wants better for me. My patience is growing thin these days. I feel my body turning against me. Undiagnosed, untreated illnesses causing my muscles to seize, my bones to ache, and my skin to itch and flake.

I point to my chest. *I want to be the test subject!*

Adam shakes his head. "It's too dangerous."

I yank my hands away and glare at him. Too dangerous for me? Or for him? He says this room is the safest place for me until Drew is found and convicted of her sins.

I'm starting to not give a fuck about Drew.

Once I can speak, once I'm free, I can tell the world what she's done. We can find her together and make sure she suffers as much as I have—rotting away in a cell, with no comforts like I've had.

I force a breath, knowing my impatience is unfair. He's lost everyone in the world dear to him—his parents; Mariella, the woman who raised him; and his son—and I know he doesn't want to lose me too.

"Darling, you need to be patient—just a little longer." Adam wraps his arms around me, and I fall against his solid chest, craving the comfort. The starched, stiff fabric of his dress shirt is like sharp nails against my flesh, but I welcome it as punishment for my annoyance with him. He smooths my hair and whispers promises. "I can take care of you. Make you whole again."

I believe him. I trust him. But with each passing day, my confidence in him is fading.

Which makes me a monster. How can I demand more from him? He is the reason I'm alive, the reason I have this life. My impatience is selfish. I'm a horrible person to want more, to have thoughts about leaving him.

I could never leave him. I love him. His love is the only thing I have. It's enough. More than enough.

All of this is Drew's fault, not Adam's. Anger weaves through my veins, and I want to hurt her for ruining the life I was promised with Adam. For taking away my future . . . our future.

"Please, trust me. Don't give up hope just yet," he pleads.

He grovels with me. I don't understand it. Rich, powerful, successful, he can have anything he wants. He doesn't have to put up with my bullshit. He allows me to push him, demand things from him, break him with my disappointment.

I'm not sure why I have that power.

Drew

"How long did the blackout last?" Dr. Collins asks.

"Just a few minutes." Long enough to have everyone's attention on me. It was the first one in so long I'd thought maybe I was getting better. It couldn't have happened at a worse time. Embarrassed, I'd blamed my blackout on low blood sugar, and as soon as everyone quit fussing and Jolie forced me to eat a Rice Krispies square, we'd left. Parker had offered us a ride home, but waking up with my head on his lap had been enough to want to put as much distance between me and that man as possible. Something in his expression had unnerved me. As though he knew what he'd witnessed. Few people recognized dissociation from complex trauma disorder. But Parker had.

That made him dangerous.

"Did something happen to trigger it?" Dr. Collins appears engaged for real for the first time. He leans forward and rests his elbows against his knees. His green eyes shine with a warped sense of intrigue. Broken brains are his passion.

I wonder if he knows he's wearing odd socks. "There was just a lot of people. I don't do well in social situations." Over the years, I've studied my condition, trying to make sense of my limitations, my inability to connect with others, my catastrophizing of events . . . My symptoms are similar to those with PTSD—my past experiences having rewired my brain to process everything as a possible threat to my safety . . . and Michael's. A defense mechanism that essentially blocks out the world—both the bad and the good.

Not that I believe good exists anymore. I thought I was a good person . . . and look what I've done.

"Did you do or say anything while you were out?"

I shake my head. The socks aren't even close to being alike. One plain black. The other red and orange striped. Were they rolled together in a drawer that way? Or did he just grab two loose socks? I picture his underwear drawer a chaotic, disorganized mess. My gaze lands on the file cabinets—were they a mess too, or were those files in order?

"How did Michael react?"

"He was disappointed that we had to leave the party." He's still upset, even though he says he isn't. I couldn't possibly feel worse. I need to make this up to him somehow, but the prickly hairs standing up on the back of my neck tell me my son has added this to the list of disappointments I've caused him.

"Why did you have to leave?"

"Should I have stayed?"

"There's no right or wrong answer. I'm just wondering why you felt you couldn't stay. If you're going to make connections in town, you'll have to open up. You need to trust that people will accept you."

"Do you have friends in town?" In the month we've been here, I've never seen him around. His house is outside of town, with just a few neighbors on either side.

"I'm an old man. You're still young. Have you ever thought about a new relationship?"

"No." Since Adam, Parker's the only man to ask me out. Until Liberty, I couldn't remember the last time I'd even had a conversation with one.

"Maybe it's time to move on."

Move on. Impossible until I can clear my name and prove that Adam is a monster. Which is what I need his help with. Dr. Collins believes I'm here to help conquer my past demons . . . and in a way I am. As Adam's former child therapist, he is the only person who could know the truth about the man I married, the only one with an inside look into Adam's psyche . . . but there's no way for me to bring it up without setting off alarm bells about who I really am. I can't trust that he will keep my secret. I'm not sure what I was expecting, but these sessions are going nowhere fast. I need to find old files or notes that he may have kept over the years . . . and knowing more about Dr. Collins might give me the leverage I'll need to access them. "Can I use your washroom?"

He checks his watch, and I think he might actually suggest I hold it until I get home. "Sure. Down the hall. Third door on the left."

"Thank you." I slip out of the office and walk down the hall. All the doors are closed. I slowly, noiselessly turn the handle on the first one.

Please don't creak.

I push the door open and glance inside. It's the doctor's bedroom. His ugly sweater collection hangs in the open closet, and his leather slippers sit next to the unmade bed. There's nothing else in the room, other than a small dresser near the window.

The next room had to have been his mother's. A handmade quilt on the bed matches the curtains hanging in the window. Two large mahogany dressers stand on opposite walls, and the tops are covered with collectible figurines. Angels. Cherubs. All shapes and sizes. Angelic-looking painted-on faces. A big picture of Jesus hangs above the bed.

It's a wonder the doctor was ever born. Who could have sex with Jesus staring at them?

But what sends a ripple down my spine are the mirrors covered with black plastic.

"Drew?"

I pull the door shut quickly. "Sorry, second door on the left?"

"Third." Dr. Collins's stare is hard as he stands in the hall and watches as I go inside the bathroom.

I lock the door and lean against the sink, count to thirty, flush the toilet, run the taps for another fifteen seconds, then open the door. I jump back as I nearly collide with him. A shaky-sounding laugh escapes from deep in my throat. "You scared me."

He's collected my sweater and purse. "I think we're done for today."

I nod. I'm not going to find what I'm looking for while he's home anyway.

OCTOBER

Drew

Billionaire donates $3.6 million to medical research.

The online news article goes on to sing Adam's praises, and my jaw grows tighter the longer I read. Bile rises in the back of my throat as I stare at his picture on the library computer screen. He hasn't aged—his dark-brown hair doesn't have a single gray strand, and the few lines around his eyes only enhance his looks. His relaxed, easygoing demeanor and charming-as-a-snake smile tempt me to throw the computer monitor across the library.

Why would he look haggard or stressed? He has wealth and power and everything he could ever want. He's not looking over his shoulder or running from the law. He's not plagued with fear. He is living the life he wanted for himself—his company growing every year, his success rising.

I'll never again have the things I wanted for myself. Success is now defined by my ability to stay hidden. He took everything from me.

I need to stop checking up on him. I tell myself it's better to know where he is and what he's doing than not, and I'm searching for anything . . . the littlest thing I can use to prove that Adam is the real monster.

Of course Adam's too smart to ever slip up, to make a mistake . . . had he revealed himself to Dr. Collins as a child?

It's torture being one of the only people on the planet who knows who he really is. The others who do are too terrified to speak out. No one would believe them. Like no one believed me.

Some are in Adam's pockets so deep they could never find their way out. They aren't looking for an exit. They enjoy the benefits of entrapment too much. Their families are taken care of. Their stomachs and bank accounts are full, and no one knows what they have to do to keep their lives that way.

I do, and I need to find a way to prove it. It's the only way I can stop running, the only chance Michael and I have at a real future.

I stare at the dark-colored eyes—Michael's eyes—and even I can't find a trace of malice or hatred in them. Over the years, I've actually come to the conclusion that Adam might actually be two very different people. The one the world sees and the one only a few of us know. Ones who find ourselves on his wrong side.

Growing up, one of my father's favorite movies was *Dr. Jekyll and Mr. Hyde*.

It always terrified me.

The ability to change from good to evil. The presence of both so deep seated in the soul. I wondered if my father could see himself in that character. If he was somehow comforted by the knowledge that there were others out there like him. And like Adam.

Or if he didn't even recognize his own behavior when he saw it.

A timed-out image appears on the screen, and I glance toward the aisle several feet away where Michael is looking for books about porcupines for his school assignment. He's sitting on the floor, a stack of books next to him.

Standing, I log off the computer and push the chair back in. "Finding anything interesting?" I ask as I sit on the floor next to him.

"Do you know that porcupines can feel their predators stalking them? They know they are being followed and watched."

There's a coolness in his voice, and I rub my arms when goose bumps surface. "I didn't."

"And right at the last minute, before they are attacked and eaten, their quills spring up to ward off their attacker . . . pretty cool, huh?"

As long as the quills spring up in time.

◆ ◆ ◆

As the weather turns cooler, I move my painting out onto the back deck. The early-October breeze blows a few strands of hair across my face, and I tuck them behind an ear as I study the canvas on the easel. The vibrant orange and yellow of the changing leaves had inspired the image of a forest on fire. Twisted trunks hold the abstract images of unreadable faces, and I try to figure out what it means.

I used to paint to tell stories, to convey emotion and thoughts, my views of the world. Now my painting reveals all the things I don't know. Each one has a hidden story that I'm not privy to. A part of my subconscious is freeing itself of its burdens, forcing my conscious mind to wander along in a state of madness, not understanding.

I sigh as I pick up the canvas and place it on the deck to dry. As I reach for a blank one, a noise on the side of the house makes my pulse jitter. I'd closed and locked the gate, but now it swings open—the loud, slow creaking of an ungreased hinge shoots fear straight to my chest. I scan my supplies as the creaking sound grows faster, followed by a loud thud of the door hitting the gate.

The spade at the end of a paint smearer is hardly an adequate weapon, but it's the best of the available options. With an eye on the corner of the house, I back toward the kitchen door. I reach for the handle behind me and then go inside and bolt it, peering out the small window. There's no one in the backyard. They still lurk on the side of the house.

Keeping an eye on the door, I back toward the drawer and grab a knife. Two knives.

I scan the inside of the house and move cautiously into the living room. My feet are silent as I creep along, but my thundering heart could give my presence away. I pause at the bottom of the stairs. I listen, but I don't hear anyone, and the front door is still bolted.

Inside the house, I'm trapped, and calling the police is out of the question, so, knives gripped tightly in my hands, I go back outside through the front door. I slowly descend the three steps and stop to peer around the corner of the house toward the back gate.

Why hasn't my heart forced its way through my chest? My veins are about to explode as the blood rushes through them.

The intruder is in my backyard.

I should run. Get in the car, pick up Michael, and keep driving. Someone has found us. But the desire to end all this running is strong, and I can't feel my legs as they propel me forward toward the gate.

I listen for the sound of footsteps on the back deck, the sound of the back-door handle turning, the rustling of feet in the grass . . .

Nothing.

They are waiting in silence for me. Hiding behind the gate.

I move closer, stepping over a graveyard of daddy longlegs, their limbs all yanked off—an unmerciful kill.

All little boys kill bugs.

Right now, I'm prepared to do far worse. I have done worse. I hold my breath as my hand reaches for the fence.

It swings open again on its own, and I flatten myself back against the side of the house, hiding behind it as it opens, knife handles clenched tightly as I prepare to swing.

But as the gate creaks closed, at my feet is a tiny kitten. My attacker—a tiny gray ball of fluff—has nearly given me a heart attack. I sink along the wall, bending my knees and resting my head against them. Several deep breaths in and out as I let the knives fall to the ground beside me.

The kitten is brushing against my legs, a tiny purring sound escaping the soft little body. I reach for it, and it backs away but then moves toward me slowly. "It's okay. You nearly killed me, but it's okay."

I pick it up, assess that it's a male, and bring him into my chest. Purring vibrates against my body—warm and soft and reassuringly calm. "Where did you come from?" I ask, petting his matted fur. Gray and black with white stripes like a tiger and beautiful big green eyes. I can feel his ribs protrude as I stroke along his side. "Hungry, little guy?"

A tiny meow answers my question. I collect the knives in one hand, then stand up and carry him inside. I pour some milk into a bowl and place it on the floor. He rushes to it, lapping it up with a tiny pink tongue.

I stare at him. What the hell do I do with him? I have no idea who owns him. I can't keep him. If Michael sees him, he'll want to. I bite my lip as he finishes the milk and turns to me, meowing for more.

I scoop him up into my arms. "I can't give you more right now, or you'll be sick," I say, petting him.

I glance outside, but no one seems to be looking for him. I suppose I'll have to make a "Found Kitten" poster . . . attracting more people to us.

I hear a car in the driveway and look outside, expecting it to be the kitten's owner, but it's Jolie's minivan. She cuts the engine and climbs out.

I wasn't expecting them so soon. My hands are covered in paint, and the paintings I'd been working on are still out on the back deck. I hurry to the front door as I see her open the back minivan door, and Michael climbs out. Jolie had offered to take the kids to the latest animated movie, now showing at the cinema in town, and I was running out of excuses to avoid a playdate. I was also realizing that Michael was safer when he wasn't with me. He was better protected within the walls of the school or with Jolie and her family—places Adam couldn't find him as easily . . .

"How was the movie?"

"Oh my God—a kitten!" Michael exclaims as he runs toward me. He takes the kitten and snuggles it. "Is he mine?"

"No. Did you have fun?"

"The movie was okay . . . can I keep him? Have you named him yet?" Michael asks, petting the kitten, who is struggling to escape his arms. He lets out a tiny hiss and nips at Michael's hand.

"I just found him in the yard. Take him inside; we will talk about it later," I tell him. Turning to Jolie, I say, "Thank you for taking him this afternoon. I hope he wasn't any trouble."

"None at all. Are you okay? You look a little pale."

Since the party, I've noticed her giving me odd, concerned looks that I hate. Like she's wondering if I can be trusted alone with a child. "I'm fine."

"Okay . . . well, see you Monday," she says, heading back toward the minivan.

"Yeah."

Jolie opens the door and climbs into the minivan. She points toward the window, where Michael is dancing with the kitten in his arms, twirling in a circle with it overhead. The kitten's going to throw up the milk it just gobbled up any second. "Looks like you have a new pet."

Shit.

"Mom, did you ask her?" I hear Jack ask from the back seat of the minivan.

"No. Michael can ask her."

What now?

"Michael's afraid to ask her," Jack says.

Jolie sends me a look. "Sorry . . . Jack just invited Michael over for a sleepover next weekend. I told them it's fine with me, but Michael has to check with you."

A sleepover? He was ready for that? I wasn't. It would be so fantastic if Jolie could talk these things over with me first so that I'm not always the bad guy, saying no.

"I told Jack not to invite him until I'd checked with you." She shoots a glare into the back seat.

"What did she say?" Jacks asks, oblivious to the look.

Jolie looks at me.

Inside, Michael's swooning over a kitten I have no intention of letting him keep. At least agreeing to the sleepover might soften the blow a little. "Sure. Saturday night?"

She smiles and looks surprised. "Yes. Great."

"Thanks again for bringing Michael home." I turn to head back inside, preparing for an argument over the kitten, but my heart beats louder as shimmering metal catches my eye in the flower bed, under the living room window. I wait for Jolie to pull out of the driveway, waving to her as she drives away; then I pick up the broken lock that used to be on my back gate.

My hand trembles at the realization that the kitten wasn't the first visitor to our yard.

◆　◆　◆

The following weekend, the kitten squirms on my lap as I stare through the windshield at Jolie's house down the street.

"Do not pee on me. We'll just stay a little longer." It's after eight, and I haven't heard from Michael yet. I'm sure he is busy having fun and that I'm the last thing on his mind, but I'd told him he'd have to check in a few times during the evening. Jolie didn't answer her cell when I called a few minutes ago either . . . or when I tried an hour ago.

I'm just here for peace of mind. It's not like I'm going to go to the front door and drag him out of his sleepover.

Both vehicles are parked in the driveway, and the lights are on inside the house.

Maybe I could say he forgot to pack something . . . but, looking around the car, I don't have anything I could casually drop off for him.

I try Jolie again, and the call goes straight to voice mail.

This is crazy. If you're going to take someone's kid, at least have the decency to answer your phone. Sleepovers won't be happening again. This one shouldn't be happening. Air constricts in my chest.

John is the town's sheriff. What the hell was I thinking letting Michael stay at his house? What if he says something? What if he tells them something about us?

A tap on the window makes me jump. I clutch the kitten tighter. His claws spring out, poking through the fabric of my sweater.

Parker.

"Hi," he says through the glass.

Great. I've been busted spying on my kid.

I force my heart rate to settle as I untangle the kitten's claws and roll down the window. He tries to make a jump for it, and I grip him tighter. "This isn't what it looks like."

"You're *not* stalking me?" He points to the house I'm parked in front of.

"That's your house?"

"Yep."

I owe him an explanation, and I can only hope it won't sound too crazy. "Michael's at a sleepover at Jolie's." My gaze wanders back toward the Casey house. "He's never slept away from home before."

"He's in good hands with Jolie. She will let him stay up late and eat all the junk food his little hands can shove into his face."

"That's not helpful," I say, but it actually does ease some of the tension from my shoulders. Jolie is the perfect mother. I've seen the way she is with her kids. Michael *is* in good hands there. With her.

"I'm kidding," Parker says. "He's lucky to get ranch dressing to dip a celery stick in over there."

I nod. "I know he's fine, but Jolie wasn't answering, and he was supposed to call . . ." Do I sound concerned or crazy? Do I even care anymore?

"Hey, why don't you come in?"

"No." I start the car. I'll try calling again when I get home.

"Why not? You clearly want to stay close in case Michael needs you—I get it. Amelia's over there too, having a sleepover with Ellie and Lila. Just come in until you're feeling okay about it," Parker says.

Being close would make me feel better, but going inside his house is not a good idea. Giving Parker any false hope that I'll reconsider his offer for dinner wouldn't be smart.

But if I go home, I'll pace the entire house, playing all the terrible, unlikely scenarios over and over in my mind.

I turn off the car.

He smiles and nods at the kitten as I climb out. "No luck with the posters, huh?"

"I don't think Michael tried very hard."

"So, you're keeping . . . what's its name?"

"Naming it means keeping it, and I'm not quite there yet."

"The kitten might have made that decision for you," he says as he opens a door that leads into a kitchen and holds it for me to go inside first.

"Would you like a drink?" Opening the fridge, he grabs a beer and offers me one.

I shake my head, my attention caught by Parker's taste in art. "These artists have destroyed famous works." The *Mona Lisa* with the zombified face has to be the worst among the offensive pieces decorating the wall on top of faded, dated wallpaper. Though, admittedly, the skill required to pull it off is impressive.

"I wouldn't exactly call them artists—just one talented asshole," he says. "My sister, Charlee."

"Your sister painted these?"

"She did. She was a fine arts major in college . . . before she decided to join the military."

My gaze is on the reimagining of Picasso's *Night Sky*. Instead of stars, Charlee had painted sperm flying through the darkness. "She's really talented, even if these are an insult to the originals."

"Was."

"What?"

"She was talented. She died in a car bomb attack overseas last year."

"I had no idea. I'm sorry," I mutter. "So, Amelia . . ."

"I'm her legal guardian." He takes a gulp of his beer. "So, you *are* interested in art?"

"I used to be."

"That sounds suspicious."

"A thing of the past, that's all." My giving up art school for Adam hadn't been as hard as I thought it would, and at the time I'd believed it was because I loved him so much.

My mother had a different opinion.

"Don't go out with him," she'd begged the night of the Roq La Rue showing as I'd gotten dressed.

"It's not a date, Mom." I'd stared through the mirror at her standing in the bedroom doorway, a glass filled with ice and vodka in her hand. She'd been carrying the same glass around all day, refilling it whenever it emptied. Her badly applied concealer and layers of foundation gave her black eyes a muddy, greenish tint. I focused on my own face.

One my father never dared to damage.

"Darling, Adam is not the right one for you."

I sighed, holding back what I thought about her relationship advice. She and my father slept in different rooms, and she used alcohol to deal with my father's demons. "I'm going to an art showing, that's all." I'd stood and left the room, but she'd followed.

"Drew, you really don't know anything about this man."

Actually, Google had revealed all.

An only child raised by his nanny, Adam had shown signs of genius from an early age, graduating high school at fifteen. He'd inherited C2 Technologies at age twenty, when his parents died in a tragic accident. He'd taken the company from a million-dollar-a-year investment to a billion-dollar entity in less than a year. He'd been named on *Forbes*'s 30 Under 30 every year since. Despite personal tragedy, he was a professional success. He'd bought my father's law firm two years before.

"I know enough, Mom. I'll be fine," I'd said.

"Drew . . ." She'd grabbed my arm, but I'd pulled away. "I'm worried about you."

I'd stiffened. "You're worried about me?" Had she seen her face? How could she continue living this way? How could she have lived this way for so long?

Over the years, I'd begged and pleaded for my mother to leave him. For us both to leave him. She'd slap me and tell me to mind my own business.

"Yes, Drew, I'm worried."

"Well, I'm fine now. I'm an adult now."

"Drew, what happened . . ."

I paused. Was she finally going to admit to the abuse that she'd tried to deny and hide all these years? Tell me I was right? Explain why she stayed and put up with this bullshit?

"Everyone makes mistakes."

I didn't know if it was a small admission of guilt for not doing what was right all these years or if, once again, she was making excuses for my father.

As I walked into the gallery with Adam an hour later, it was a challenge to shake off the pleading look she'd sent my way as I'd left the house. But I forced it aside as I focused on the main reason I was home.

"I can't believe you were able to get tickets for this event." Though, knowing then who Adam was and that he practically owned Seattle, it shouldn't have surprised me. But that evening, standing in the Roq La Rue surrounded by fifty of Seattle's most influential, felt surreal.

I'd spent a lot of time around people like this—the rich and elegant. Damn, I'd tried my hardest not to become one of them, but I was having trouble keeping up my disdain for the wealthy. I was a hypocrite for doing it anyway, so I relaxed and enjoyed the atmosphere. Not easy to do when my date was a multibillionaire. One my mother claimed I should stay away from.

But Adam was nothing like my father. I avoided men like my father. I would have seen those traits in Adam. Recognized the desire to hurt.

"It wasn't easy," Adam had said, taking a champagne flute from the waiter's tray and handing it to me.

"You don't drink champagne?" I'd asked, sipping it, eyeing him over the rim of the glass. He could almost steal my focus and attention from the exquisite art, in his dark suit and light-blue dress shirt, opened at the top to give a glimpse of a thick, solid neck that led into a muscular build.

"I don't drink at all," he'd said.

"Never?"

"I like to remain in control."

The look he'd sent me should have had me running. I hadn't had a real relationship—my lack of trust in people being deep rooted. I'd had a few casual dates over the years, but the moment someone got too close, I'd pull away. That night, I'd moved a little closer as we made our way beyond the lobby into the showing area.

My hand trembled slightly on the flute, and I clutched it so hard for fear of dropping it that I risked smashing the glass into my palm. On the walls in front of me hung the new, exclusive, final collection of an artist I'd tried to emulate for years. "I don't even know where to start."

Adam's hand was on my lower back, guiding me to the left. "I believe the 'Artist Journey' begins this way."

"Artist Journey?"

He lowered his head. "It was on the sign in the lobby."

"Oh." I'd been too preoccupied with him to notice.

Stay focused on the work. This is not a date.

"Do you see one you like?" Adam asked as we perused the collection.

"One? How about all of them?"

Adam's laugh was deep and rich, and my knees weakened. Everything about him was magnetic. His passion, his dedication to success, his ambition—all things I usually found off putting were drawing me to him.

"I'm glad you agreed to join me tonight," he'd said. "I don't think anyone else I could have asked would be enjoying this as much."

No doubt he'd had a little black book full of women, and the mix of jealousy and pleasure that I was the chosen one surprised me. "Thank you again for inviting me." I scanned the eclectic selection of red-and-orange hues on the wall in front of me. "It saddens me that this collection will be broken up. They tell a story together." But it would take a multimillionaire to afford to buy the entire collection.

"Tell me the story." Adam moved closer.

The scent of his cologne was subtle, but it filled my senses. The rich, confident smell could have been designed with Adam Crenshaw in mind. "Oh . . ."

"Come on, I'm fascinated," he said, his dark eyes burrowing into mine—a silent challenge.

I raised the glass of champagne to my lips, my mouth suddenly parched, but just a drop trickled out onto my tongue. I lowered the glass just as Adam reached for another and replaced it with the empty one in my hand. "Go on."

"Okay . . ." I took a deep breath and pointed to the first one on the wall—a scene of a burning building, the swirling smoke rising from it spiraling in the shape of abstract dollar signs. "The entire collection is a commentary on capitalism. It begins with the destruction of power, as is suggested in the crumbling of the building . . ." I moved farther right, gesturing to the next painting—a mother sitting on the ground outside a slum apartment, her baby sucking on her exposed, bruised breast. "This shows the contrast between the developed world and the poor. The ever-increasing gap between economic growth and individual poverty . . ." I paused. Talking about art with my friends in New York had never felt this intimate.

"Please continue," he said, his eyes not on the canvases but on me while I spoke.

"You need to look at the paintings."

He smiled. "Sorry—you're distracting when your passion shines through," he said, but his gaze shifted to the next painting, leaving me to soak in his compliment in private.

I quickly learned he was good at that. The moving forward, then backing off, that only made me fall harder, faster.

J. M. Winchester

Two days after the showing, Adam was on the front page of the daily newspaper.

> Multibillionaire Adam Crenshaw buys entire Walter Bax collection to donate to the Seattle Museum of Art.

My eyes couldn't read fast enough.

> Five million dollars . . . the collection will be moved once the exhibit at Roq La Rue ends.

But it was why he'd bought them that had me dazed.

A good friend insisted that these works tell a story and they belong together . . .

"Good morning, darling."

My mother's voice that early had surprised me. She was not a morning person, but that day she was already dressed in her tennis gear. Her injuries sufficiently healed to return to the country club.

"Early lesson today?" I hid the newspaper.

"Yes . . . do you have plans?" Her usual soprano voice was scratchy that morning, as though she were coming down with a cold.

"No . . . I thought I'd paint." Since the showing, I'd been itching to get to the canvas. Inspiration had been all around me those past few days, competing with thoughts of Adam.

No one had intrigued me this way before. Or provided a deep sense of inspiration. I had been drawn to the complexity of him. The inner struggle I imagined he faced, taking over his parents' company at such a young age, after their untimely deaths. I had been so taken with him that I was seeing things that weren't really there.

"That's wonderful." She added a shot of brandy to her mug, and I frowned. It was a little early, even for her.

"Everything okay, Mom?"

90

She nodded toward the paper. "Be careful, okay, sweetheart."

"I will, Mom. It's nothing."

"He bought an art collection for you."

"It's not for me. It's for the museum of art."

"It was for you, darling."

The words had the opposite effect of her intent, warming me through my very core. Of course Adam was a billionaire—he could afford big gestures like this—but it had meant something to me. He hadn't bought them for himself or, worse, to impress me, and that made my soul scream with approval.

She kissed my head. "You've always been turned off by things that shine too brightly . . . trust your instincts, sweetheart," she said, and I could smell alcohol on her breath already, so I dismissed her credibility on the subject of my life.

"Where are you and Michael from exactly?" Parker asks, bringing me back to the moment.

I shake off the cobwebs of the past. "Here and there. My family used to be in Seattle."

"Used to be?"

"Dead."

The solitary word is void of the usual emotion associated with death, but I don't know how to fake emotions I no longer feel. "Is that her—your sister?" I ask, pointing to the picture of a woman in her air force uniform hanging on the wall.

"Yes. That was Charlee's graduation picture from sniper school."

"I didn't know the US military allowed female snipers."

"They don't. Charlee was only the eleventh woman to pass her sniper training. The air force allows qualified women to train. Unfortunately, they still wouldn't put her out in battle."

And yet she'd died anyway.

"Do you want to sit? In the window maybe?" Parker asks.

I let out a slow breath, petting the yet-to-be-named kitten sleeping in my arms. An effort to relax. I know my actions, my overprotectiveness, must be raising flags, but I don't know how else to live. We've survived this long because of my inability to let my guard down, my lack of trust. "I know it must look strange, the way I am with Michael; it's just . . ."

"Drew, you don't need to explain. It's okay. I get it."

"You do?"

"I do. Parents protect their children at all costs." His softened, understanding expression makes my nerves tingle. "The good ones anyway."

The good ones. "Um . . . I should get going. I'm sure Michael's fine."

Parker follows me as I head toward the door. "What's happening here? Did I say something wrong?"

"No. Nothing. I just have to go." Coming in had been a mistake. Getting close to him or anyone in town is not the right thing to do. Michael and I need to remain ghosts in the towns we pass through—insignificant background shadows on the daily lives of the people around us.

The connections we've already made in Liberty could be our downfall.

◆ ◆ ◆

I'm in a dark room. I hear Michael calling out to me, but I can't find a door to get out. There are no windows. No way to escape. His screams get louder and more desperate. I bang on the walls and call out to him, but my voice is drowned by the sound of a gunshot. Blood bleeds from holes in the walls, filling the room, continuing to rise until I'm drowning in it. I'm sinking lower. Dying.

I can hear Michael calling to me, but I can't save him. I can't save myself.

A low hissing wakes me from my unsettling sleep. It's pitch black outside. The last thing I remember seeing was dusk.

My bedside lamp is off, and the room is enveloped in darkness. My eyes take a moment to adjust enough to see the kitten sitting on the edge of the bed. His back is stiff, his ears are down, and his tail is thick, standing straight up. The hissing continues as he stares toward the corner of the room.

My gaze follows, and I blink several times before a dark shadow crosses the corner.

My heart stops.

My hand finds the knife, and I toss back the covers. I scan the room, but the shadow is once again concealed in blackness. The kitten comes to stand next to me, and his yellow-green eyes glow in the dark. An eerie feeling wraps around me, one of being watched, of being in the presence of danger.

"Hello?" I stand up and edge toward the door.

The kitten turns quickly on the bed and lets out another hiss. This time toward the window.

A figure passes in front of the glass, illuminated by the moonlight.

I drop the knife, narrowly missing my toes, and let out a yelp as I stumble backward, closer to the door. Someone is outside. Someone might be in my room.

My hand fumbles for the light switch, and chills run up and down my spine. My nerve endings are tingling, and my pulse is sprinting.

The shadow is gone.

I blink, but there's nothing there.

Like always. No sign of an intruder; just the prickling sensation creeping up the back of my neck.

I bend slowly to pick up the knife, and the atmosphere in the room makes me tremble. I don't believe in ghosts. So either someone was there, or I'm losing my mind.

I force a breath. I refuse to believe it's all just paranoia. I know what I saw.

The kitten is rubbing against my legs.

I pick him up and seek comfort in the soft, tiny bundle. He'd sensed the presence of something in the room too. I'm not crazy. At least not about this.

"You saw the shadow too, right?"

He purrs against me, and I slowly walk back toward the bed. I refuse to look at the window. I pet the kitten, and in that moment I name him. "Good kitty, Shadow." Slowly, my heart rate returns to normal, and the haunting atmosphere in the room disappears. Shadow's tiny eyes close, and mine feel heavy.

The silence-shattering sound of my cell phone ringing has both of us leaping off the bed. I drop the kitten, my hands flying to my heaving chest. "Jesus."

It's Jolie. "Hello?"

"Hi, Drew, I hope I didn't wake you."

She doesn't sound panicked, so I keep my voice steady, my concern light. "Everything okay?"

"Oh, everything's fine. Michael's just missing you, I think."

"Does he want me to come get him?" I'm still fully dressed, and I'm already heading down the stairs.

"You're probably settled for the evening. I'll get John to bring him home."

It will sound odd if I insist on driving back toward the other end of town, so I say, "Okay, thank you."

I wait in the living room and get up to answer the door once John's headlights stream in through the open curtains. He climbs out with a wave. He's wearing pajama pants and a sweatshirt with the sheriff department's logo on it.

I haven't forgotten how close to danger I am, but seeing the logo has my body twitching. Though, in that moment, I'm almost tempted to ask him to search the perimeter of my house . . . it's only fear of what he might uncover that keeps me from asking.

He opens the back sliding door of the minivan and lifts Michael out.

I wrap my cardigan tighter around my own body as he comes up the walk. My sleeping little boy looking weightless in his arms.

"Hi. He fell asleep the minute we left the house," he whispers, coming inside.

"Thank you for bringing him home," I say. "He's never done a sleepover before. I was fairly certain this might happen."

He nods. "Where's his bedroom? I'll carry him in for you."

I hesitate, not liking this man in our home, in our space, yet feeling a little better that he's here.

He's a friendly neighbor. A husband and a father.

A law enforcement officer. Can he sense my guilt? Smell my crimes?

"Just upstairs—the first door on the left," I say and follow him up. Once Michael's on his bed, I see John out. "Thanks again."

"No problem. Listen, is Michael trying out for any of the school or community sports teams this year?"

"I don't know." Another way to tie ourselves to this place is not something I'm eager to pursue, but Michael is more vocal these days in his own desires, so I doubt the decision will be mine.

"He was playing street hockey with the neighborhood kids in the cul-de-sac tonight, and he was incredible with the stick. Says he's never played before, but I think if he can learn to skate as quickly as he learned to navigate around with the ball, he'd make the boys' Junior League team this year. Jack tries out each year."

I nod, my gut tightening. It shouldn't surprise me that Michael's talented in sports without ever really having played . . . he's built like Adam—solid and strong for his age. So much like his father already.

"If he wants to . . . no pressure," John adds.

"Yeah, no, thank you. I'll be sure to talk to him about it."

"Okay. Well, good night."

I wave and close the door. After locking the dead bolts, I slide the chain across and go upstairs to Michael's room.

He stirs as I pull back the comforter and place it over him. "Hi, Mom."

"Hi, sweetie. Did you have fun?"

He nods sleepily, reaching for my hand. "I thought maybe you might be lonely here by yourself."

I pull the blanket back and climb in next to my thoughtful, caring, sweet boy and realize I'm wrong.

Michael is nothing at all like Adam.

"Hey, Mom?"

"Yeah?"

"Who was that man?"

My blood chills. "What man?" I'm already scanning his dimly lit bedroom, but all I see is Shadow sitting in the hallway outside the bedroom door.

"The one standing on the side of the house. He ran away when we pulled up."

I swallow hard, wrapping my arms tighter around him. "What did he look like?"

He murmurs something unintelligible, and I know he's drifting off.

I lie awake. Ears tuned for any sound of danger. Knowing, in our half-asleep states, that my little boy, the kitten, and I couldn't possibly all have imagined a person watching us.

Drew

We need to leave Liberty, but I'm not sure how without raising suspicion. Of all the friends Michael could have made here, his connection to the sheriff's son is already making things more complicated. If I leave town with Michael now, without a word to anyone, would John attempt to locate us or alert other authorities?

Our missing person files have been cold cases for years. Risking new investigations is something I need to avoid.

And, with each passing day with no further incidents, it's easier to convince myself that the broken lock was nothing and that the person lurking around our home was just a random intruder—one scared off by John's presence the other night who won't be returning.

If it had been Adam, if he'd found us, then he would have returned. I'd be in jail by now . . . or worse.

I've left three messages for Dr. Collins, hoping to schedule another session, but he hasn't returned my calls. So, I drive to his house.

I stare through the frantic windshield wipers toward the dark house, looking for any sign that he's home. Wind rattles the old windows of my car, and the howling sounds like ghosts. I glance in the rearview mirror and shiver at the sight of the heavy thunderclouds moving in over the woodsy area across the street, threatening to give way to a full storm.

This neighborhood with its old, decrepit homes is unsettling.

I get out and hurry through the rain to the front door, my foot slipping on the wet, peeling, decaying top step. I ring the doorbell and hear it chime inside the house. I scan the interior of the house through the frosted windowpane on the side of the door, but I don't see him. I take my phone from my pocket and dial his number again.

The old landline phone rings inside, but no one answers. His archaic machine picks up, and I disconnect the call. He's never given me his cell phone number.

I knock. I wait. I don't see or hear him moving around inside.

I go around the side of his house and look in through the living room window. He's not there. I reach over the back gate and, opening the latch, I head into the overgrown backyard. I peer in through each of the bedroom windows, but I don't see him. His office is empty too.

I wait a few minutes longer, watching through the office window for movement, straining for any noise inside, but, other than the rain beating against the house, all is quiet.

He's not home.

The single-pane window in the old, rotting wood should have been replaced years ago, so wiggling it open is easy, and, two minutes later, I'm hoisting my body up onto the ledge and crawling inside. The house is dead silent.

I have to be quick. I need to find what I'm looking for before he comes home. He has to have kept files on his previous patients. He's written books that had to have been based on Adam—evil minds, babies born without a conscious, manifestations of abnormal desires . . . his books reference his studies from exactly the time he would have treated Adam, in the early eighties . . .

There had to be something. He'd never destroy the evidence for his theories.

As before, the desk drawers are locked, so I grab a paper clip and insert it into the hole. Seconds later I hear the turning of the lock. Adding breaking and entering to my newly acquired skills doesn't bother me. Since our first day on the run, survival has outweighed morality.

I yank the drawer open, and a small scream escapes me. The smell of the dead, decomposing mouse inside makes me gag. It's the only thing inside the drawer, and who knows how long he's been trapped there, buried in dust.

I close the drawer, holding my breath as I check the one below it. An abandoned spiderweb stretches across the empty space. The mouse's last meal before karma found him?

Shutting it, I scan the desk's surface. He has to keep the keys to the file cabinet somewhere. Maybe he carries them with him. Either way, there's nothing on the desk.

I take the paper clip and go to the cabinets, but, as I place a hand on top, the thing shifts away from the wall toward me. I move it back and forth, and a hollow rattling sound comes from within. Empty.

This makes no sense. Where are his notes from when he was practicing?

I approach the book shelves and scan for anything that looks like a binder, notebook . . . nothing. Just extra copies of his own books and other psychotherapy titles line the dusty shelves.

I open the boxes on the floor, but it's just more of his mother's junk.

There has to be something somewhere. Dr. Collins's obsession with the warped, twisted minds of psychopaths wouldn't allow him to just get rid of the evidence that supports his years of research.

A stack of envelopes on the table near his old chair catches my eye, but it's just a lot of bills . . . most marked *Final notice* or *Overdue*, confirming my suspicion that the doc isn't doing so great financially.

I open the office door and move into the hall. I'll search every room in this place if I have to.

Then the sight of his slippered feet sticking outside the bathroom door has my heart beating against my chest. He is home. Something's wrong.

My wet shoes squeak against the hardwood floor as I move slowly toward the bathroom. His feet don't move. He's not making a sound. He's lying facedown on the floor, empty pill bottles scattered all around him.

Jesus. How long has he been here like this? Is he already dead?

I strain to see if his back rises and falls . . . any sign of life. I glance toward the front door. My car is in the driveway. My fingerprints are all over his office, and there's no record of me being a patient of his. I'm not supposed to be here.

His motionless body starts to blur in my swimming vision.

I should get out of here. No one can know I was here.

But I can't leave him. On my knees, I struggle to roll his body over. Dried blood on the floor where his head hit increases my panic. If he overdosed, he could be dead, and I'll never get the answers I'm searching for. Could I somehow be under suspicion in his death? This time, I know I'm innocent, but who would believe me?

I check for a pulse at his neck and find one. Thank God. I shake him. "Dr. Collins. Can you hear me?" His body is limp.

I stand and turn on the taps. I grab the cup next to the sink that holds his toothbrush, fill it with cold water, and throw it at his face. "Wake up . . . please wake up."

He moans, and his head moves from side to side, but his eyes stay closed.

I throw more water. I slap him. I continue to shake.

Finally, his eyes open. He sees me, and fear registers in his groggy expression. "It's okay. You took too many pills," I say. Like three bottles too many. "I need to get you to a hospital." I can drop him off and leave.

He shakes his head, pushing me away. His eyes droop closed again.

"Dr. Collins, wake up. We need to get you some help."

"Get out," he mumbles, rolling to his side. He coughs, and a white milky substance drips from the corner of his mouth.

I move closer and lift his body beneath his underarms.

He tries to protest, wiggling to free himself from my hold, but he's too weak. "Leave me," he says.

"No. I can't do that. So either cooperate, or I'm calling an ambulance." An idle threat.

He pushes at me, but I don't budge. I lift him as high as I can and drape his body over the open toilet. "You need to vomit."

His head rolls to the side, and I slap him again.

"Go away," he says, slumping forward. His head hits the edge of the porcelain, causing the gash to start bleeding again.

"You need to get sick. Now." I grab his toothbrush and extend it to him. "Stick this down your throat."

He mumbles as his consciousness is stolen again.

I open his mouth and ram the toothbrush down. I don't know how long ago he took these pills, but it's the only chance of saving him without calling an ambulance. I can't do that.

The toothbrush does the trick, and he vomits. He's more alert now, and he grips the edge of the toilet, emptying his stomach's contents.

I look away, fighting the urge to get sick myself.

Five minutes later, I help him to his room. He lies on the bed and stares at me, as though trying to figure out who I am.

"Just rest," I say, grabbing a blanket and placing it over him. I'm desperate to get the hell out of there. He should be fine now. There's already a water glass beside the bed, and I'm not staying a second longer or leaving my prints anywhere else.

"Drew," he says weakly.

"Yes. Just rest. You'll be okay." I have to go. I'm hoping when he gains full consciousness, he'll forget I was ever here. I know I won't be mentioning this.

He grips my wrist with surprising strength. "My son is dead because of me."

"You need to rest, Dr. Collins. You're confused right now."

"No. It was my fault. He died nine years ago today."

Nine years ago . . . the same time I was living my nightmare. "How was it your fault?" If I can get him talking about his son in this drugged state, maybe I can ask him about Adam . . .

His eyes roll back, and his grip loosens on my arm.

"Dr. Collins, tell me about your son."

"My fault . . ."

"I don't believe that. I'm sure you must have tried to help him . . . like you've helped others over the years." I pause. "Other boys . . ."

"He's gone. My son's gone . . . nine years . . ." He drifts off, and I shake him gently.

"Dr. Collins . . . wake up." In this lucid state, I could ask him about Adam, and maybe he'd never even remember the conversation. "Dr. Collins."

Nothing. He's out. His body has gone limp, and I see only the whites of his eyes. Damn it!

I turn to leave, but his hand wraps around my wrist again. "Wait. How did you get in?" His half-open eyes are suspicious. His expression: not the least bit thankful I saved his life.

"The front door was unlocked," I say, removing his hand from my wrist.

He shakes his head, but his body sags limply against the bed. I hurry out of the room, but I hesitate and then go back to his office. I remove my wallet from my sweater pocket. I take out $500 and slide the money between the overdue bills, then leave through the open window.

Catherine

I fix my witch's hat on my head and lace up the knee-high boots. The costume is too big, but Adam found the smallest one they carried at Freaky Freddie's. The sound of the doorbell has me hurrying to the desk, where a television is set up so I can watch through the security camera as the kids come to the door.

It's barely dusk, but our first trick-or-treaters are a ninja and a ballerina. I touch the screen, wishing I could be the one filling their bags with the full-size chocolate bars Adam gives out. I can see him at the door now, talking to the kids. He's dressed as a vampire—his dark hair gelled back and fake blood dripping from the corners of his mouth. His cape is real velvet, and the tuxedo he wears beneath is the one he wore at his wedding to Drew. I was angry when I saw that he still had it, but he insisted it was nothing more than a Halloween costume now.

He won't be wearing it when we finally get married.

On-screen, the ninja does a spinning kick, and the ballerina does a twirl, her tutu circling around her.

I clap and cover my mouth as a silent sob wells in my chest. They look about eight or nine.

Dylan would be about that age. I wonder what he's dressed as for Halloween. I bet it's something brave, like a firefighter or police officer. He's strong like Adam. I could always tell he was strong. I wonder if he even gets to go trick-or-treating, or if that monster keeps him locked up, hidden away from the world.

Like Adam does to me.

I shake my head.

That's not the same. Dylan was abducted. *I'm* safe.

The door closes, and the kids hurry off toward their parents waiting at the end of our driveway. They wave to Adam, and the dad scoops up the little boy and hoists him over his shoulders as they walk down the street.

My heart breaks for Adam. He should have that with his son. He would make such a wonderful father.

It was on Halloween night that Adam first kissed me, after my last performance at the Seattle Opera. My contract was up, and I wasn't sure what was next for me. An understudy who'd gained only minor recognition filling in for Seattle's prima donna, I wasn't in high demand or being asked to stay on for future productions.

I was crying when Adam came to my dressing room. He said the overly harsh critics knew nothing, that I was as talented as I was beautiful. He'd touched my cheeks, brushing away the makeup-stained tears, and when his lips had touched mine, I'd given in to the kiss. I knew he was married, but he said his wife was mentally ill. He said he hadn't known about her psychosis before their marriage, and now ending things with her would be cruel.

He took me out a few times—dinner, the ballet . . . I fell for him. He told me he loved me, said he would help me with my career. He had contacts and money.

I was devastated three months later when he told me his wife was pregnant.

I'd been offered a position to perform that spring with the Atlanta Opera as an understudy for the principal female lead. But Adam had a different proposition. He wanted me to be his son's nanny. Come live here with him, raise his son with him. He promised a life much more fulfilling than traveling the world and rehearsing songs I'd only get a chance to perform if, by some miracle, the lead couldn't.

So, I'd said yes. It was the right decision. Drew could never have taken care of a child . . .

My chest tightens as more children run toward the front door.

I failed to take care of him too.

Drew

I've always hated Halloween. I used to love the fall harvest and the changing of the seasons. Gold, orange, and deep-purple leaves turning the countryside into a vibrant oasis. Cooler days offering a reprieve from the smoldering heat of summer and the anticipation of cold winter's shortened days. But Halloween in its haunting spookiness was my least favorite day of the year.

Unfortunately, Michael wasn't on board with my boycotting-Halloween idea. He's excited to celebrate his first ever. Dressed in his vampire costume from Walmart, he races around the front yard, waving his red-and-black cape behind him. Plastic, fake blood–soaked teeth keep falling out of his mouth when he speaks. "Can you text Ms. Jolie and see if they're on the way yet?"

"No. They'll be here soon." I scan the street, but there's still no sign of their minivan.

Come on, Jolie.

I want to get this mandatory trick-or-treating out of the way. It warms my heart to see Michael looking so happy, but I can't shake my ever-present nervousness.

Wind blows through the leaves at my feet, sending them on an upward spiral around my legs. The chill in the air makes the hair on my arms stand up beneath my thick, bulky sweater. A full harvest moon is perfect for Halloween night, but to me, it's daunting, like a bad omen—glowing big and bright orange in the sky, keeping the dark clouds in the distance at bay.

For now. Another thundershower looms on the horizon. Which means the kids need to hurry up, get some candy, and get inside before the storm hits.

A gust of wind blows my hair into my face, blocking my view, but I hear the minivan approach.

"There they are!" Michael calls out.

His excitement over this makes me increasingly guilty. The more freedom I give my little boy, the more I realize how much of a prisoner he was before. My attempt to shield him, keep him safe, has bordered on kidnapping. I can't change the past. I can only move forward, but my priority will always be keeping him safe.

I pull my hair back into a low ponytail and use the elastic around my wrist to secure it as the minivan is pulling into the driveway. We decided our neighborhood was best for trick-or-treating because of the duplexes—the kids could cover more ground faster. I look at Michael's pillowcase and wonder how the hell I'm going to carry it when it's full.

Luckily this isn't Jolie's first time.

Her children jump out of the van and immediately open the trunk to retrieve a red wagon to pull behind them once their loot gets too heavy.

Will I ever have parenting figured out as well as Jolie does?

She climbs out of the van, and her wildly inappropriate Catwoman costume makes my eyes bulge. Skin-tight black leather with white stitching hugs every curve of her five-foot-eight frame, and the envy tastes bitter on my tongue.

"Where's your costume?" she asks, spinning to give me a better view of hers.

How she's going to walk a thousand blocks in the six-inch skinny-heeled boots is beyond me. "I'm Poison Ivy before she turned sexy," I say.

She laughs. "Sorry we're late. John took one look at me in this, and into the pantry for a quickie we went," she whispers.

"Remind me never to eat at your house." I'm certain the pantry isn't the only place Jolie and John have had sex. The jealousy I feel for Jolie is almost enough to make me hate her. I want to. She has everything. A wonderful, devoted husband who still desires her enough for quickies among their breakfast cereals. Smart, talented, polite children. The beautiful house, the cars, the clothes, and damn, the body. But she's also kind and the closest thing to a friend I've had in years. Her ability to make me feel bad about myself has nothing to do with her and everything to do with me.

"Oh . . . and I hope you don't mind, but I invited Parker and Amelia to join us."

Shit. Seeing Parker's truck turn onto our street, I reach up to yank the ponytail out, refusing to question why. If Jolie notices, she doesn't say anything.

"Okay, kids, who's ready for a sugar coma?" she asks.

The streets are crowded with children in costumes and parents cradling their coffee cups at the end of driveways as their children go door-to-door. Parker and Jolie seem to know everyone, and by default, I'm introduced to more of my neighbors than I'd care to know. I've purposely kept to myself since moving into the house, avoiding the family in the house on my right and ignoring the older woman on our left, pretending not to hear her when she says hello in the morning as Michael and I leave for school.

Now I know all about her seasonal arthritis, and I have an open invitation to tea anytime I want to stop by.

"She's sweet," Parker says.

Well, he could have tea with her. "Mm-hmm . . ."

A group of older kids rush past us on the sidewalk, dressed as zombies, and the sight of blood, gore, and dead, vacant eyes makes me shiver and look away.

"Not a fan of Halloween?" Parker asks.

"I think it's for children. Those teens seem a little old to be out here. But Michael's enjoying himself—that's what matters."

"You do know it's okay for you to enjoy something sometime too, right?"

My gaze is on the kids as they run up to another house. How much longer do we need to do this? Going up to strangers' homes makes me uncomfortable. I know no one could possibly recognize us, but I don't like how familiar we're getting with the neighbors.

"Jolie's having fun," he says. "I'm actually surprised she was able to leave the house. John isn't a jealous man, but shit, that outfit she's practically painted on would make any guy protective."

"Jolie is pissing off every wife in this neighborhood." The edge in my voice surprises me, and it's gone as I continue. "She looks amazing, and she's gotten into the spirit. I think that's great."

"Hey, about the other night . . . I'm sorry if I said or did something . . ."

I shake my head. "It had nothing to do with you." At the door, I see Michael step inside a stranger's house . . . what is he doing? I told him not to go inside.

"Look, Drew, I'd really like to get to know you. And Michael."

I nod, not fully listening. The homeowner has handed out cups of hot chocolate and cookies to the kids, and I shake my head. What did I tell him about accepting things like that from strangers? Wrapped candies only.

"I'm not going to pretend to know what you're running from—"

I stop and swing around to face Parker. "Who says we're running from anything?"

He holds up his hands. "Figure of speech. Metaphorically, I guess. I just meant that I'm a good listener, that's all. And if you ever want to talk . . ."

"I don't." Too blunt. "But thank you."

He stops walking. "Meaning butt out?"

Exactly. "I'm just a private person, Parker. I choose to deal with my own battles and let others deal with theirs."

"So, you won't get involved with anyone; you won't open up?"

"No. My life is and will always be just me and Michael." I'm not sure how to say it any more clearly. I don't even know why he insists on trying to be friendly. I've made it as clear as I can that I'm not interested in friendship or anything else from him.

The kids exit the house and run across several lawns to one farther down the street. Where the hell is he going? I can barely see him in the crowds of children in costume. Jolie's no longer right behind them. I see her on the other side of the street, talking to some women I recognize from the school. I quickly sidestep a group of parents to keep Michael in view.

"Michael's going to grow up. Then what?"

Parker's still talking. He doesn't know when to quit.

"I'll be alone . . . Michael, wait up!"

Parker shakes his head. "Not every person will hurt you."

"Please don't. I don't need life lessons. I need to be left alone to live the way I want to live." Michael has disappeared inside another house. Goddammit!

"You're putting a lot of pressure on Michael."

He's hit a nerve. "How dare you? You have no idea what we've been through, yet you think it's okay to judge us?"

He takes a step closer and touches my arm. "Not at all. That's what I'm saying. That I'd like to know. I'd like to help if I can." Concern and a million questions I'll never answer reflect in his eyes.

"Jesus! What is it with everyone? Just because we live in the same town and our kids go to school together doesn't mean we all have to be up in each other's business. I'm fine. Michael and I are fine." I walk away to get Michael as he exits the house.

I've had enough.

His first trick-or-treating experience is over.

Rain beats against the roof of the house, hitting the skylight in the kitchen downstairs so hard that I expect the glass to shatter. Howling wind outside my bedroom window rattles the thin panes of glass. Tree branches whip back and forth across them, the scratching sound like a wild animal trying to get in.

After a teary argument over the unfairness of his night being cut short, Michael is asleep in his room down the hall, while I struggle with mom guilt. Letting my argument with Parker and my own anxieties ruin my son's night was wrong, and it reinforces why I can't get involved with these people . . . with him.

They don't understand. They could never understand.

Their kindness and willingness to help only make things worse.

Our time in Liberty is short lived. I can feel the itch to move on, the impending inevitableness of the situation weighing heavily on my mind.

Shadow, sleeping like a log despite the noise outside, stirs on the bed near my feet. I guess his days as a homeless kitten have made him oblivious to the noise. He feels safe here with Michael and me.

Silly kitten.

I have to make things up to Michael. He's such a good kid, and he doesn't understand this life we live. I need to figure out a better way.

Not for the first time, the thought of hiring someone to murder Adam crosses my mind, but the idea is laughable. I'm a fugitive on the run, and Adam is one of the most successful businessmen in the world. Also one of the deadliest.

No one could take on Adam and win.

The old house creaks and moans, struggling not to collapse under the pressure of the storm, and I force several deep breaths, trying to quiet my mind. Sounds of the tempest make it impossible to hear any noises from an intruder.

Tonight would be the perfect night for Adam to find us.

I close my eyes just for a second, and when I open them again, everything is black.

I bolt upright, and immediately my hand goes to the knife in the bedside drawer. I moved the weapon once Shadow started sleeping with me at night. Grabbing my phone, I get up and peer through the bedroom window. The neighborhood is dark.

A power outage.

My failure to plan hits me like a brick to the forehead. I'm prepared for an intruder to try to murder me in my sleep, but I'm not ready for an attack by Mother Nature. Using the phone screen's light, I search my room for a candle, a flashlight left behind by a former tenant, a light source of any kind.

Nothing.

I go into the bathroom and rifle through the drawers.

Nothing.

Damn it!

Howling of the wind and pounding of the rain against the roof have amplified in the darkness. My chest hurts as I fight to control my rising anxiety.

I leave the room and carefully make my way downstairs, suddenly grateful for that big harvest moon that provides the only stream of light as it reflects off the living room hardwood floor. I use the wall to guide my way, my eyes growing accustomed to the darkness.

I go into the kitchen and open several drawers. I find a small flashlight.

A loud crash and the breaking of glass make me jump and spin around. A tree branch from the big maple tree in the yard has smashed through the kitchen window.

My knees unsteady, I reach behind me to support myself against the counter. Gales of wind threaten to blow the curtains from the rod, and rain pours in through the shattered glass.

The sound must have woken Michael, but he doesn't come downstairs or call out.

My heart pounds even faster. I turn on the flashlight and run upstairs to his room. His door is slightly ajar, and when I push it open, my world stops.

His bed is empty.

Saliva fills my mouth, and the room closes in around me, spinning . . . the floor unsteady beneath my feet. I blink and swallow repeatedly in a matter of seconds. Tightness wrapping around my chest makes me gasp for air. Next I'm screaming, "Michael? Michael!" I run through his room, tossing bedsheets aside and looking under the bed, in the closet . . . but he's not there.

Hearing Shadow's fearful meowing, I run back down the hall to my room, not feeling my legs beneath me.

Except for the frightened little kitten, my room and bathroom are empty. My body shakes, and I drop the flashlight. It rolls under the toilet, and I retrieve it quickly, but it blinks several times, then goes dark.

"Michael! Where are you?" I run back downstairs, missing the last step and twisting my ankle as I fall over it. Pain shoots up my leg, and a tingly sensation spreads throughout my foot, but I keep moving.

The living room is so dark. I yank back the curtains, desperate for more light. "Michael!" If he's hiding, I'm going to lose it. Unfortunately, the hollow feeling in the pit of my stomach tells me my son is not in the house. I check the kitchen again. Wind blasting through the broken glass has scattered papers and towels all over the counters and floor.

I grab my sweater from the hook near the front door, and, as I reach for the top dead bolt, I see it's already unlocked. All three are.

A loud knock sends me scrambling back away from it, injuring the painful ankle even more. Eyes wide, I stare at the door.

I have no knife. I have no flashlight or anything hard to use as a weapon. Even my cell is useless. Who can I call? I'm alone. I'm defenseless. And whatever false sense of security I thought I had vanishes.

I can't hide. I need to do everything in my power to find Michael. I turn the knob and prepare for whatever's out there.

Parker and Michael stand on the doorstep, dripping wet and huddled under the awning.

Overwhelming relief has my entire body trembling. Once again, my world goes black.

◆ ◆ ◆

"Sorry I couldn't catch you," Parker says, wrapping a plastic bag full of ice around my ankle.

I sit on the couch, my leg propped up on the coffee table, another ice pack against my forehead, where the swelling and bruising are nothing compared to the damage done to my pride. I'm embarrassed, I'm confused, and I don't like that Parker is still in my house, insisting on helping me.

"And I'm sorry I ran away," Michael says for the tenth time. He is sitting so close to me our legs are touching. He's squeezing my hand tight, a worried look etched across his young features. Worried about me or about being in trouble, I'm not sure.

He doesn't have to worry about either. I'm fine, and I'm so relieved he's safe that I can't be angry at him for a second. This is all my fault. I ruined his night, and he was upset.

Enough to run to Jolie's house and ask if he could live with her.

That hurts the most.

"It's okay. We will talk about things later." Once Parker leaves. Which I really need him to now. He's too caring, too tender. I'm not used to being taken care of, and the last man to touch me did so out of hate and a desire to inflict pain.

Parker's healing touch has an even more unsettling effect on me.

"I think we're okay now." I remove the ice pack from my head. "Thanks again for bringing Michael home . . . and for the candles."

He'd brought a bag of them from Jolie's, correctly assuming I might need them.

Unfortunately, they are scented tapers from Jolie's sex-therapy practice. Right now, the combined scents of Midnight Sensuality and Inner Goddess are making me feel nauseated, and I feel incredibly awkward as I slowly get to my feet.

"Don't get up. What do you need? I'll get it," he says.

"Nothing. I'm fine. I was just seeing you out so I can fix my kitchen window."

He frowns as he stands. "Right. Okay. Um . . . there's not much you can do about the window tonight."

"I can clean the glass from the floor and put something in the frame to prevent more damage." I have no idea how I'm going to get the large branch back outside where it belongs or even if I have any wood or cardboard I could use as a temporary fix, but the sooner Parker leaves, the quicker I can get to it.

I take a step, and my ankle gives way.

His hands are quicker this time, catching me around the waist as I fall.

My blood pressure soars to an all-time high. He shouldn't be here. I don't need him. I don't want to need him. And I certainly don't want his hands on my body.

But damn if these fucking candles aren't messing with my head.

What the hell is in them?

I remove Parker's hands from my waist and step away, but again the ankle won't support my weight.

"Whoa . . . easy," he says. "Look, I know you're worried about the window, so why don't I at least fix that before I go?"

"It's after eleven. Don't you have to get back to Amelia?"

"She's spending the night at Jolie's. It's fine."

He doesn't wait for me to answer but heads to my kitchen.

I sit next to Michael, knowing any other protests are a waste of breath.

Michael picks up my leg, settles it back on the table, and replaces the ice pack. "I'm sorry," he says again.

Shadow is snuggling in close to my hip, seeking refuge from this terrifying night.

"It's okay, sweetheart. I'm sorry I ruined your night." I glance toward the kitchen as I see the tree branch being lifted. "And I'm sorry that you feel living with Jolie would be better." I touch his cheek, grateful for the noise in the kitchen to drown out our words, giving us privacy.

"I didn't really," he says. "I was just angry at you."

"I'm angry at me too." I pull him in for a hug. Things have to be different from now on. I saved Michael from one tragic life; I won't force him to live another.

NOVEMBER

NOVEMBER

Drew

The surprise call from Dr. Collins this morning asking if I wanted a session today was something I couldn't turn down. My money is apparently tempting enough for him to put aside his suspicion and distrust. Though we've obviously both come to the conclusion that we're not going to talk about what happened the last time I was in his home, uninvited. He's accepted my bribe, and I'm fine not knowing why he tried to kill himself.

I just need answers now, faster than before. If his next suicide attempt is a success, I'm screwed. With no files anywhere in this house, I need to somehow get the information I'm seeking directly from him. Sitting on the couch in Dr. Collins's office, I stretch my leg out in front of me. My ankle is still swollen and throbbing inside an ugly-looking boot that the doctor at the local medical center suggested I wear for a few weeks. "Michael ran away."

The doctor's eyes widen.

"Not for very long. Just an hour or so . . . he was upset."

He nods. "Has he ever run away before?"

"No. I'm worried about him."

"Why?" The bandage on his forehead is tinged with blood, and one end hangs loose. The gash was deep and could have used stitches. His hair is disheveled today—not slicked back over the balding patch—and his cardigan is buttoned up wrong.

We're an unsightly pair.

"He's withdrawn and moody." Even before the drama of the previous night, he'd been acting a little strange. He doesn't want to talk about school or tell me stories about his friends. I worry about him. He is Adam's son. I can't forget that Michael's DNA is tarnished by psychotic genetics.

"With his friends or just you?"

His teacher had told me that morning that he was doing fine at school. "With me."

He's siding with Michael. I can see the judgment in his eyes. "He's finding his own independence. It's natural that he moves away from you as he develops his own individuality. It would be concerning if he wasn't."

"What do you mean?"

"The Oedipus complex is something I'm sure you've heard of."

I nod. "A boy's obsession with his mother."

"At Michael's age, it's common for a boy to move away from that and start to develop more of a bond with the male role model in his life. In the absence of one—as in Michael's case—the infatuation with the mother can manifest itself into a dangerous obsession. While the boy is essentially in love with her, his own masculine identity growth is being thwarted, leading to an unhealthy reliance."

Michael has spent most of his life with just me. He's never had a male role model. "Do you think that's happening to Michael?"

"I've never met Michael."

There's an odd note in his voice, and his stare chills me. "But you've seen it before . . . in other patients?" My heart is racing. Adam was raised by his nanny. His father worked long hours to build C2 Technologies, and his mother rarely had time for him . . . he seemed to have forgiven his father, but his hatred for his mother had been obvious—the exact opposite of the complex the doctor is describing . . . or another, more dangerous level perhaps?

"Yes."

"Can this result in cruelty later in life?"

"Toward the mother?" He studies me more intently than before. I'm not sure what he's looking for.

I nod, needing him to continue. This is as far as we've come to discussing what I'm really here to learn about.

"Possibly. Genuine affection for an alternate caregiver could grow as much as the hatred toward the mother does. A different connection is formed . . . more often the patient will become violent toward his wife once he sees her as a mother, fearing she will abandon their child."

Therefore, hiring a nanny. Adam's affection for his own nanny had indeed been transferred to Catherine . . .

"What about the absentee father? What role does he play?" If Michael does have issues, I refuse to accept all the blame.

"As I mentioned, that could be the main source of the problem. Children typically succeed better in adulthood when there has been influence from both parents in their upbringing."

Good. Adam is at fault for not being in Michael's life, for not being there . . .

But Adam didn't abandon Michael; I took him away.

"Really think about what I said about making connections, allowing other people into your lives; a new relationship could be good . . . for your son's sake."

Connections. A new relationship . . . for Michael's sake.

I sit in the car outside Parker's house.

His tow truck is parked on the street in front of me, and his pickup is in the driveway. All the lights are on. Part of me had been wishing he wouldn't be home.

"Are we going in?" Michael asks from the back seat.

"Um . . . no. It's dinnertime. Wait here. I'll be right back," I say, climbing out of the car.

"Can I go down the street to Ms. Jolie's house to say hi to Jack?"

"No. Wait here. And lock the door behind me," I say, shutting the driver's side door and walking up Parker's front steps.

His surprised expression when he answers shakes my confidence. "Hey, Drew. How are you?"

"Hi. Well, it's not broken—just sprained." I gesture to my foot, and he eyes the boot.

"Damn, that sucks. Want to come in?"

"No, I can't. Michael's waiting in the car," I say, pointing to the vehicle.

Parker waves to Michael, and he rolls down the window. "Hey! Is Amelia home?"

Amelia appears in the doorway. "Who is it?" She leans under Parker's arm to look outside.

Michael waves.

"Why don't you go say hi?" Parker says.

Amelia hesitates, sending Parker an annoyed look. "I'm doing my homework."

"It'll just take a second," he says.

She shakes her head no.

Watching the exchange has me even more uncomfortable. "We have to get home . . . I just wanted to thank you again for the other night."

Off the hook, Amelia hurries back inside.

"It was nothing. It was the least I could do, since the whole thing was my fault." He leans against the doorframe and folds his arms, and I try not to be affected by the sight of the muscles straining against the fabric.

Terrifyingly strong and overpowering.

"No, it wasn't."

"Well, not the power-outage part, but I was just as much to blame about ruining Michael's night as you were."

I shake my head. "No, it was a bad parenting call . . ."

"But I aggravated you by being an ass . . ."

"But I kinda deserved it." I hesitate, thinking about Dr. Collins's warnings about Michael's isolated life, free of male influence.

"Either way, I was out of line." He stops. "We're arguing again."

I laugh, and the sound carries on the wind. I'm not even sure it came from me. I haven't smiled in so long. Annoyance, anger, stress, and worry—all emotions I balance daily. But never something close to happiness.

"What?" I ask, the smile fading as Parker continues to stare at my mouth.

"Nothing. I . . . uh . . . nothing. You sure you don't want to come in?"

"I can't . . . not today, at least. We need to have dinner, and then I'm taking him to hockey tryouts . . . but another time?" It takes all my strength to say the words. Inviting this man into our lives is the most dangerous thing I've done in years.

And when he smiles, I instantly regret it. "Yeah. And I'm going to hold you to it."

Drew

A turkey-shaped invitation inviting us to Thanksgiving dinner at the Caseys' house was my only reminder of the holiday.

I'd been avoiding Jolie as much as possible since the Halloween incident, but I can't stop thinking about Dr. Collins's unspoken warning about keeping Michael isolated, so I accepted the invite. Michael likes Parker and John, and male role models are apparently important.

I'm trying to undo any damage I may have already caused my son, knowing his genetic makeup might be my worst enemy, my hardest battle.

"Can you hand me a casserole dish from that far-left cabinet?" Jolie asks, her hands buried up to her elbows in oven mitts. She can even make domestication look sexy, and I'm rethinking my choice of skinny jeans and sweater as I watch her move effortlessly around her kitchen in a red knee-length dress and skinny heels. She opens the top oven and removes a baking tray covered in tinfoil, setting it down on the pot holders on the counter.

I retrieve the casserole dish and hand it to her. "What is that? It smells delicious." I can't remember the last time Michael and I celebrated Thanksgiving. I wouldn't know how to cook a turkey successfully if my life depended on it.

"Baked brussels sprouts with shaved bacon," she says as she scoops the steaming vegetables, made deliciously unhealthy with the addition of bacon, off the tray and into the casserole dish. She covers it and slides it back into the bottom oven, where I assume everything is staying warm.

I've never been interested in cooking, but right now it's added to the list of normal things I want to learn how to do. I make a mental note to pick up a cookbook the next time I'm at Walmart. Michael and I have lived on "don't give a shit" packaged meals long enough.

I feel proud of my resolution to do better. Be better. Maybe that's all Michael needs.

Small victories.

Like the skinny jeans and the pale-pink sweater. The new additions I've made to my wardrobe have had a profound effect on my nonexistent self-esteem. Everyone has noticed the new clothes, but no one has said anything. Probably afraid they'll spook me back into beige.

"The turkey is almost done." She removes the oven mitts and stands on tiptoes in the precarious heels to reach a platter on top of the cupboard.

"Here, let me," I say. She's taller, but she could break her neck in those heels, and I feel like I should do something since she's feeding us.

"Thanks. You sure your ankle is okay?"

I nod. The boot for the sprain came off the day before.

"Be careful; I think there might be a smaller dish stacked on top," Jolie says.

I reach as far as I can, and my fingers touch the platter. "You want the bigger one?" I ask.

She doesn't answer.

A quick glance over my shoulder, and I catch her expression. Her gaze is on my exposed side as my sweater is raised over the top of my jeans. Several scars are visible, and I quickly grab both platters and set them on the counter. "There you go."

"Thank you," she says, busying herself with wiping the bigger platter free of dust. "Can you put the other one back?"

"Sure." I do so quickly and once again feel her eyes on my exposed skin. An explanation feels needed. "I . . . uh . . . had an accident years ago."

She nods. "Looks like a bad accident. Was anyone else hurt?"

I hate talking about my past. I can't without lying, and I admire and respect Jolie. She's as close to a friend as I've had in so long. But I nod. "My husband—Michael's father—died."

Her expression is full of sympathy but also a slight disbelief. "I'm sorry. That must have been so tragic. Was Michael in the car?" She pours gravy into a porcelain gravy boat without spilling a drop, her gaze on me.

"No. Luckily not."

"Thank God for that," she says. "And you're okay? Now?"

Emotionally or physically, I'm not sure which she means. Either way, the real answer is no. "Yes. Years have a way of healing, right?" It's the standard claim.

She shakes her head. "Not always."

I've never wanted to be honest with anyone ever before, but I'm tempted right now, because I sense she knows it's not the truth, and I also sense she might still be there for Michael and me if I do tell her. I clear my throat and glance around the kitchen. "Is there anything else you need help with?" She has everything so under control; I'm searching for anything at all. I want to help, but I also want to be out from under her caring scrutiny.

"I think I'm good. Do you want to bring those bottles of wine out to the dining room?" Almost as though she could sense my need to escape.

"No problem."

In the dining room, I set the bottles down in the middle of the beautifully decorated table. A tablecloth of multicolored fall leaves lies beneath a set of gold-toned dishes. Long-stemmed wineglasses are set at each place setting, and a wreath in the center of the table completes the festive harvest theme.

It's so warm and welcoming that I almost feel relaxed. Like we belong here, celebrating with Jolie and her family and Parker and Amelia. Like we finally belong somewhere.

My gaze wanders toward the living room across the hall. Parker is lying on his back on the floor, wrestling with the two boys and his tomboy niece all at once. The kids are squealing in glee as he tickles them and pretends to body-slam them onto the couch. Music playing throughout the house creates a happy, peaceful environment. A real home. Real families doing normal family things. Something I've never had. Something I've never been able to give Michael.

My heart is so thankful for Jolie and her family on this first real Thanksgiving we've ever celebrated.

◆　◆　◆

"Hey, Drew, do you have a sec?" Jolie asks as I push through the school doors the following Monday.

"Sure." I zip my coat higher as the cold wind hits my face. It's been snowing for three days, and the heavy clouds don't look close to being finished.

"I hate to even ask this . . ." Her chest rises and falls, and her expression is pained.

"What's wrong, Jolie?"

"Jack can't find his autographed Sidney Crosby hockey card. He noticed it missing on Friday. He says he was showing Michael his collection on Thanksgiving . . ." She sighs. "I can't believe I'm even asking. I'm sure it will turn up, and I'll be a terrible friend for even thinking . . ."

"That Michael took it?" Was she serious? Michael hadn't even made the Junior League team this year. While John was right about his stick-handling skills, his balance and speed on skates just weren't there yet. The tryout results had been posted the week before, and he hadn't seemed disappointed.

"I'm sorry, Drew. I'm sure he didn't mean to . . . but if you could just ask him if maybe he borrowed it?"

"*Stole it*, you mean?" Cold wind pierces through my thin winter coat. "I'll ask him."

Jolie slides her hands into expensive leather gloves. "Drew, I really don't mean to offend. And if he has it, it's no big deal—Jack just wants it back."

If Michael stole his friend's card, it's a massive fucking deal. "I'll find out tonight."

"Thank you," she says. "Hey, I don't have any appointments today—want to do some early Christmas shopping?"

"No." I hurry away to the car. I want to get home and search for the card. There won't be any Christmas presents this year if I find it.

At home, I check his room and the small toy bin in the living room, and I'm relieved not to find the card. I feel bad for even thinking he could have taken it. If I want Michael to trust me, I need to trust that he's the kid I believe him to be. Not accuse him of things.

Still, the minute we're home after school, I ask him. "Hey, buddy . . . do you know what happened to Jack's Sidney Crosby hockey card?"

He shakes his head, glancing up from his math homework. "No. He showed it to me at Thanksgiving, but that's it . . . Amelia had asked him to trade cards with her, but he said no."

Amelia. I release a sigh of relief. Parker's niece was definitely an odd one. Her mother dying overseas . . . never knowing a father besides Parker . . . makes sense that she might be acting out. "Okay. Thanks, honey."

Later, I call Jolie and tell her. She apologizes for even thinking Michael could have taken it.

Michael

Amelia was crying her face off at school today. Jack yelled at her on the playground monkey bars for stealing his hockey card.

I flick the corner of the card with my finger. It got bent when I was looking at it. Jack would be so angry if he knew. He told me not to take it out of the plastic case, but I wanted to see if the signature was real or just a fake stamp, like on the cards Mom bought me at Walmart.

The signature is smeared. I believe him now.

Then I had to hide it. Jack would never play with me again if he found out I've ruined his card.

I don't know why he cares about it so much anyway.

It's just a stupid card. He has so many other toys and cool things to play with. I don't have many toys. Every time we move, there's no room in the car to take a lot of stuff, so we end up leaving my things behind.

This is Mom's fault.

Drew

"Michael! Come on, or you'll be late for school," I call up the stairs.

"Be there in a minute," comes his reply.

I grab our coats from the back of the hook near the front door and climb the stairs to his room. I knock once on the door and push it open. "We have six minutes until bell . . . what are you doing?"

Shadow squirms in one hand as Michael's tiny fingers try to pry the kitten's mouth apart.

"Nothing. He ate something of mine," he says, quickly setting the kitten back on the floor.

"What was it?"

He looks away. "Nothing. It doesn't matter." He reaches for his coat, but I pull it away.

"It does matter. A toy could make him sick or get stuck in his intestinal tract." A vet visit isn't something I want to deal with. I pick up the cat. "What did he eat, Michael?"

Silence.

"Michael!" I poke a finger in Shadow's mouth, and his sharp teeth scratch my flesh as I search around. Feeling paper, I pull it out of the kitten's mouth. "Is this it?" I look at the soggy tiny piece of paper in my hand.

Michael nods. His gaze is on the floor.

I squint, trying to see why it was so important. "What was it?"

"It's not important," he says. "Can we go now?"

"Okay . . ."

He grabs his coat and passes me, but I see his hand clenched tight. I stop him. "Is that the rest of it in your hand?"

"Let me go." His glare is a silent warning, and I know in my gut what it is. I study the piece in my hand, and my grip on his arm tightens.

"Ow, Mom. You're hurting me."

My pressure doesn't ease up. "Michael, open your hand."

"No."

"Now." I can feel my fingers tighten around the small bone of his forearm, but I don't release him. He'll have to wear a sweater to hide the print of my hand, but I don't care. He stole and he lied to me. "Michael, I won't ask again."

The determination in his stare is almost threatening, but he slowly opens his hand, and the mangled, chewed pieces of Jack's hockey card fall to the floor.

"I think that covers every block from here to Springfield," Parker says the next day, climbing back into the truck. He shakes snow from his hair and turns on the windshield wipers to clear the window.

In the passenger seat, I'm holding back tears. It's just a cat. One I didn't even want to keep in the first place. But Michael is devastated that Shadow is missing, and I'm surprised at how anxious I feel. A tiny, defenseless kitten out in this weather.

"I thought I'd locked that kitty door before going to bed, but it was open when I got up this morning." I still can't understand how he escaped. I'm so diligent about keeping the house secure.

"He's been on his own before. He's a tough kitten," Parker says, reaching across the seat and touching my hand. I don't move it or pull away, even though the contact feels like a hot iron burning into my freezing hands. He dropped everything to help me today. I didn't know who else to call.

No one. I should have called no one. A missing kitten cannot be our downfall.

But Michael was so upset . . .

"But that was September, not November." The cold snap in Missouri this week doesn't bode well for survival, especially after nightfall.

"How's Michael?" he asks.

"He's a mess. I could barely get him to school this morning."

"Well, let's try not to worry just yet. Shadow could be waiting on the back step for all we know."

I glance at the pile of "Lost Kitten" flyers on the console between our seats, and I feel ill. Michael loves the kitten. He'll be devastated if Shadow isn't found.

"Hey, we still have a bunch of these left . . . why don't we drive a little further in the opposite direction?" Parker asks, squeezing my hand. I know why he's suggesting it. He likes this time with me, despite the circumstances. He likes feeling needed. His hand tightens around mine, and my anxiety only gets worse, but I nod.

Mentally, I'm already packing. The feeling that someone is watching us is back with Shadow's disappearance. I know I locked that kitty door. He didn't escape. Coming to Liberty in search of answers was a mistake. Dr. Collins is old, and his own mental state is questionable. Even if I did tell him who I am, and he agreed to help me prove that Adam is one of the soulless psychopaths he loves to write about, who on earth would believe a woman on the run, wanted for murder, and a retired psychotherapist who couldn't even prevent his own son's suicide?

We will stay through December . . . Michael deserves to spend one Christmas season here with his friends, but in the New Year, with or without answers, we'll keep running.

DECEMBER

Drew

The lack of holiday decorations in the doctor's home is a welcome relief. It's barely December, and the entire town of Liberty has been transformed into a winter wonderland. Michael loves it. All he can talk about is Santa . . . and why he's never had a visit from this amazing toy-yielding elf before.

To me, Christmas is another day I need to survive. The end of another year quickly approaching without answers, without clarity, without hope.

"Have you found your lost kitten yet?" Dr. Collins asks, sitting in his chair, placing a newspaper he was reading on the table next to him.

I frown.

"The posters," he says.

So he did leave the house. "No. Not yet." I scan the office, and almost all the clutter is gone. Except for the desk and file cabinet, which I know are empty, and his chair, everything is gone. "Where is everything?"

"Decided to clean out the office." He studies me. "You seem more on edge today than usual."

"It's the kitten . . ." I take a deep breath. "Also, Michael's been lying." He's still grounded over the hockey card, and I haven't told Jolie the truth yet. Our lives here are getting too complicated. We will be gone soon, so I need to get answers fast.

I need to tell Dr. Collins who I am. But I haven't decided how far I'm willing to go to make sure he doesn't tell anyone else. He must have seen the news, read about our disappearance and the nanny's murder. Like me, he must have kept tabs on Adam all these years . . . but will he believe me when I tell him I had no choice?

"Lying about what?"

"Does it matter?"

"There are different kinds of lies. Those we tell ourselves. Those we tell others. Lies can deceive or protect. Either way, if Michael feels he can't be honest with you, there's an underlying cause."

Or maybe he's learned to lie from me. Maybe I've inadvertently taught him that lying is okay.

He stands. "Give me a sec; I have a book that might help. It's not mine. It's by a former colleague. It's in a box in the hallway. I'll get it for you."

As he opens the office door wider, the breeze blows through an open newspaper, its pages scattering to the floor. The front page of the business section lands beside my feet—a glaring headline stealing my ability to breath.

"Adam Crenshaw marries Paris runway model Isabella Barnet in a private ceremony on December 1."

I stare at the article, my breath coming in labored gasps. The image of Adam in a tux standing next to a beautiful, stick-thin, twentysomething model has created a vacuum effect around me.

How the hell could he have gotten remarried?

He's still married to me.

I'm stuck in this depressing, spiraling time warp, unable to move forward, unable to remember the past, and he's going on with his life?

I pick up the paper with a violently shaking hand.

The couple met less than six months before and kept their relationship a secret from the media. The union comes just after C2 Technologies' acquisition of competitor Movement Tech, owned by Barnet's family.

Adam hated Movement Tech. Said he despised the unethical way they operated. The name of the company is circled . . . Dr. Collins has seen this article. Was he still keeping tabs on Adam too?

> Married next to a twenty-foot Christmas tree, outside in the snow, the two followed up their vows with a winter sleighride through the trails behind the billionaire's log home on the lake.

I want to stop reading, but I soak in every detail. My gaze continues to flit back and forth between the words and the brilliantly blinding beauty in the pure white gown and fur-trimmed cape in the photo. She looks so vibrant, so happy . . .

She glows.

> The couple then surprised guests with the news that they are expecting their first child in July.

The room around me starts to spin, and the paper crinkles in my hand.

Expecting their first child . . .

Finding out I was pregnant was the best and worst day of my life. Knowing I was going to be a mother, that I had life growing inside me, gave me the briefest light of hope in what had become a dark existence. Then it went out like a flickering flame in a thunderstorm.

This was Adam's baby too.

The one thing that would tie me to him forever. Even if, before, I'd somehow found the courage to leave. Even if my broken brain could stop blaming myself for the abuse, and I could summon the courage to pack my things and get as far away from him as possible, I now carried his child.

What should have been the most exciting news was now a life sentence.

Abortion had been something I'd passionately fought against . . . now, faced with this, my overinflated moral ground slipped from under my feet. The thought of killing my baby made me feel nauseated. The thought of bringing this baby—Adam's baby—into his twisted world made me vomit in the medical clinic's wastepaper basket.

"A little early for morning sickness. You feeling okay otherwise?" the family doctor Adam insisted I see asked, handing me a tissue to wipe my mouth.

"Yes. I'm fine. Just surprised . . . in a good way," I lied.

"Well, Mr. Crenshaw is thrilled."

His words made the room teeter. "Adam knows already?" I'd just found out.

"I called him before coming in with the news. I know it's customary for the wife to tell her husband, so I apologize for robbing you of that opportunity, but Mr. Crenshaw insisted he be notified of the results of your appointment today, directly."

My palms were sweaty, and my mouth was full of saliva I couldn't swallow fast enough.

Adam controlled everyone. Going to his doctor had been a mistake. I couldn't trust anyone. And this doctor had robbed me of the opportunity to keep this to myself until I found a way out for my baby and me.

"He's naturally hoping for a boy," the doctor continued.

If my husband wanted something, he usually got it.

And, four months later, the ultrasound revealed that Adam even had the power to control my womb.

I put my energy into the baby. My only reprieve came from thoughts that in a few months, I'd have a beautiful baby boy to take care of. My days wouldn't seem so long and lonely. I believed that once the baby arrived, Adam might be different. It was a foolish hope, but I clung to it to keep the darkest thoughts at bay.

He may have hurt me with his anger and intimidation, but he wouldn't hurt the baby.

I had to believe that.

He told everyone how proud he was to become a father. He bragged about it to his colleagues. He presented me like a trophy at events. He even acted like he loved me whenever we were out in public, and of course I knew better than to act anything other than the glowing mother-to-be, so grateful that my husband had planted his powerful seed in me.

We were happy, life was wonderful, and this baby was a blessing.

Alone, he called me fat. He said the baby couldn't weigh more than a few pounds, so why did I look like a cow?

"Even your face is fat." He spat the insult as he removed his tie and hung it in its place on the rack. Everything had a place. His obsessive-compulsive disorder hadn't bothered me before. Until it extended to me. I had a place too, and I didn't dare stray from where he put me.

He gripped my upper arm and squeezed tight. "Stop eating so much. This isn't an excuse to let yourself go."

I winced as his fingers reached all the way to the bone. It wasn't the physical pain but the emotional wounds that seared through my heart. Gone was the loving, adoring, lust-filled gaze he'd once had when he'd look at me. Now, it was just pure disgust at the extra weight I carried.

I believed him when he said I was getting fat. I felt ugly. The swelling in my legs and arms and the puffiness in my face were something I'd never seen before. My ever-expanding waistline and my never-ending morning sickness made it difficult to do the simplest of exercises, and I struggled to catch my breath after walking up a flight of stairs.

It was hard to accept the changes to my body when I resented feeling so tired and sick all the time.

The only benefit to being unattractive to Adam was that he left me alone.

At night, he'd sleep in one of the spare bedrooms. He never came to me. He never wanted sex. Which should have been the greatest relief. No more painful intercourse. No more having to do things I didn't want to do.

Yet, it burned a hole in my heart, and I sickeningly wanted him to force himself on me again. I wanted to feel wanted, even if it was in a hateful, demeaning act that I derived no pleasure from.

Maybe I was sick. Maybe I was the crazy one Adam often said I was.

Maybe that's why I'd entered the room the day Adam brought home the new nanny. I'd watched as he'd led her upstairs. To my bedroom. The one where I slept alone.

He wasn't trying to hide it. He'd found a new way to torture me, while pleasuring himself. I knew he was cheating. He was never home before midnight. A man like Adam doesn't go without sex, and if he wasn't getting it from me, he'd look elsewhere.

But in my house? In my bed? The bed he once shared with me?

That day, I got undressed in a spare room down the hall and stared at my naked body in the mirror, comparing these new thicker curves to the thin, tiny-breasted, hipless woman I'd seen entering the house. I was hideous. She was perfect.

I couldn't fault Adam for wanting her and not me, could I?

But what if I offered myself to him? Gave in to anything he wanted. Would he choose me once again?

Fueled by an irrational jealousy, I wrapped a silk robe around my body, tying the belt over my belly, and walked barefoot, quietly down the hall.

The moans coming from inside the room were growing louder. Hers. His. The creak of the bedsprings and the sound of the headboard beating against the wall.

I hesitated at the door but then opened it.

The young girl was on all fours on the bed, her hands clenching the bedsheets. My bedsheets. Her long dark hair was a curtain blocking her face—silky and smooth. Her thin shoulders, small breasts, tiny waist, and smooth hips and thighs were all visible. She was beautiful.

She heard me enter and swung her hair to the other side. Her gaze locked with mine, her expression unreadable. She was a stranger, but yet she looked hauntingly familiar. I felt like I'd seen her face somewhere before.

This woman. Our soon-to-be nanny was perfect. I was fat and ugly. Of course Adam wanted her. I was a fool to think otherwise.

She had replaced me.

I stare at the news article in my hand, hearing Dr. Collins's footsteps approaching down the hall. I want to hide it, but I'm numb.

He enters and stops. I glance up at him, and he is staring at the clenched newspaper article in my hand. Recognition—truth—registers in his eyes. My cheeks are wet, and a salty tear leaks into my mouth through the corner.

"You're her," he says.

"Yes. I found you because I needed your help, but I just wasn't sure I could trust you."

"Get out," he says, throwing the door open wide and moving away from it. "Now."

I stand on shaky legs and walk toward him. "Dr. Collins . . . he's a monster. You know that. You were his therapist. You write about him in your books. Adam was the subject for *Inside the Evil Mind*, wasn't he?"

"I think you need to find someone else to treat you . . . I'm not getting involved in all of this."

He's afraid of Adam. I know that feeling. "You know him."

"That was a long time ago. I've left all of that in the past."

"How?" In nine years, I've relived every last second of my life with Adam . . . I'm desperate for the freedom Dr. Collins thinks he's found. "And besides, I don't believe that. You've been watching Adam too. You circled the name of that company in the article . . . why? What are you looking for?"

"I'm not looking for trouble, which is what you're bringing. I need you to leave."

"Look, I know what the media said about me—I'm crazy, I'm a murderer, child abductor—but I did what I had to do to protect Michael."

He stands firm, unwavering. "Drew, you need professional help. Help I'm not qualified to give you."

"Dr. Collins, please! You know the truth about how dangerous Adam is. You know!" I reach for his arm, and he pulls back quickly.

"I can't help you, Drew. I don't even remember treating him. I won't let you bring your problems on to me."

A lie. He'd based theories, written articles and books on his work with Adam—narcissistic tendencies, psychotic behavior—how can he not believe me now? "Please, Dr. Collins . . . he's going to find me, find us . . ."

"Drew, you are a criminal. You shouldn't be here."

"I'm not a criminal. I didn't abduct Michael the way the news reports said. We escaped for fear for our lives. You know Adam is dangerous."

"You killed a woman."

Damn it! Back to this again. No one believing me. "I had to, and I honestly don't remember much about that night. That's part of the reason I'm here."

"I thought it might be you. Your eyes . . . something about your eyes matched the eyes of the woman in the papers. The murderer."

"Dr. Collins, please. Adam will find Michael and me and kill us. You need to help me."

"Michael is Adam's child . . . he has more than death to be worried about."

More fear. More confirmation that he knows exactly what I'm talking about.

What the hell is he saying? "Michael's a child. He is nothing like Adam . . ."

"Are you sure about that? The lying . . . the unusual behavior. Where's your kitten, Drew?"

My entire body chills. "No. Michael is not Adam."

"I thought it might be you, but I couldn't be sure . . ." His voice trails off, and an eerie vibration radiates down my spine.

Was he the one watching us?

"Dr. Collins, did you come to my house?"

"I don't know what you're talking about. You broke in here."

So he does remember some of that day . . .

"I'm not a bad person. I just need answers and for someone to believe me and help." I'm completely desperate and at his mercy.

"You need to leave."

"Help me, please. You must have notes about him that prove that he's dangerous, that could confirm that he has always been this way. Help me prove that anything I may have done was out of self-defense. A need to protect myself and Michael."

"Please leave." He moves into the hallway, and I follow. "Get out, or I'll have to call the cops."

An ultimatum? Not both?

I stare at him for a long moment, but I know he won't help me. Letting me leave is probably more assistance than he'd like to give. Anyone else would report me for abduction. Once again, I'm all alone in this.

I run out of the house. I slip on a light dusting of snow that's been covering the ground since I've been inside, but I don't feel the big, wet, blowing flakes as they hit my bare arms. I'm numb. The image of Isabella Barnet's face is all I see as I climb behind the wheel, tear away from his house, and drive through the blowing snow toward home.

Home.

What home?

Tears blind me as I hit the gas harder. I need to escape. This town. My mind.

The wipers swish back and forth, not clearing the windshield fast enough. My hands clutch the wheel, and my foot presses the gas pedal to the floor.

My car spins, spiraling on the deserted road. It hits a stop sign pole on the corner. My head snaps forward and hits the wheel, the impact breaking me out of my trance.

Ten deep breaths are supposed to help. I make it to four before I see the lights of a truck in the rearview mirror. It stops, and Parker gets out.

I'm out of the car and in his arms before I can think better of it. I almost want Dr. Collins to call the police. I want this nightmare to end . . . I choke on a sob, knowing all of this was for nothing. I'm a murderer, a child abductor, a crazy woman . . .

"Hey . . . shhhh, it's okay." Parker's voice is calming. The feel of his strong arms around my body is unexpectedly comforting. "It's okay. You're okay," he says, whispering the words against my hair as the snow falls all around us.

I have no right to need him. Being in his arms goes against everything I've done until now to keep Michael and me safe.

But this man, these arms, and the feel of the cold snow falling on my face are the only things that remind me that I'm still alive, that I made it out of the hell that was life with Adam.

But at what cost?

Catherine

Adam's home. He was gone so long this time that I started to wonder if he was coming back. Sometimes my mind wanders to dark places when he's gone so long. Without hearing his voice, I start to hear whispering around me, telling me that I shouldn't be here.

As if I have anywhere else to go.

Sitting at the mirror, I apply a deep-red lipstick to my dry lips. They still look cracked and slightly shriveled by the colder weather approaching, but at least they look a little prettier. Adam likes my mouth.

I brush my long dark hair, ignoring the handfuls of strands that come out of my head with each stroke. I take a black marker and color in the white patches of scalp showing through.

I smile. Seeing lipstick on my teeth, I scrub it away with a finger as I hear footsteps on the stairs.

He's coming.

It takes all my strength to push myself up from the chair, and my knees wobble slightly. The last few months, it's felt as though my limbs aren't connected, as though the joints want to snap apart, leaving me just a sad-looking marionette lying on the floor, unable to move.

But I can't give in to the pain or desire to lie in bed. I have to pull it together. Adam's home.

I'm already naked as I wait for him.

I hear his voice, and my heart beats loudly. He's home. I've missed him more this time than the last time. I hope he's home to stay for a while. My mind wanders when he's gone . . .

Another voice. A woman's. My smile slides from my lips, and my heart is echoing even louder against my ribs. Who is that? An employee? A new housekeeper?

The woman laughs, and my hands clench.

It's not a casual laugh. It's a flirty, playful laugh. A lover's laugh. A *wife's* laugh.

I can't laugh.

I try, but my face just does a noiseless grimace that makes me look crazy.

I wait, moving closer to the door so I can hear.

Talking. More laughing. The closing of a door down the hall.

I sit on the floor near the door, like an obedient puppy waiting patiently, calmly, for its master. I can't act on the anger in my chest. I can't bang on the door or the wall between the rooms. This woman can't know I exist. I have to be calm and patient and quiet.

Time passes, and my rage is almost at its worst when he opens the door.

I'm still on the floor, but I hope my eyes are full of pure disgust as he enters the room. I hope he can feel the loathing. I hope he understands my silent hatred.

Who is she?

He bends and lifts me off the floor, his hands under my armpits. He cradles me in his arms and carries me to the bed. When he lays me on my back, I slap him hard across the cheek. Once. Twice. Three times . . . I lose count.

He takes it.

When my arm is tired and my palm sore and red, I stop.

"She's my new wife," Adam says calmly.

I glare at him. I point to my heart. *I* want to be the wife. He doesn't need her. I can follow through with this pregnancy. I can be a wife and mother—everything.

He takes my hand and kisses it. Then he shakes his head. "No. You will never be the wife. You, my darling, are the nanny. You are what I desire."

I shake my head. I don't want to be just the nanny. I want to be the wife and mother. He can't put me in the role I don't want.

"Shhhh . . ."

How cruel of him to pretend he can hear my thoughts. How cruel of him to try to silence them. Aren't I silent enough?

"Trust me: the nanny is the one you want to be. The others mean nothing to me. Once she has the baby, we will be done with her."

She's pregnant?

Done with her? What does that mean?

He grabs both of my wrists and places them over my head, and I can see his erection in the front of his pants. He follows my stare. "This is what the nanny does to me—no one else."

I calm down. My confusion disappears.

I do that to him. No one else.

I smile, hoping my bright-red lipstick is still in place.

Drew

Oh no.

As I pull into my driveway the next day, the blinding glow of twinkling holiday lights trimming the roof of the house and around the windows and door makes me cringe.

May as well put a neon sign above the place with a big flashing red arrow that says, "They are hiding right here."

"Wow! Our house looks sick," Michael says, unbuckling his seat belt before I've put the car in park.

I could be sick.

Parker is carrying a ladder to his tow truck. The sheepish expression on his face when he passes us suggests he'd been hoping to make his exit before we got home.

"Parker did all of this? He's the best," Michael says, peering through the front seats to get a better look.

"Yeah, the best," I mumble as he gets out of the car and runs toward the house.

Now, I can't tell Parker to take them all down. Everyone thinks my reluctance to embrace holidays the way they do is because I've never had an opportunity before or that I come from a background that didn't offer me the chance to enjoy these things.

They're not wrong, but it's not as though I can tell them about my past. Unfortunately, they keep trying, which makes things so much harder for me. I already feel guilty that Michael hasn't experienced things the way other kids do, the way he deserves . . .

And damn, the sight of the lights makes me shiver. Christmas was always the worst in our house. Not because my father's abuse toward my mother increased but because it stopped. For several weeks over the holidays, he was a different man toward her. Kind, caring, compassionate. He never raised a hand to her or said a harsh word.

My mother cherished the attention he was giving her. It healed her slightly. Gave her a glimmer of hope. Made her believe that things could be different, that he'd changed. Christmas miracle and all that. But this person he pretended to be terrified me more than the angry, abusive person he was. I knew it was all just another form of mental and emotional torture he bestowed on my mother.

She couldn't see that, and for so long I thought she was weak.

"Are you getting out of the car?" Parker yells through the window. He's dressed in a heavy ski jacket and scarf, but his hands are bare and red, the skin cracking from the cold.

He's done all this for us.

"Still thinking about it."

"Holy cow, Mom! You have to see the backyard!" Michael is jumping the height of himself as he comes running back through the gate.

Jesus. I ignore the bitter cold as I climb out and shoot a look at Parker as Michael takes my hand and drags me through the back fence.

Holy *Fucking* Cow.

My entire backyard is a winter wonderland. Big, light-up inflatables cover every last square inch of the space, pegged deep into the frozen ground with large spikes. I squint in the glaring brightness to see a Santa train with reindeer heads sticking out the windows, an oversize animated snow globe, and characters from the latest children's holiday movie, which Michael has watched four dozen times so far this season.

"Isn't this amazeballs?"

God, I wish my kid wasn't picking up so much slang at school. "It's something," I say.

Parker's warm breath is against my cold, bare neck as Michael runs off to get a closer look at the freaky-looking snowman-thing. "I couldn't resist."

His nearness makes me shiver, not the cold. My need for comfort I felt on the street has somehow spiraled into a semirelationship. I know I'm not ready for this, but I'm not sure what to do about it. He's being so wonderful with me and with Michael . . . and a part of me appreciates the caring attention, even if I know I can't accept it, that I don't deserve it.

He turns me around to face him. "You're not really mad, are you?"

I shake my head. "Not mad . . . just . . . it's a little over the top." It's a beacon for danger. I can only hope that the rest of the neighbors get into the spirit so my house doesn't stick out so much.

"I wanted to go big. Michael said you two have never decorated before." He smiles and touches my nose to soften the accusation, but I hear the note of judgment in his voice.

What mother doesn't make an effort at Christmas for her child?

"We have decorated. Just not like this." I glance around again. The three-foot evergreen we always buy from some gas station parking lot that we cover with handmade decorations on Christmas Eve doesn't even measure up to this. But how can I explain to Parker that the holidays and all their magic were ripped away from me at a young age? My backstory is as damaging as my current one.

"Well, Michael's excited. Look at him. Loving it."

He's running from one inflatable to the next, his little feet leaving footprints in the snow. "He *is* loving it. Thank you."

Parker smiles. "Wait till you see the inside."

My mouth gapes before I realize he is kidding. He doesn't have a key to my home. "That's not funny."

"It was a little funny," he says, moving closer, grabbing my hips to draw me in to him.

My body tenses, and I press my hands against his jacket to keep him at a distance. "Parker . . ."

The lights disappear around us, and we are standing in complete darkness. "What the . . . ?"

"Shoot. Must have blown a fuse."

I raise an eyebrow. "Can you admit that maybe it's a little too much now?"

"Nah, we just need to hit the breaker. It will be fine. And I'll pay your power bill this month."

I hadn't even thought of that. The landlord will probably shit when he sees the monthly bill for this. "Come on, Michael!" I watch him dodge the quickly deflating inflatables.

I lead the way back to the front door and unlock it.

"Where's the fuse box?" Parker asks.

I shrug. I've never had to find it before. I look around the house quickly. Besides the breakfast dishes still left in the sink, I don't think there's anything embarrassing to discover . . . still, I hesitate before letting him in.

"I think it's downstairs," Michael says.

"Great. Want to grab a flashlight and give me a hand?"

"Sure!"

"No . . . you know what," I say. "I'll do it." He can't go down there. Parker laughs. "Do you even know how?"

"How hard could it be?" I block the door to the basement.

His eyes narrow as he moves closer. "What's in the basement?"

"Nothing. I just have personal things stored down there." A huge bag of cash and an incriminating scrapbook hidden under a floorboard.

"Maybe it's time I see some of these personal things." He steps toward me, a look in his eyes that doesn't take a genius to decipher. I'm going to need to put a stop to whatever is happening before things get out of hand, but the idea of returning to a lonely, solitary life is depressing. I'm not ready for a relationship, but the alternative doesn't appeal to me either.

"Ready," Michael says, returning with the flashlight.

Luckily, Parker lets the more uncomfortable conversation drop. "I'm not allowed to go in the basement. What's your mom got down there?" Parker asks Michael, but his gaze is still locked on mine—daring me to open up, let him in a little more.

"Dead bodies," Michael says.

Michael is deadpan, and a shiver runs along my spine, images of two different dead bodies flashing in my mind.

Why would Michael say that?

Parker moves me away from the door. "Look, if it *is* dead bodies, I promise not to call the police—deal?"

Would he keep that promise if he knew the truth?

I'm not getting around this. The money is out of sight . . . it's just the other things that aren't that have my palms sweating. "Fine." I open the door to the basement.

Michael rushes ahead of us on the stairs and stops at the bottom. He puts the flashlight under his chin and says, "Spooooky . . ."

It is actually. With his tiny face illuminated by the dull light, his dark eyes appear sunken deep into his face. Chilled, I shiver as though someone walked over my grave. I've only ever been down here in the daytime. Even then I run back up the stairs, fearful that a hand will reach out from under them and grab my leg.

It's a very real possibility in this version of a horror movie I'm living.

As we reach the bottom, Parker takes the flashlight and shines the light around, and I hold my breath as the beam illuminates several paintings along the wall. "Ah, so this is your secret," Parker says, moving closer.

"Um . . . I think the fuse box is over there." I squint and see it on the left wall. Away from the paintings. Away from one of a million secrets I keep.

But Parker's studying the canvases. "Wow, there's a lot. You did all of these?"

This selection is only a fraction of the paintings I've done over the years. All of them hidden away and then burned or destroyed before we move on. I can't take them with me—there're too many of them, and we take only what we need. These are my therapy, and destroying them each time we move on is another step in the recovery.

I can't be an artist anymore. These paintings will never mean anything to anyone but me.

Luckily most of them are simple abstract portraits of Michael . . . the only "photos" I capture of his life.

Parker shouldn't even be seeing them.

Yet a small part of me feels a tiny surge of pride as he says, "These are fantastic, Drew."

"It's just a hobby. Can we get the lights back on?"

"This is an impressive hobby. Why are they all down here? You should have them displayed."

"She thinks they suck," Michael says.

"They don't."

"I know that," he says. "Tell her."

Her. "That's Mom to you," I say. Reprimanding him is easier than dealing with the compliment from Parker. "Come on, guys—lights." I dance from one foot to the other, my arms wrapped around my waist. The chill in the basement and the darkness continue to creep me out. But I also don't want to go back upstairs alone.

Hair stands up on the back of my neck, and I move closer to a wall and lean against it as Parker finally goes to the fuse box.

I peer through the dark as he lifts Michael to see inside. Watching him show him how to reset the breaker does things to my insides. In a short time, Michael has learned a lot from Parker. He's patient with him. He's the only male role model Michael has ever had to look up to, and while that was my goal, Parker's influence on my son also terrifies me.

The fact that my little boy has made a connection with Parker is paralyzing. The way he's come to love Jolie and her family and his friends and teachers. He's created his own little village of people he depends on, people he needs. We can no longer pick up and move on without consequences.

The lights come back on, and I rub my arms for warmth. "Great. Let's go back upstairs."

Michael hurries up ahead, but Parker lingers, his gaze on my paintings once again.

"Coming?" I ask.

"I'll be there in a sec," he says.

I hesitate, but a spider dangles from the ceiling on a long stretch of dusty web in front of me, and I swipe at it as I run back upstairs, leaving Parker with a million questions he knows I'll never answer anyway.

Catherine

Adam brought me a tree. A tiny three-foot one with a small bag of shatterproof ornaments.

He couldn't stay to help me decorate, though. He's going away again. With her.

That's why he brought the tree. A consolation prize for spending another Christmas alone. He always finds a reason not to be here. I know why. As a child, he never celebrated the holidays. His father was too busy to take time off work, and his mother was a horrible woman who took no joy in anything, except stealing her son's happiness.

Only Adam's nanny, Mariella, made any attempt at all to make the season special for him. On Christmas Day, she'd sneak in one small, inexpensive toy, wrapped in a brown paper bag, disguised as her lunch. His mother never noticed, and Adam cherished those little gifts. He kept the ornaments, superhero figurines, and tiny toy cars and trucks in a display case in his office.

He told me about them once when I asked, but after that, discussions about Christmas or his troubled childhood had been off-limits. He doesn't like to think about those days. And the holidays are too hard on him.

I understand.

I heard him talk about skiing in the Alps with Isabella. That sounds fun. I hope they have a good time. I hope she doesn't fall and break her neck.

End up useless like me.

Adam will love her more then. He loves the weak, broken.

I put the bulbs in order of color on the floor beside the tree. Six red ones, six green ones, six gold ones. Traditional colors. Like the ones on my family's tree across town. Sixteen blocks away.

What would they do if they knew I was so close? Still alive. Not missing. Not dead.

They can't know. It's not part of the plan. Adam says we need Drew to be convicted of murder so that she'll stay away forever. But I can't stop thinking about my family lately . . . the time of year, I guess.

It's December twentieth. My mom would have had her tree decorated for three weeks by now. By December first, our nine-foot tree would have been erected each year. She'd let my brother and me help put the ornaments on, but then she'd move them all around later so that the same colors wouldn't be clumped together on nearby branches.

I need this tree to be perfect. Like hers.

I start with the red ones and strategically place them all around the tree. Plastic branches scratch my arms, but I need to push the bulbs in far enough so they won't fall off if I get angry someday and knock the tree over.

Next the green, then the gold. It doesn't take long, and I stand back to stare at the pathetic little tree.

My mom would be proud that the decorations are spread out at least.

Dylan is old enough to help decorate a tree. I know if he were still here, Adam would celebrate the holidays with us. He'd find new joy in the season because of his son. I wonder if Drew lets him celebrate holidays, or if she's just as damaging to Dylan as Adam's mother was to him. I hope wherever he is, he is enjoying the sights and sounds of Christmas, the displays in storefront windows, and visiting Santa at the mall. I wonder what his favorite Christmas song is. I bet it's "The Little Drummer Boy." I tap the beat of that song against my belly, and the baby reacts. It's his or her favorite song too.

Tears wet my cheeks, and I wipe them away. No sense crying about things. This was the life I wanted—with Adam, in this house, with our child.

I touch my stomach. At least I'm not completely alone.

I wonder what I'm having. I hope it's a girl. That way Adam won't look at this new child and only see the one he lost.

Once the baby is born, this way of life will end, and we will be a normal family.

Next year, we will have a big nine-foot tree, and Adam will help me decorate it. And when this baby is old enough, he or she will help too. My child will put all the same colors together on the same branch, and I won't move them.

Drew

"So, when do I get to see these paintings that Parker keeps raving about?"

I should have known he wouldn't keep my secret. To him, telling Jolie about them is simply a demonstration of pride and admiration. To me, it's a violation of trust. "They are nothing. This tape roll is out. I'll grab more," I say, climbing up from my perch on the living room floor, where we are wrapping Christmas presents together.

We'd shopped together earlier that day. Whatever she bought for Jack, I bought the same for Michael. The two kids are such close friends now and share a lot of similar interests. Though I can't help but wonder if Michael is simply mimicking Jack to ensure the two remain friends.

But Jack is a great kid, and if Michael's going to imitate anyone, it could be worse.

I haven't told Jolie about the hockey card. It's gone, and I can't replace it. I don't want to risk the boys' friendship. Michael needs his friend.

I open the drawer in the kitchen and take out two half-used rolls of tape. Who knows how long they've been there. I didn't buy them. Using things that once belonged to other people should bother me, but Michael and I are used to not owning things. Simply borrowing from our surroundings until we move on.

When I return to the living room, Jolie is gone.

The basement door is wide open, and a second later . . .

"Holy shit, Drew! You need to sell these!"

I want to be mad, but I can't. I knew why Jolie wanted to wrap gifts here instead of her place, and I knew she'd find a way to see the pictures.

The only person I'm pissed at is Parker, and even then, it's hard to stay mad at the people making my life here feel relatively normal.

I don't go downstairs. I return to wrapping, but when Jolie comes upstairs carrying two big canvases, I shake my head. "Forget it."

"How much?" She holds out the pictures. I don't have to look to know which two she's chosen. I'd painted images of the boys together from memory. Abstract and conceptual of friendship, but I know she understands what they represent.

"Not for sale." I tear a piece of tape from the roll and secure the wrapping on a new remote control car that cost more than my usual entire Christmas budget.

"I need these pictures in my life. So, either you display them here, or I want them."

I swear she's about a second away from a temper tantrum if I say no. "I'll put them up."

"You're lying."

"Jolie, these aren't that great. I just paint for fun." I secure the ends of the gift and set it aside.

"Bullshit. These are amazing. I'm taking them." She grabs her keys from the end table and heads toward the door, struggling with the large canvases.

Jesus, she's serious. "They're mine."

"You can visit them anytime at my place," she calls, hurrying through the snow to her minivan.

Standing, I go to the door. "What about your presents?"

"Finish wrapping them for me—I'll come back," she says, climbing in behind the wheel and driving away with the only solid proof of my existence.

By Christmas Day, the pictures are professionally framed and mounted above Jolie's fireplace. "I can't believe you took down the pictures of Laila." Jolie's old deceased family dog had occupied that space on the wall. Now, my paintings are up there.

I can't stop staring at them, seeing every flaw, wishing I'd known their eventual fate so I could have painted them better.

Or destroyed them faster.

Though the image of the boys speaks to me as well. And, if they had to be hanging somewhere, I'm reluctantly glad they are here in Jolie's home. No matter what happens in the future, my son and his best friend will have these shared memories preserved.

"I have a friend who is opening a new medical clinic in Springfield," Jolie says, hooking an arm through mine as she hands me a glass of wine. Nonalcoholic. My thoughtful friend knows I don't drink. "She's on the hunt for artwork . . ."

"It's Christmas, Jolie, and my holiday wish is for everyone to stop talking about my paintings," I say gently but seriously. The dream I once had has been gone for a long time. These paintings are the only ones that won't eventually meet a fiery demise.

She looks ready to argue but nods. "Okay." She clinks her wineglass to mine. "To letting the subject drop because it's Christmas."

I accept the toast and take a sip of the bitter-tasting liquid, knowing the subject will come up again but taking my reprieves where I can get them.

As she walks away, I turn to see Parker staring at me from across the room. He is sitting on the floor beneath the Caseys' nine-foot Christmas tree, assembling a walking, talking, four-foot robot for Jack, the only item I didn't duplicate for Michael, thinking the $400 price tag was too high for a robot that would no doubt spook me somehow.

His gaze is on me as he works. Intense, warm, and lust filled.

He looks amazing in the new sweater I gave him that morning as we opened gifts together at my place under our tiny tree. The deep red suits him, and the soft fabric that cost more than I've spent on any one item in years hugs his muscular body. It was Jolie who reminded me to get something for him. It's been so long since I've had to think about anyone other than Michael and myself that the thought hadn't even occurred to me. I'm grateful she suggested the sweater. My experience shopping for a man is limited, and otherwise, the beautiful earrings he gave me would have embarrassed me. They are heavy in my ears, and I feel the weight of their significance in my chest.

He winks at me, and I take another sip of my drink.

Over the last few weeks, we've spent a lot of time together. Too much time. At first I found his surprise drop-ins after work intrusive, but then I found myself ready for them, accepting of them.

Michael adores him, and he's been happier and doing better in school since Parker started coming around more often. He and Amelia have put aside their differences and have gotten closer.

All around me in this living room are temptations of a better life. One I know I don't deserve. One that could be ripped away with the slightest whisper of truth.

Parker smiles at me when my gaze lands on him again, and my pulse races as I glance at the clock on the wall. It's after seven p.m. It will soon be time to go home.

◆ ◆ ◆

Nine years without sex is one hell of a dry spell, but I don't miss it. I'm relieved that sex is not a part of my life. Or at least it wasn't until tonight.

Parker's lips drop to the hollow at the base of my neck, and I close my eyes tight. My body tenses, and my hands close into fists at my sides. How do I tell this man that I don't want him? That his gentle touch reminds me of a harsher caress. That his kiss only makes it hard to inhale, and not in a breath-stealing kind of way but in a constricted-airway, panic attack–inducing way. I want to want him. I want his kiss to fill me with a desire, a need I haven't felt in a long time.

Maybe I don't know how to feel it anymore. Maybe Adam's damage has severed any ability I have to feel it ever again.

But time has run out. I can't keep holding him off, satisfied with hugs and kisses. It's either I break things off with him or I give in to whatever he thinks is happening between us.

"Drew, I want you . . ."

I can feel that he wants me. The look in his eyes terrifies me. I don't want to be desired in this way. The last time left me used, broken, and hurting. I don't say anything, and the abused wimp who still lives inside me says that I have to do this. It's been a month that we've been *dating*. He has been moving in more and more—more touching, more kissing. More of everything that makes me ill, but I pretend to want.

I'm useless in this department, but there's nothing I can do. I can't be normal anymore, so the only thing left is to keep pretending. Keep pretending I can have a relationship with a man, keep pretending Michael and I fit into this small-town life, and keep pretending that I'm not completely messed up.

He kisses me again. This time, holding me firm against his body, his fingers digging into my waist. I'm returning the kiss on autopilot, and if he senses zero passion from me, he doesn't show it. I don't want the kiss to stop, only because then we will have to move on to more. I'm prolonging the inevitable, and I'm hoping for my body to show any sign of being ready.

He is breathing harder when he pulls away. "Drew . . ."

The pleading questioning in his voice has me nodding. I'm agreeing for him. And I instantly shut down inside. Preparing for the worst.

I suddenly wish Michael was home and not spending the night at Jolie's. It would give me an excuse.

He takes my hand and leads me down the hall to my bedroom. I'm in a fog as he reaches for me again and pulls me into his chest. "We really don't have to rush this," he says, but I can tell he needs this.

In the end, Parker is just a man. He can pretend to care about Michael and me, but all his thoughtfulness, caring, has to be with a purpose, a goal . . .

"It's okay," I say. "I'm ready." It's a lie, but he won't care. He just wants sex.

He reaches for the waistband of my leggings and yanks them off quickly. He's obviously worried I'll change my mind. His hands run the length of my thighs, massaging gently.

All I feel are Adam's fingers biting into my flesh, leaving a trail of dark bruises. When I glance at my thighs, the purple marks aren't there, yet I can feel them throbbing.

This is Parker. Not Adam.

He undresses quickly and removes the rest of my clothes. I don't make a move to stop him. I say nothing. My boring white underwear and bra fall to the floor at his feet.

If my silence is bothering him, it doesn't show.

I don't know what he wants from me, so I lie there waiting for orders.

I wait for his commands. I hate that I am this woman once again. Why am I here? Why am I doing this?

What sick, twisted part of me thinks this is the right thing to do?

Parker's gaze takes in my naked body, and I want to shield myself, hide all the ugliness. I can't look at him. I can't see his disgust and still go through with this.

I feel him lie on the bed next to me, and the back of his hand caresses my cheek. "You are beautiful, Drew."

Lies.

"So soft . . ." His fingers trail along my collarbone, but I barely feel them. I'm successful in my ability to shut down completely and go numb.

His touch finds the scars on my side, and I hear him swallow hard. "I'm sorry for what you've been through . . . I can't pretend to know your pain . . ."

Does he believe my lie about these scars? Does he believe any of my lies? Would his gaze hold all this love and compassion if he knew he was lying next to a murderer?

"I wish I could make it better for you, Drew. If you'd open up to me, let me in . . ."

I feel my chest constrict, and I need him to get on with it. Kindness and concern in his voice and the desire and want in his actions are confusing me, weakening me.

I can't be weak right now. I may be lying here exposed, naked . . . but I'm not vulnerable. I refuse to be. He can touch every inch of my body, but he won't reach me where it matters . . . where he could inflict damage.

I finally look at him, reaching for his body.

In that moment, I hate him, I hate myself, and I hate Adam for taking away any pleasure I might ever have.

Fuck Adam.

Somewhere deep within, a defiance surfaces, nearly strangling me with its strength.

I'm not letting Adam control this. Control me. Not anymore.

Once more, I need to find a way to escape him.

Catherine

This must have been what Drew felt.

Maybe that's why she went crazy. Adam says Drew was insane before I entered their lives; it's the reason he came looking for me, needed me.

But hearing Adam and me make love had to have had an effect on her.

Listening to the sound of Adam and Isabella down the hallway has me rocking back and forth, my hands covering my ears, praying, wishing it would end.

It's the same thing every night. I'm not sure why he keeps sleeping with her. She's already pregnant.

After she has the baby we won't need her. His words replay in my mind, and I don't know what they mean. What happens to Isabella after she has the baby?

Being alone more these days, I've been remembering. I don't like the images that are resurfacing about the night Drew escaped with her child.

My child.

Drew's child?

Damn. I'm confused.

I've been feeling worse lately. I haven't eaten much in days. It's hard to get out of bed now, but migraines and nightmares keep me from sleeping, so I just lie here, my muscles aching and my skin itching against the bedsheets.

I want to scream, but I can't.

I lift my hands away from my ears and hear that they've stopped. The sound of footsteps follow, then water running. Adam always showers afterward.

With her. Not with me.

Never with me.

Why am I different? Why does he have both of us? What does he mean when he says we won't need Isabella anymore?

And what if he decides to keep Isabella and not me?

I feel my stomach beneath the bedsheets. This anxiety, this stress, is not good for the baby. Damn Adam for putting me through this. Putting the baby through this. I press against the small hump.

Move. Please move.

Nothing. I push harder.

Wake up. Just a tiny motion. Anything to give Mommy peace of mind.

A tear slides down my cheek, and I roll to my side, clutching my aching head. I'm not sure how much longer I can survive this way.

FEBRUARY

Drew

I thought we'd been careful, but the two pink lines in the display window of the stick blur together before it falls to the floor with a loud clatter.

This can't be happening.

Delaying my plan to move on after the holidays had been a mistake, but I'd started to believe we could stay here in Liberty a little longer. With each day that passed without Dr. Collins revealing our secret, with Parker becoming more and more a part of our lives, I'd allowed myself to believe we might be safe here.

Every day, I still woke with the same feeling of panic in my chest, but, as the days went on without incident, without us being found out . . . I'd started to relax. I'd smile at the other parents at school pickup. I'd invite Parker and Amelia to have dinner with us. And I'd let Parker get close, accepting his kisses, his touch, more willingly . . .

My pretending to be normal overshadowed common sense.

And now I am pregnant.

A baby would be the worst thing right now. New life growing inside me would only be another entrapment. An eerie sense of déjà vu washes over me. Nine years ago, I'd struggled with similar conflicting feelings. There had been nothing I could do back then. This time there was.

This time there wasn't a question about what I had to do.

But damn, if only this time I could feel happy. Like other pregnant women. I want to cry happy tears instead of ones of dread and apprehension. I'd known in my gut that I was pregnant, but I'd lived in denial, hoping I was wrong. Or perhaps wishing an ill fate would save me from having to make this decision.

I hate that I'm thinking that way again about an unborn child. My child. Parker's child.

God, I know how badly he wants a child. The father figure he is to Michael and Amelia tells me I'd have nothing to worry about. He'd love this baby as much as he loves Michael and me. He'd love me more for it. He'd be so happy once he found out. He'd hug me, tell me everything would be okay. This pregnancy would be so different from the first. I'd have the love and support I'd craved the first time . . .

But haunting memories of past pain chip away at any little bit of happiness I might feel, erasing any doubt about what I have to do.

I've let our lives become complicated enough. I've opened us up to danger and the truth coming out. I can't have another baby. Someone else whose life would be at risk. Someone else who could be hurt because of the lies I live.

The walls of the bathroom close in around me, and, picking up the stick, I wrap it in almost a full roll of toilet tissue before burying it under other garbage in the wastepaper basket. Then, taking the bag out, I tie a knot and bring it directly to the dumpster in the alley behind the houses.

No one can find it. No one can know.

I need to deal with this immediately.

I drive two hours outside town to a small medical clinic that performs abortions for a hefty fee. They will keep my secret. They will keep me and Michael safe. Wallet clutched in my hand, I drive past the clinic, parking the car several blocks away.

I walk on numb legs, unseeing, unfeeling. I want to get this over with as fast as possible, yet I'm barely moving. As I walk up the sidewalk toward the front doors of the clinic, I'm accosted by a group of picketers. Words on their signs swim together, and I quickly avert my eyes from the gruesome images portrayed.

I'm pushed and shoved. *Murderer, sinner, child killer* echo in my brain. They don't understand. I'm doing this to protect Michael.

They block my entry to the clinic, and several security guards come outside, shoving them all back, allowing me to pass.

"Do you have an appointment?" an older woman asks as I approach the desk. I'm relieved to see that the waiting room is beyond the admittance desk. Walking in to a roomful of women—there for their own reasons—would have shattered my resolve.

I have no choice but to be here. Maybe they don't either. Still, I'm relieved not to have to stare into the faces of the same women I used to judge unfairly.

"No." I scan the hallways to my left and right. Doctors and nurses pass, going from one room to the next. How many of us are here to fix our mistakes today? How many before me? How many after? A nurse catches my stare, and her neutral expression hides judgment, disdain, prejudices.

"Ma'am." The woman behind the desk snaps her fingers, and I jump.

"Sorry. What?"

"Health card and ID?" she asks, reaching out a hand through the opening in the glass around her. There's a large crack in it directly above the sign that says PROTESTORS WILL BE ARRESTED.

"I have cash," I say, opening my purse.

"We still need identification," she says.

"Can I fill out a form or something?" There's no way I'm providing my real name . . . or rather, the fake name I've adopted.

She studies me for a second. "Name?" she asks.

I hesitate. "Lisa." I hate myself even more right now, and once again I'm forced into this spiral of pain, regret, and sorrow. I'll live every day knowing I've done another horrible thing. First Catherine . . . now this child . . . how can I ever look at Parker again after this? My breath feels stuck in my mouth, like it can't wedge its way past the lump lodged in my throat. My ribs expand, but no air makes it to my lungs.

Once again, Adam has control over my life.

The room spins around me. Anger—real, dark, deep-seated anger—spurs through my veins. How dare he still ruin my life?

"Last name?" The woman's voice sounds far away.

It needs to end. Adam's hold on me has to be severed.

"Last name, miss?"

I wish she'd stop talking and let me think. I grip the edge of the counter and lower my head, willing the ground beneath me to stop heaving, shaking me off-balance.

No matter what I've done in the past, I deserve a life. I deserve freedom. I deserve to have this baby surrounded by love and support.

Parker. The one thing that makes this impossible situation possible. If I can trust in Parker just enough.

I'm backing away from the desk. My legs have disappeared. The clinic around me feels like a tunnel closing in. I'm moving, following the beam of light on the dirty tiled floor before the opportunity to escape vanishes.

"Ma'am . . . you okay?"

I keep walking until my back hits the door.

"Ma'am? Do you need assistance?" She stands at the desk, and the two guards move toward me.

I must look crazy, not responding, but my body is numb as my mind tries to make sense of the decision I've just made.

One that could truly put everything at risk.

Catherine

Sharp, gripping pain started an hour ago. Pacing, I clutch my stomach, willing this child to stay inside. I need this baby. Adam needs this baby.

Soundless sobs escape me as I walk around the room, feeling the walls moving in on me. It's too small in here. I can't breathe in this stale air. Hail beats against the roof, and the loud clap of thunder makes me jump.

I've always been terrified of thunder. The loud, jolting noise that follows the lightning's flash. Adam usually comes to me when there's a storm like the one tonight. He holds me and talks to me, easing the anxiety.

He hasn't come to me yet.

Another stab across my midsection has me buckling as the door opens.

"It's okay; it's only the weather," Adam says, coming toward me.

I shake my head, holding my stomach with one hand as I point to the note I've left him on the vanity.

He picks it up, and his shoulders pull back. "No hospital. You're going to be fine."

I lunge at him, fragile fists pummeling his chest.

This baby needs help. I need help. This one can't be taken from me too.

"Come lie down," he says.

I shake my head. I need to pace. The baby won't move. Hasn't moved in days.

Adam supports my back with one hand and holds my hand in his other and paces the room with me. "It's going to be okay."

Why can't I give him this one thing he's always wanted? The thing we had and lost? Why can't I do this and free myself from all of this? If I can just give Adam a child, all of this will be over. We can forget about Drew and Dylan and Isabella . . . and just be together. I have to believe that. I'm broken, I'm damaged. To the world I'm dead. Only Adam still cares about me, loves me, wants me. Only he can still see value in me. I have no one else.

Thunder claps, and I grip his hand tight.

He kisses the side of my head. "It's going to be fine," he says.

He repeats it over and over until I don't hear the words anymore. I don't hear the soothing of his voice; I just walk in a trance, jumping and tensing at each loud menacing clap.

Then the pain stops.

I stand up straighter and look at him in relief. He's right. I'm going to be fine. The baby's fine.

But the carpet feels damp beneath my feet.

No! Not again.

My knees weaken, and I clutch at Adam, willing him to make this stop, praying it's all just a nightmare. But the gripping pain around my midsection starts again, and I know it's devastatingly real.

I've made it so far this time.

I grip Adam's hand and point to the door. Maybe it's not too late if we get help, if he takes me to a hospital. Maybe we could save this baby. Save me.

Adam shakes his head no as he supports my fragility.

I silently plead with him, but he refuses.

He doesn't want me to have a baby.

Realization causes my world to shatter once more, a soundless sob escaping me. He doesn't want me to ever be a mother. My heart is breaking, the truth ripping me apart, while Adam is calm and undestroyed.

"See, that's why we have Isabella," he says. "She will have the baby you can't have. Then, you will truly be the nanny again."

Drew

The timer on the library computer screen ticks away my minutes.

I have three minutes left, and my fingers type as though on autopilot. I know I need to stop this. This searching, this chasing, this stalking. I'm trying to move on. Trying to forget the past that hasn't caught up with me yet.

One that may never catch up with me.

I should focus on the possibility of a new future with Parker and Amelia and Michael and this new baby.

But what if the past doesn't continue to leave me alone? What if I start to live again, and Adam does find us? It would be the end of so much more now . . . it isn't just Michael I have to fear for now.

The search engine loads articles about C2 Technologies, and I scroll through, looking for one I haven't seen before. There has to be something . . . somewhere that could help me remember. Page after page of business news—all reports I've already read.

One minute left on my time.

Come on: there's got to be something new, something I've overlooked, something I've missed . . .

I stop at one dated nine years ago that sets my pulse racing.

"Twenty-five-year-old CIO David Collins commits suicide; found in CEO Adam Crenshaw's office with a gunshot wound to the head . . ."

The picture of him in the top-right corner of the article is small, but it makes me slightly dizzy.

I keep reading, pulled in to the article. The truth is here. I can feel it.

"Everyone at C2 Technologies will mourn the tragic passing of David Collins. He was a good man. We only wish we'd known about his internal struggles in time to help him through these obvious tough times."

The article from a local Seattle newspaper goes on to focus on the internal investigation into Collins's involvement with a competing technology company—side deals and divulging confidential C2 information—and my heart falls deep into my stomach as the "Time's up" message flashes on the screen.

Suicide. Gunshot wound to the head.

David Collins didn't commit suicide. I know what really happened to him.

Flashes of blood; the sound of a gunshot rings in my ears.

I remember now. I know where the images of the dead man are coming from.

David Collins. The doctor's son.

Adam killed him. It wasn't like in the movies. It wasn't dramatic at all.

It was actually quite calm and civilized. Other than the plastic covering the floor in his penthouse office, nothing was out of the ordinary. Impeccable suits, shiny leather shoes, a business meeting that would end in the murder of the company's latest inside snake.

So normal. So real. So absolutely bone chilling.

I'd finally gotten the courage to leave Adam. I'd filed for divorce, and my hand was trembling violently as I held the papers in a manila envelope and entered his office. Later, those papers mysteriously disappeared . . .

Adam was so relaxed, so professional. If holding a gun to his CIO's head and pulling the trigger a second later made him the least bit uncomfortable, fazed, it didn't show.

I saw the man's blood before I heard the gunshot, and my eyes were unable to look away. The same way people can't tear their eyes from a train wreck as it happens, I was transfixed on the execution and the aftermath.

I remember feeling Adam's hands on my arms, lifting me from the floor when my knees had given out unnoticed. "This had to be done," he'd said. "Don't feel bad for him. He knew it had to be done."

The calm tone, meant as reassurance, paralyzed me. My organs froze, my muscles seized, and my heart stopped beating—just like the dead man on the floor. Adam, on the other hand, was at peace with what he'd just done. He believed murder was the right thing. He was actually a dead-hearted son of a bitch. A sadist, a narcissist, a sociopath. A wealthy, influential man who had the means to get away with anything he wanted.

Even murder?

Turned out even murder.

"What did he do?" I'm not sure why it mattered to me, or even where the strength had come from to ask the question. It shouldn't have mattered, but I needed to know.

Maybe to avoid a similar fate.

"He had developed a ransomware product. He was hacking our clients' accounts, then blackmailing them into paying him for the information. He was cheating people, Drew, and impersonating me to do it." Anger rose in Adam's tone, but his voice remained steady, quiet, as he spoke, as if even his anger knew better than to overcome him. "All my hard work and success into making this company great, then a snake like him threatens to destroy my reputation. Stealing. Cheating." He spat the words as though they were a million times worse than *abuser, murderer*.

"This is business," he said. He rubbed my numb arms—not as a gesture of comfort but of control. I felt nothing. "And, like the other information you've been privy to, I expect that this will remain confidential."

I swallowed hard and nodded, tears burning my eyes. "I understand. I won't say a word." I had to sound convincing enough to make it out of that office alive and not wrapped in plastic like the limp body on the floor.

"I believe you," he said, placing a hand on my six-month-pregnant stomach.

A gesture that in most situations signified a loving, caring, fatherly touch. Not this one. This one was a warning. I felt the silent threat cut through me like a knife were pushing into my stretched stomach, not his fingers. It wasn't only my life at risk if he decided he could no longer trust me to stay silent.

Seeing the envelope still clutched in my hand, he nodded toward it. "Was that for me?"

"I . . . uh . . ."

He took it and opened it, his eyes scanning the documents inside. When he looked at me again, his expression revealed disappointment . . . disappointment that I could have been so stupid. "Don't worry. You made a mistake. I'll take care of these," he said, tossing the papers onto his desk.

My stomach heaved violently, and I threw up at his feet. The oatmeal I'd eaten for breakfast came up looking exactly like it had going down. Now splashed across his polished Armani shoe.

My escape was not going to happen.

He reached for a tissue from his pocket and handed it to me to wipe my mouth. "This pregnancy has been rough on you. I think maybe you need more rest."

I nodded blankly, knowing more rest meant I was about to become a prisoner in the big, expensive hell I used to call home.

After the murder I'd witnessed, I wasn't allowed to leave the house, and no one was allowed to come see me. Calls came in for me that I wasn't allowed to take. No computer. No cell phone.

Isolation.

I was so lonely in that house. All day. All night. Seven months pregnant, and each day felt torturously long. Adam had canceled the daytime cleaning service, replacing them with a nighttime crew when he was there. They'd move throughout the night like shadows. I tried once to catch their attention, but they kept their heads down, unseeing as they roamed throughout the halls of my home. They'd been warned not to talk to me. The gardeners had been let go; the pool went uncleaned. The new nanny kept her distance, avoiding my gaze if we accidentally crossed paths in the hall. He told everyone it was me. In my depressed state, I was going mad—forcing everyone away. That I was hysterical, and he feared the effect my stress was having on the baby.

Eventually, I was confined to the bedroom. For my safety, he told everyone as he'd locked the door from the outside.

The only person I saw was him.

How quickly the sight of someone who'd once sent my pulse racing had changed and now did so for an entirely different reason. I was terrified. His smile held no sincerity. His words held no warmth. His touch was brutal and demanding—whenever he did touch me.

How had this happened?

How could he have fooled me into believing he was something he wasn't? How had I not seen this monster? How could I have been so wrong about my instincts? About the passion and love we'd shared?

Around and around my thoughts would go. Ending at the same revelation—I couldn't trust myself anymore.

And I couldn't trust him. I couldn't trust family and friends. Everyone had abandoned me. The only person who came once a week was my mother, and her unseeing eyes, unhearing ears, could never help me. I'm not sure why she came. I'm not sure why Adam let her come.

She wasn't a threat perhaps. She was weak, abused, an alcoholic, self-absorbed.

Not someone who could save me.

One day, I almost got my savior. A neighbor who came to deliver mail that had accidentally been put into her mailbox.

From the bedroom window, I saw her pull up to the gate. She hit the intercom, but no one answered. She got out and came through the gate door, which for some reason was unlocked.

Adam never forgot to lock the gate, so I labeled it a miracle.

Up the walkway . . . up the stairs. She came closer, scanning the yard.

The bedroom door was locked from the outside. I was only allowed to leave the room when my mom visited, so I waved from the window that Adam had bolted shut.

She didn't see me.

I pounded on the glass, not caring if Adam heard. This was my chance to get the hell out of this nightmare.

The woman didn't look up.

Adam intercepted her at the door. I could see her smile and laugh at whatever he said, and I looked around for something heavy. I knew I might never get this opportunity again. She was there, but she was leaving.

My heart pounding, I had one shot. I grabbed the antique vase that had once belonged to Adam's own childhood nanny—something he prized more than just about anything. The one item heavy enough to break the window flew from my hands and smashed against the glass seconds later.

I ran to the window, cutting my bare feet on shards of glass, and waved my arms through the opening. The feel of the hot sun burned into my flesh as I called out, "Help . . . call the police, please!"

The woman glanced up, the shocked expression on her face turning to one of uncertainty and fear.

"Please—you need to help me! I'm being held hostage. Please, please, call the police." I heard how crazy I sounded, but I was desperate.

She continued to stare, and I continued to beg for help.

But then Adam walked toward her, and, without a glance in my direction, he touched the woman's arm and said something to her.

Her gaze fell on me again, and a flash of pity reflected in her eyes as she nodded once.

What the hell had he said? "Don't believe him! Please, please, call the police!"

I could feel my one shot dissipating as she walked away slowly. Down the stairs. Down path. Back through the gate, which Adam then locked.

The woman glanced at me once before driving away, and my eyes pleaded with her not to believe him. To rescue me.

But she drove away.

The only person who came to me was him, and that's when the cutting started.

When the bedroom door swung open, there was nowhere to hide. No escape. My chance of getting out was gone, and now I had to face the consequences of my actions.

Adam's eyes held storm clouds desperate to release their thunder.

How long had he been waiting for an opportunity to hurt me? I hated that I'd given him a reason. Up until now, the abuse had been sexual, mental, emotional . . . he'd never crossed the line into physical. And, even in my muddled mind, I know how sick it was that even I was considering that his next actions might be justified.

I was bad. I deserved to be punished.

This is fucked up, my brain had screamed.

It was silenced by the self-loathing I'd embodied.

He stalked toward me, and I saw a shard of glass from the broken vase in his hand. My pulse raced, and my heart was in my throat. "Adam, I'm sorry . . ."

"Shut. Up." He reached for my arm, but I placed both behind my back, backing up quickly until I reached the wall. Cornering myself between the dresser and the open door, I was trapped.

"Give me your arm," he said, suddenly calm, as though whatever he were about to do had extinguished his anger.

Calm Adam was worse. Goose bumps surfaced on every inch of my skin as I shook my head, knowing that if he wanted my arm, he'd get it. Delaying the pain was only making it worse. The fear of what was about to happen was making me nauseated. It was better to give him my arm and let him inflict the pain, and then it would be over, but a sense of fight or flight wouldn't allow me to surrender.

"I said, give me your arm."

"Adam, please. I can fix the vase . . . or find an antique store that might have one." As if I'd ever be given the freedom to leave the house. The reality of my future, caged up with him, made me wish for death.

I stared at the sharp, pointed edge of the fragment. Would he consider slitting my throat with it instead? I'd welcome the relief of death. I wasn't sure how much longer I could survive this way.

My baby shifting inside my belly reminded me why I hadn't found a way to take my own life yet. He'd moved a lot in those last few months, and I was terrified that he could sense my fear. Feel my anxiety. Did he know the world I was bringing him into was full of hate and darkness?

"I don't have time for this." Adam grabbed my shoulders, pulled me away from the wall, and threw me onto the floor at his feet. He knelt on the hardwood next to me and forced me onto my back. As he put his right knee on my chest, I gasped, trying to suck in as much air as possible before the heavy weight of him made it hard to breathe. His other knee pinned my one arm to the floor as he reached for the other one.

Without hesitation, he sliced through the skin at my wrist.

I cried out in pain. Was he trying to kill me? Slit my wrists? But the wound was only surface deep, and the thin trickle of blood that appeared began to clot right away.

The next one was a little deeper, just below the first one, and I clenched my teeth together as tears streamed down my face.

What the hell was he doing?

I'd expected him to punch me, kick me, beat me, stab me with the shard . . . but not this.

The third slit . . . then the fourth, fifth, sixth . . . all ran parallel, and the blood seeped up my arm, staining the cap sleeve of my shirt. I gasped for air, and my body started to tremble on the floor.

Adam lifted my wrist to my face, showing me the wounds. "Why did you do this to yourself?" he asked, so eerily calm.

And the realization of what he'd done had my core shriveling.

"You . . . you . . . did this to me." I struggled with the words. The terror of the situation and the numbing sensation in my arm made it difficult to focus, to think clearly about his words.

I realized the intent behind his actions, but my damaged mind couldn't quite grasp reality.

Adam moved closer, his grip tightening on my arm, forcing the blood to ooze out from the wounds. "Who the hell will believe you?"

After Adam left, I lay there on the floor for a long time. Or at least it felt like a long time. It might have been just a moment. Time had no relevance to me then.

But when the bedroom door reopened, I scrambled to my feet and ran into the en suite bathroom. I tried to shut the door, but Adam blocked it.

"Let me help," he said, entering with the first aid kit we kept under the kitchen sink.

"No." The word was barely more than a whisper on a trembling breath. I didn't want him to touch me again. I didn't want him anywhere near me.

I reached for a facecloth and wet it, but he took it from me.

"I don't understand why you couldn't just listen to me and stay here until the baby is born. Then we can get you the help you need," he said, taking my right arm.

The help I needed was never coming. I remained silent as he pressed the cold, wet cloth to my bleeding wrist.

"I give you everything you could ever want. This house, nice things . . ."

The bile rising in my throat made it hard to swallow as he continued to list all the things he gave me.

Everything but the things I craved most. Love, security, freedom . . .

"So much like my mother. She never appreciated what my father gave her either. Never understood the long hours he put in. She was never home either . . . at least he was working. Making the company a success." His words were harsh, but, in contrast, his touch was now tender, and it frightened me more than the violence he'd just displayed moments before. He wiped the remaining blood from my arm, and, taking a container of alcohol, he applied it to a cotton ball and dabbed the wound.

I flinched, and he blew on it to ease the sting.

I stared at him. Not believing. Not understanding.

I'd seen this drastic change in a person once before—in my father—and my mind and body went numb at the realization that I'd walked straight into the same trap my mother had. We were the same. We shared the same hellish fate. I'd learned nothing from years of witnessing her abuse.

"I know what you're thinking," Adam said.

I didn't think he possibly could.

"You're wondering how I can go from cruel to caring like this."

I stilled. I had no idea what would set him off next, and that was most terrifying of all.

He took the bandages from the case and slowly wrapped my wrist. "I don't know really. I think I was born this way. My mother was the one who took me to see Dr. Collins as a child. He said the pain I inflict on others doesn't have enough of an impact on me to have a lasting effect—to rewire my brain in a significant enough way. I don't derive as much pleasure from it as my victims suffer pain." He taped the bandage closed and put the tape away. "He tried a lot of different therapies with me . . . some of them very unconventional. My mother basically gave him permission to do whatever he wanted. She just wanted a normal child."

"Did he . . . hurt you? Is that why you killed David?"

Adam looked at me as though it was the dumbest thing I could have suggested. "No. I killed David because he was trying to destroy my reputation, take away everything I've worked hard for." He paused. "I guess, in a way, I've gotten revenge on the old doctor . . ."

"What happened to him?"

"I don't know. He couldn't help me—fix me—so I stopped going to see him after my parents died." He handed me several painkillers, and I took them with a violently shaking hand.

My blood was cold in my veins, and my arm felt numb. I didn't need the painkillers, but I took them anyway, as Adam instructed.

I wanted him to leave. For once, I craved silence, being alone. But first, I needed to ask. "Adam, what happened to your parents?" I'd read they'd been found dead in a ravine—an apparent car accident. It was a topic he refused to talk about; therefore, I'd never asked him about it before now.

Now, it was the only thing I needed an answer to.

Adam put everything back into the first aid kit. "What do you think happened to them?"

I was ice cold at the casual way he said it.

"Of course, my father's death was a mistake. He wasn't supposed to be in the car that day. I'd only meant the accident for my mother. Her demands on my father were taking him away from the company, and I had no need for her." He stood and approached the door. "I never did have any need for her. I had Mariella, my nanny."

MARCH

Drew

Dr. Collins won't answer my calls. Three days in a row now he hasn't been home. The first day I waited an hour. Yesterday, I waited a little longer. My desperation is rising . . .

I know the truth now.

Tangled, fragmented images that have haunted me for years are starting to become untwisted. One body and murderer identified.

Now the memories are getting clearer. I can distinguish from the day David Collins died and the night the nanny was murdered. I'm remembering more—for better or worse. Now I need to keep going. Keep pushing my reluctant mind to recall everything.

My stomach is in knots as I think of what I need to tell Dr. Collins. That his son didn't commit suicide, that he was murdered.

That I'd witnessed it.

Will the truth cause him more pain? Or give him a sense of peace? Will it be enough for him to want to help me?

I knock on the door again and wait. A new desperation trickling through my veins. If I can tell him what really happened, he will believe me about Adam. He'd know that his instincts about his former young patient had been right.

But will he be brave enough to do the right thing? To help me?

I knock again, but there's only silence from inside the house. I peer around the side, toward his office, but new metal bars have been added to all the outside windows. I knock once more, then try calling him, but the phone just rings inside the house.

Where the hell is he?

"Drew?"

I jump and spin around at the sound of John's voice.

"Sorry, didn't mean to startle you." He studies me as he comes closer—in full uniform. Badge and gun at his waist. I've only ever seen him in it that one time on the side of the road when the car broke down. Most of the time he's in civilian clothes, and I can almost forget that my closest friend is married to a law enforcement officer. "You looking for Dr. Collins?"

Shit. How do I explain this? I nod slowly. "Yeah . . . he, um . . ."

"None of my business . . ." He hesitates. "We just received a call from the neighbors about a car being here a few times this week . . . a woman hanging around . . ."

My mouth is dry as I nod. "I guess I got the appointment time mixed up."

He nods, surveying the house. "Yeah, well the neighbor said he's been gone for about a week, asked them to keep an eye on the place."

"Right. He might have told me, and it slipped my mind." I force a laugh as I descend the steps and pass him on my way back to the car. This is embarrassing and unnerving.

Will John mention this to Jolie? To Parker?

It probably wouldn't surprise any of them to know I've been seeing a therapist, but it complicates things.

I pause before opening the car door. "Um, John?"

He moves closer and opens the door for me. "Don't worry, Drew. I won't say anything." He pauses. "But, you know, we are all here for you and Michael. Whatever you two need, okay?"

I swallow the large lump in my throat. He has no idea what he's promising. "Thank you."

I climb into the car and give an awkward wave as I drive away.

I'll have to try again in a few weeks. When I know the neighbors aren't home watching . . . and John's not on patrol.

Dr. Collins deserves to know what happened to his son, and it's the only thing I have that might convince him to help me.

MAY

Drew

I stare at the moving van outside our house as Parker carries the last box upstairs to my bedroom—our bedroom now.

All around me are boxes. New boxes. Not the old tattered ones I've reused for our things over and over again. These boxes contain Parker's things and Amelia's things . . .

He's selling his house and making an offer to my landlord to buy this one. We've combined the furniture—choosing the pieces in the best shape, getting rid of the rest. His dishes were newer, not chipped and mismatched, so mine are in the dumpster behind the house.

Moving in together makes sense.

How many times has Parker reassured me of that?

With the baby on the way, it's the natural thing to do. Live together. Be a real family.

And Parker would be right, if we were a normal couple. If I weren't hiding so much from him.

"Well, that's the last of them," he says, reappearing in the living room. His jeans are torn and dirty, and his old T-shirt is faded, with little holes around the collar. He's sweaty when he wraps his arms around my waist. "We are officially living together."

He sounds so happy.

"Hey . . . don't worry, okay?" He bends slightly at the knees to look at me. "This is the right thing—with the baby coming. It's going to be great."

I nod, staring into his kind, caring eyes. He was over the moon when I told him about the baby. He's so trusting. So . . . oblivious.

What would he do in this moment if I told him everything? Revealed who I am and confessed to murder? Would he believe me? Understand? Still want to have this baby—this life—with me?

"Parker . . ." I clear my throat. It's there. Everything I've been hiding. Temptation to unburden myself with the truth bubbling up inside my chest.

This pregnancy is weakening me, doing things to my mind. The room spins, and the floor feels unsteady beneath my feet. I haven't had a blackout in months . . . but the threat of one is never far away.

"What's wrong?" he asks. "More second thoughts?"

I can never tell him the truth. Parker's far too good to ever understand. I nod. "Yeah, I guess so . . ."

He pulls me in tighter and kisses the top of my head. "Everything is going to be okay. I promise."

If only I believed in promises.

He backs away and checks his watch. "I have to get the rental van back . . . you'll be okay?"

"Yes. I'm fine."

"Don't worry about unpacking anything. I'll do everything when I get back."

"Okay," I say as he leaves the living room. A moment later, I hear the moving van driving away from the house.

Alone again, I look around. So many boxes. I'm claustrophobic standing in the middle of my living room, surrounded by the trappings of the next logical step in our relationship.

A wave of morning sickness has me rushing to the bathroom.

A reminder that I don't really have a choice in any of this anymore. Running away again with another man's baby is not an option.

Jolie and Parker share a birthday—both born the second of May—and the weather is perfect the next day for their annual outdoor BBQ in the Caseys' backyard.

Unfortunately, the smell of grilling meat is making me feel nauseated. Faking smiles and talking to the fortysomething guests in the yard is a challenge when, at any moment, I might get sick, giving away the secret my oversize blouse is hiding.

With Michael, I'd barely shown until I was well into the pregnancy—five months at least. But this baby is demanding notice. I've gained twenty pounds already, and there is definitely a stomach protruding through the shirt whenever I sit, so I remain standing.

"You okay?" Parker asks as I untwist the cap off a bottle of water and guzzle before sneaking several Cheerios from a bag in my pocket. They are the only thing that tames the nausea. I was never sick during my first pregnancy. Maybe a higher power thought I was suffering enough and gave me a break.

So far, this pregnancy has been so different from the first—both equally terrifying, for different reasons. I'd longed for Adam to be a kind, caring, excited father to be . . . now, Parker is driving me crazy. He worries about me all the time and dotes on me, and the way he places a hand on my belly . . . makes my spine chill. I know it's out of love for this baby, but it feels like possession.

Parker is nothing like Adam. The baby and I are safe with him.

For now. As long as the truth stays hidden. I look across the yard, where John is playing catch with Michael and Jack. He's kept my secret about Dr. Collins, and, once again, the temptation to confide in someone—take a chance that someone might believe me, might help me—is strong.

Maybe it's the time that has passed, or maybe it's the faint glimmer of hope for a better future, that has me lowering the protective walls I've built around Michael and me . . . Either way, I need to pull it together and stay guarded.

"Do you need anything?" Parker asks, not looking at the hot dogs he's grilling.

"I'm fine," I say quickly as several of Jolie's friends approach with open hot dog buns. We haven't told anyone about the pregnancy yet, and I'm happy to not say a word. Ever. But Parker's itching to tell his family.

"Hey . . . you okay?" Parker leaves the grill to stand in front of me.

"I'm just not feeling great."

He kisses my forehead. "Ten more minutes, and then we are out of here."

"Thank you."

Jolie clinks her wineglass, capturing everyone's attention. "I have an announcement to make, and since everyone is here, I think now is the perfect time . . ."

Parker stares at me and hesitates just briefly before interrupting. "Wait a second—we have one too."

What? I swing to look at him, but he's grinning so widely, and all eyes are on him. "What are you doing?" I hiss.

"I don't think we're fooling anyone anyway, Drew," he whispers.

Knowing looks on the faces of the neighbors I barely know say he's right, and there's no point denying it. My loose blouse has hidden nothing, so I nod reluctantly.

"Drew and I have some exciting news," Parker says.

Now it's Jolie's turn to interrupt. "Oh my God . . ." Her high-pitched squeal hurts my ears as she hugs me. Then she pulls back quickly. "You *were* going to announce you're pregnant, right?"

Parker laughs. "Yes, I was. Thanks for assuming and stealing my thunder. Maybe I should spoil your news," he says.

I glance at him, buried in another hug from Jolie. He knows what Jolie was about to announce? He hasn't told me anything. *She* hasn't told me anything.

"What's going on?"

She pulls away. "I'm so happy for you guys!"

Something's up. Tears gather in her eyes. My stomach knots even more. I'm not going to like what she's about to say.

"Damn. This makes my news a lot harder. Thanks a lot, Parker." She hits his arm and brushes the tears from her eyes as she wraps one arm through mine and turns to address the crowd. "Well, my news isn't as exciting as Parker and Drew's . . . but I've been offered a position at the University of Seattle—teaching sexual-therapy classes. We are leaving at the end of the school year."

Jolie's words hit me like a freight train. While the other women rush to congratulate her and immediately start planning a girls' getaway weekend for the fall, I'm frozen.

Fuck my customary forced smile. How I really feel has taken residence on my face.

She's moving to Seattle. The one city I can never visit.

A champagne cork popping makes me jump, and a second later a glass of the bubbly liquid is in my hand. Then taken away by Parker. "I'll drink for both of us," he says, wrapping an arm around my waist. I'm grateful for the support as my knees feel wobbly and my chest feels tight.

A toast to us. A toast to Jolie.

She's leaving. Now. When my life is becoming even more complicated. How could she do this to me? How can she just abandon me? Seattle. May as well be the moon. The support I was hoping for from her during this pregnancy and beyond vanishes.

"Drew? You okay?" Parker asks, looking worried.

No, I'm not okay. "I'm fine. Just too much excitement, I guess." For everyone else but me.

Michael

I thought there was something different about Mom. I thought she was sick. She throws up a lot, and she's always tired. She spends a lot of time in bed, but that's not really different. Her headaches are back. I thought she was getting better. I thought everything was getting better.

But things are getting worse. She's having another baby.

I sit in the new rocking chair in the room the baby will sleep in. Parker bought it and surprised Mom with it today.

At first, it was great having Parker and Amelia living here with us. He's like a dad. Only he's not my real dad . . . but he will be the new baby's real dad. He plays with me and listens to me, and I feel safer with him here. But lately, we talk about the baby all the time.

Amelia says she's excited to be a big cousin. She doesn't understand. Parker's going to have his own kid soon. Then he won't love us.

They ask me if I'm excited to be a big brother, and I lie and say yes.

They talk a lot about baby names. It's like the only thing they talk about.

They like the name Gregory if it's a boy. Jessica for a girl. At least Parker does. Mom doesn't seem to care what they call the new baby.

I think both names are dumb.

I stare at the mural Mom has started to paint.

Animals.

Stupid.

They spend all their time getting ready for the baby. No one has noticed that I lost a tooth. It's gross and bloody and starting to smell bad under my pillow.

No stupid tooth fairy either. Shoulda known that wasn't real.

What else has Mom lied to me about?

Is she telling the truth when she says she will still love me when the baby gets here?

No one seems to care that I'll be losing my friend soon too. Jack's moving away. He's my only real friend. The other kids at school either avoid me or tease me.

Mom and Parker only care about a baby that isn't here yet, and Jack is leaving.

Soon, I'll have no one. And no one cares about that.

Catherine

I watch Isabella through the security-camera monitor set up in the room. I can only see her when she's outside, but she spends most of her time there. She's brought the garden back to life. We haven't had a gardener for years, but now the yard is blooming again—so colorful and bright.

She swims in the pool, and I stare at her perfection. That used to be me. I sometimes feel like she's *my* replacement, but Adam assures me it's the other way around.

I'm the important one. The one he wants.

I watch now as she climbs out of the pool, and the sight of her tiny baby bump has me mourning again for something I'll never have. Adam says no more trying for a baby. He came in two days ago with a needle. Birth control.

I was far too weak to fight him off.

Afterward, he held me while I cried. He's right. I can't try again. My body can't take another pregnancy, and my emotional state is so fragile already that I've been having dreams about leaving. About running away, getting help.

Which is unfair. Adam is helping me.

Isabella wraps a towel around her body and slides her feet into a pair of flip-flops before disappearing from my view.

A moment later I hear the back door close and her footsteps on the stairs. I hold my breath. My door is locked from the inside.

Will she try the door handle? Doesn't she wonder what's in here? What has Adam told her?

Her footsteps pass the door, and I listen to the sound of water running in the en suite bathroom down the hall.

I get up and go to the door; I unlock it and open it slowly. Adam is out of town. It's just me and Isabella here in this house. I don't want her here. I liked it better before she came. I want it to just be me and Adam again.

I tiptoe toward the sound of the water. I hear her singing, terribly off-key. Like cats being tortured. She'll never sing to her baby. I won't let her.

I stop outside the open bedroom door and look inside. I've never seen this room where Adam sleeps with her. It's painted a boring beige color. The four-poster bed is covered by a white duvet, and everything in the room is of maple wood. Light and bright. Unlike my dark-blue room, with the mahogany bed and denim-colored bedsheets. The sun shining through the open blinds hurts my eyes as I move in farther, scanning the clothes in the walk-in closet—hers on one side, Adam's on the other.

I quietly remove a soft, light-pink cardigan from a hanger and put it on. It's too big for my skeletal frame, but I fasten the ties around my waist and pull it back up over my shoulders. I turn to finger the row of Adam's suits. They are in order of color—beiges, grays, navies, and different shades of black. The dress shirts are all white—starched and impeccably pressed. A row of dress shoes are lined up on the floor underneath, but on top of the closet is a lone shoebox.

I take it down and open it. Adam's personal things. An old watch . . . a few family photos. One catches my eye. I pick it up out of the box and stare at a face that looks just like mine but slightly older. Long dark hair. Dark eyes. High cheekbones and porcelain-white skin . . .

Turning it over, I see the name and date on the back.

Mariella. 1996. His nanny. I shiver as I stare at the face that is hauntingly a reflection of my own.

Is this why he loves me?

I tuck it into the pocket of the sweater and close the box, putting it back exactly where I found it.

Then I head toward the bathroom.

Isabella is still singing, and I hear the popping sound of a shampoo bottle opening. I peek inside and see the steamed mirror, her naked body blurry behind the frosted glass. I scan the vanity. All her makeup and hair products messy on the counter. My stuff is neatly arranged. Disorganization like this drives Adam crazy. Doesn't she know that? Doesn't she want to make him happy?

She doesn't deserve him.

I creep inside, staying by the door, hidden from sight, as I pick up her lipstick.

It's a pale-coral color.

I wipe the steam from the mirror and twist off the cap. Then I apply the pale shade to my dry lips. It's not my color. Adam prefers red. Doesn't she want to make him happy?

This adventure of mine outside my room is making my pulse race, my body hot, my hands clench and unclench. I don't feel safe out here. There's too much . . .

I reach for a tissue to remove the lipstick and drop the lid into the sink with a loud clatter.

The singing stops, and I freeze.

"Hello?"

I hold my breath, sliding farther out of sight, toward the doorframe.

"Adam? Is anyone there?"

I slip out of the room as I hear the shower door start to open. On my fragile legs, I run back to my room and close the door as quietly as I can, locking it again.

I inch backward toward the bed and sit on the edge, my heart thundering in my chest. I wait. I hear her footsteps just outside the door as she tries the handle.

Should I let her in? What would happen if she knew about me?

Should I tell her that we won't need her soon? Demand that she leave now?

How? How could I tell her those things?

I stare at the door but make no move toward it. Footsteps disappear down the hall; then the water resumes.

I lie on my back, my heart pounding in my chest.

I left the room. Could I do it again? Could I go farther next time?

Drew

The room next to Michael's will be the nursery. I feel guilty that the baby gets its own room while Amelia is sharing Michael's for now until Parker renovates, adding in another bedroom for her. But he says it's only temporary. He's determined to make the perfect home for all of us.

One big happy family.

Now that everyone knows about the baby, it suddenly feels a lot more real, and this room will have to be ready in six months. The only thing in here so far is the rocking chair Parker bought for me.

I flick the light switch, but nothing happens. The bulb is burned out beneath the light cover that serves as a disgusting cemetery for dead flies.

I'll need to clean in here before I can set up the furniture. I wait for any excitement to surface, but I'm numb. Jolie's news has my mind in a mess. I stand in the middle of the room, trying to envision how wonderful it could look, but all I see are the walls of another nursery, Michael's nursery, closing in around me . . .

"It's lovely."

My mother's praise that day so long ago was the first thing to have filled my heart with any joy in months. Adam was away on a business trip, and I was relieved to have the time without him to put together the nursery. Of course, I wasn't alone. Besides my mother's weekly visits, I now had twenty-four-hour surveillance while Adam was gone.

My mother seemed impressed that Adam had gone through the trouble to "protect" his crazy wife.

The large, scary-looking guard was almost as terrifying as Adam. I avoided him as much as possible. The way he eyed me gave me chills. When my mother wasn't there, I locked myself in my room voluntarily.

But the nursery furniture I'd ordered had arrived that day, and I constructed the crib and changing table and dresser myself. Despite doctor's orders, I lugged those heavy boxes up the stairs one at a time, determined to do this project alone. I didn't want or need Adam's help. Though I was reluctant to believe he would help, even if I'd asked.

It would perhaps have been something else he'd want to control.

Which made taking the opportunity away from him that much sweeter.

"Really?" I'd asked, sitting in the big, oversize rocking chair in the corner of the room and observing my work.

The large mural on the wall had taken four hours to paint, but the vibrant jungle scene turned out better than I'd hoped. I wanted this room to be a safe zone for the baby. I wanted the colors to be bright and happy and uplifting.

"You did a great job, sweetheart."

"Thanks, Mom."

Over the last six months, she'd been in and out of rehab again; therefore, I'd kept my marital issues to myself. She had no idea how unhappy, alone, and scared I was. Or that my marriage had turned into a hell. And, like everyone else, she believed I was suffering from mental illness. Funny how she took no ownership for my possibly fragile state of mind.

"Adam will love it," she said.

The mention of him erased any happiness. No, he wouldn't. And I couldn't help but suspect that somehow, someway, I'd be punished for this.

"Mom . . . ," I started, with no idea what I was about to say.

She ignored me; she went to the window and closed the drapes. The brightness of the mural faded. "You don't want neighbors knowing your business."

Her home was always dark and dreary. The curtains all drawn tight. No sunlight. No fresh air. No window for the outside world to peer inside.

"Mom," I tried again. "Can I talk to you?"

"Of course," she said, but she'd opened her purse and retrieved a flask.

"Adam has changed," I said carefully.

"All men change."

I fought for the courage to continue. "He's abusive. Like Dad." Instinctively, I pulled the sleeve of my shirt lower, hiding the scars that had yet to fully heal.

She ignored my reference to my father. "Adam has a lot on his mind right now."

I nodded.

"He's stressed."

I bit my lip, knowing that I was getting nowhere with her. "He's been a little rough with me lately." Understatement, but I was treading slowly, carefully . . .

Her forehead wrinkled, and something resembling understanding flashed in her eyes before it was gone. "He's a powerful man. Sometimes, powerful men don't know their own strength. He hasn't gotten to where he is in life, in business, by being soft, Drew."

Obviously the story she'd repeated to herself all those years.

She gestured to the room around us. "All of this . . . none of this would be possible if he wasn't the person he is. Sometimes you need to put him first. Understand the pressure he's under."

It sounded like my father's words coming out of her slightly swollen, bruised lips.

"Besides, I do remember warning you, darling," she said quietly, sipping from the flask.

The kick to the gut was delivered with precision. "You're right. You did," I said, knowing I didn't have an ally in her. My mother was struggling with her own darkness. I couldn't expect her to be a light in mine.

Adam came home early the next day. His wild expression as he stormed into the nursery had me scampering down the ladder and putting it between us as he stalked toward me.

"You're home a day early." Maybe he was upset about work. Maybe his mood had nothing to do with me or something I'd done.

I'd be the one to pay either way.

He grabbed the ladder and tossed it aside, the metal making me jump as it crashed against the wall, leaving several large dents. "What the hell, Drew?" he asked.

My mind was frantic, desperate to think of what I'd done wrong. "Adam, what's wrong?" I asked, backing away until my body hit the wall. Nowhere to go.

He ripped the paintbrush from my hands. He'd yet to tear his angry eyes from me to see the painted room or the assembled furniture. "I asked you a question."

He was expecting me to know what I'd done. Trying to manipulate me into a guessing game, in which I could potentially reveal a list of sins deserving punishment. "I don't know what you mean."

He grabbed my hair and twisted my head up and back. "That corner. See that camera."

My neck hurt, and I could feel strands of my hair being torn out. I winced as I tried to nod. We'd had the security system installed in the nursery the week before; I'd wrongly assumed it wasn't being monitored yet.

"I've been watching you every day. Listening."

I swallowed hard. I hadn't said much.

After my mother dismissed me, I spent the night thinking maybe she was right. Adam was just stressed, and he was a powerful man—one with needs and desires. A wife should please her husband, right? Maybe he had a right to be angry right now.

I was bad. I never should have said anything bad about him to my mother. To anyone. "I didn't do or say anything, Adam. I swear."

"That's right. Because there's nothing to do or say." He released my hair, and I massaged my kinked neck.

He stalked to the middle of the room and looked around for the first time.

I waited.

Please, God, let him like it.

"This is garbage."

That hurt more than the hair pulling.

"I mean, you're not a great artist anyway, but this is really shit, Drew. You actually want my baby sleeping in here?" He kicked the leg of the wooden crib. "Look at this junk. You have the shittiest taste, Drew."

Tears burned the back of my eyes, and he smiled, seeing the pain he was inflicting. "Oh, come on, you didn't think you did good, did you?"

He picked up a can of red paint I'd been using and approached the mural.

"Adam, please don't . . ." I'm not sure where I found the voice to say anything.

"Don't what?"

"Don't destroy it." I hated how weak I was, but, in my next thought, I was wondering if he were right. Maybe it was garbage.

"This will be an improvement," he said, throwing the paint at the wall.

A small gasp escaped me, but I knew better than to utter another sound. I pressed my lips together, and my hands balled into fists at my sides.

Big, red smears of paint dripped down the wall, covering hours of work. Erasing the love and energy I'd put into creating something I thought was beautiful for our child. The splatter ran in streaks to the baseboard, then creeped over the edge, staining the animal-print rug.

Destroyed.

Next, a can of green paint stained the wall . . . then blue. All the images I'd carefully drawn and painted disappeared beneath big ugly smears of color. Finally, he threw the can across the room, narrowly missing my body. I yelped as it hit the wall next to me, paint seeping into the carpet at my feet, splatters ruining the light fabric of the rocking chair, where I'd envisioned nights rocking the baby to sleep . . .

He looked around for other things he could use to damage and destroy, and my chest was aching so badly that I believed my heart had shattered into a billion pieces.

"Get out," he said.

I hurried out into the hallway, and he shoved me away from the room as he closed the door behind us. "Stay out of there, and, next time, remember I'm watching, listening. All the time. To everything."

The next day, a professional painting crew arrived to redo the room the way Adam wanted.

Desperate to use these workers to help me escape, I waited until I heard Adam's study door close and his voice on a conference call before creeping down the hall toward the nursery. I carried a small bag with barely anything in it—a change of clothes and a toothbrush. I'm not sure why I didn't pack anything else. My mind wasn't working properly.

"Hey," I whispered through the open door.

The two men turned to look at me but continued painting the walls a dark denim blue. The same dark, powerful shade that Adam had painted his offices.

"Hey, please . . . I need help," I said, daring to step a little closer. I eyed the camera in the corner, hoping I was out of range of the shot.

The two men ignored me.

"Please . . ." I begged. "Just toss me the keys to your van." It was parked in front of the gate leading to the house. I'd seen it pull up. I'd have to make a run for it, but, hearing Adam's voice in the study, I knew I could make it, relying on my desperation and need for survival to propel my legs. "Hey!" I said a little louder when they continued to ignore me.

One man glanced my way again, and a brief look of consideration flashed on his face before the other guy shook his head. *"Loco,"* I heard him say.

Loco. Crazy.

Adam was telling everyone I was a nutcase. And everyone believed him.

I glanced down at my body, realizing for the first time I was still in my bathrobe. My feet were bare, and my "go bag" was a pillowcase.

I believed I might actually be crazy. I certainly looked the part.

I slunk away from the door and was walking backward toward my bedroom when Adam's study door opened.

His menacing stare is still burned into my mind as he took in everything, knowing what I'd been trying to do.

I turned and ran.

He chased.

The slam of the bedroom door echoed throughout the house, and the next twenty minutes of my life were beaten from my damaged brain.

I remember lying on the floor for a long time after I heard Adam's car leaving the driveway and the big iron gates close. I struggled for consciousness, in a dreamlike state. I couldn't believe he'd left me alone. He must have thought he'd left me for dead.

I didn't feel dead. Death wouldn't hurt that much. My right arm was definitely broken, and I could feel blood trickling down both cheeks. Swollen eyes made it impossible to focus on the door. I tried to sit up, and pain radiated through my core. If I was still pregnant after this, it would be a miracle.

Or, more likely, a curse.

He'd never hit me in the stomach before. Was he, too, regretting this unborn baby? If I lost it, if I was no longer of use to him, would he set me free?

Never.

I didn't have much time. Adam had probably called in a cleanup crew to come dispose of me. I had to get out of there. I pulled myself up against the edge of the bed; blood dripped onto the comforter, the red seeping into the embroidered white floral design, fading to pink as it reached the ends . . .

I lost consciousness for several moments, and my eyes flew open in panic. I listened but heard nothing.

I stood up and fell against the post of the bed. I used it to steady myself and closed my eyes as I rested my head against it to try to stop the spinning of the room. My head throbbed. The pain wasn't isolated to one spot but spiraled through my brain, making it hard to think . . . to breathe . . . to focus.

I needed to get out.

The door was a million miles away beneath my unsteady feet. If he came home now, he would kill me. For real.

For all I knew, this could have been a trap awaiting me. Adam could still be in the house somewhere. Or waiting just beyond the gates of this multimillion-dollar prison.

I swallowed a lump in my throat, the metallic taste of copper making my stomach turn as the thick liquid seeped down the back of my throat.

If I stayed there, I would die.

I opened the door, and, not trusting my legs, I fell to my knees and crawled to the stairs. I went down them on my ass, like a two-year-old finding independence. The front door was unlocked.

My heart pounded loudly in my ears, and the sound threatened to cause my brain to explode. A noise in the kitchen made me jump, and

I sat motionless, not breathing, waiting for that monster to appear with a knife or some other weapon he could end my life with.

Then I heard the sound of the fridge opening and the familiar humming of our housekeeper. She usually came at night. I had no idea why she was there that day, but my mind spun with indecision.

Could I trust her? Would she help me? The neighbor hadn't. The painters hadn't. I couldn't take the chance that she would.

I shuffled down the rest of the stairs and hurried toward the door. I gripped the handle as she appeared in the foyer behind me. "Miss Drew . . ."

I swung open the door and ran to her vehicle, the one Adam had bought for her to run errands in. It was still running, the smell from the back seat revealing she'd just come from the fish market. Master Adam only ate fresh fish.

He'd probably prefer it if she brought the things home still breathing, so he could be the one to end their lives.

I slammed the door, turned the key, and hit the gas. I saw Lucinda in the driveway, waving at me, but I ignored her. I'd learned to trust no one.

The car was headed straight for the gate. I reached up to unlock it and hit the button attached to the mirror. It opened slowly. So painfully slowly. In the mirror, I saw Lucinda chasing after the car. She was surprisingly fast for an older woman, but the thing that chilled my core was the look on her face.

Not worry or concern but determination and anger.

I was right not to have trusted her.

The gate was barely out of the way before I'd driven through it, wiping blood away from my eyes as it dripped down my forehead. The red liquid stained my hands as I gripped the steering wheel tight. My wedding ring was covered in it, and I let go of the wheel long enough to tear it off and throw it into the back of the car.

I was getting the fuck out.

I wasn't stopping until I got to the police station, and then there would be no going back. Ever.

Adam couldn't control everyone in this city. Someone had to be able to help me. The thoughts fueled me to drive faster as I approached the end of the hill. I sped past the stop sign. There was never anyone around there during the day. They were either slaving away at jobs they hated to afford their luxurious lifestyle, or they were lying by the pool reaping the benefits of someone else's sacrificed life.

This was not me. It never was. It wouldn't ever be again.

I was getting the fuck out.

My determination kept me from blacking out as I drove the eight blocks to the community policing station.

Relief flowed through me as I pulled into the lot and got out of the car.

Safety awaited me inside. A way out of this hell. I still couldn't believe Adam had given me this opportunity, and it was the only thing nagging me as I stumbled inside. The pain in my stomach was the worst of it all, and I was convinced I was having a miscarriage.

I could feel blood trickle down my leg, and I glanced down to see a red line all the way to my ankle, dripping onto the police station floor. "Help . . . please help," I managed to say before my body collapsed to the floor.

"Hey . . . I need some help over here," I heard a deep voice say. It sounded distant. The whole room seemed far away.

But then I felt two arms lifting me off the floor, and I closed my eyes, giving in to the darkness . . . knowing I'd awake to light.

I was safe.

I did awake to light. Bright, glaring, hot lights pointed directly at my face. I shut my eyes tight and lifted a hand to shield them from the glare. I heard voices all around me, and the smell of iodoform told me I was at the hospital.

My body sank back into the bed; my muscles relaxed for the first time in months, fear and anxiety drifting away as I realized I'd made it. I'd gotten out.

"Drew . . . can you hear me?" a female voice said to my right.

Eyes closed, I nodded.

"Can you open your eyes for me?" she asked as she stood over me, her body blocking the light.

I opened them. "I'm at the hospital." It wasn't a question; I just felt like I had to say something to let them know I was conscious.

She nodded. "The police brought you in. You're in pretty rough shape."

But I was at the hospital. Away from Adam. Somewhere they could help me. "How's the baby?" I asked first. I wasn't sure what answer I really wanted to hear.

"He's fine. We've run some tests, and he's doing great," she said. "Were you trying to end your pregnancy?"

I frowned. "No. Why would you think that?" I felt my sense of security slipping away by her accusatory tone.

"Because you drove straight into the iron gates on your property," she said, checking my eyes for signs of concussion or lies—I couldn't tell.

"I didn't run into the gates."

"Your crashed vehicle says otherwise." A new voice spoke to my left, and I turned my head slowly to see two police officers standing in the room. "A 2015 Audi S4?"

I shook my head, and a wave of nausea hit. "No. I was driving the housekeeper's car."

"That's not the one that was at the station." He came forward and showed me a picture of my Audi—damage to the front that looked like the vehicle had crumpled like an accordion on impact.

"I didn't do that. I wasn't driving that car." Was I? My brain hurt, and I was suddenly confused. Doubting.

"Well, where did all of these injuries come from?" the second officer asked.

Adam. I blinked several times, and the events of the last few hours became clearer again. I had to stop getting confused. Now was my chance. "My husband. Adam Crenshaw did all of this to me."

The police officers exchanged looks, and the monitor to my right started beeping. "Her blood pressure is going up. Can we do this later?" the nurse asked. "She's obviously confused, and she may have suffered a more serious brain injury than we'd thought."

They didn't believe me. Tears burned my eyes as panic set in, making it difficult to breath. "It's true," I yelled. "My husband is abusive. He tried to kill me . . ." My shrieking voice was convincing no one that I was anything but crazy—I could see it on their faces. "Please . . . you have to believe me."

The taller, older police officer moved forward. "Look, Mrs. Crenshaw, you've had a really bad accident. You are confused."

"Why don't you believe me?"

"Ma'am . . . you are accusing your husband of some serious crimes. And, unfortunately for you, all of the evidence points to self-harm."

"Self-harm?" What evidence? My gaze flew to my wrist, where the cutting scars were just healing over. Faint purple marks in neat rows indeed made me look like a victim at my own hand. "I didn't do this," I whispered. "It was Adam. All of this was Adam."

They exchanged looks.

"What the hell is going on?"

My nightmare went from bad to worse as Adam entered the room.

"No! Get him out of here!" I tried to back away, as high on the bed as possible, but the monitors and tubes had me trapped. Who the hell let him in? Why won't they believe me?

"Darling, darling . . . it's okay . . . shhhh," Adam said, approaching. "It's okay. I'm here now. Everything will be okay." He took my hand, and I tried to pull back, but his death grip wouldn't let me.

He kissed it, and I tasted vomit in my mouth.

The look in his eyes that no one else could see but me was one of pure pleasure. "I'm here now. You're safe." He had my wedding ring—now free of all signs of blood—and he slid it back onto my finger.

Tears poured down my cheeks, and I turned to the nurse. "Please. Please help me. You have to believe me." She was my only hope. I prayed that this woman could see through Adam and his bullshit.

"I'm sorry, Mrs. Crenshaw, but you are safe now. We will get you the help you need."

The help I needed was to be away from Adam.

Defeated, I sank back against the bed, my body going limp. How long did I have left to live? It depended on when the hospital planned to release me.

"Dr. Bishop is here too," Adam said as another man entered the room.

Who the hell is Dr. Bishop?

An elderly man dressed in a tan suit appeared in the crowded room beside Adam.

"Dr. Bishop is a highly trained psychotherapist. He's here to help."

The doctor stepped forward. "Drew . . . how are you?"

How the hell do you think I am? I wanted to scream. I wanted to run away. But Adam, the police officers, and this doctor would never let it happen. I looked away from them all.

"I'm sorry that you felt you had to do this to yourself, Drew," the doctor said. "But we will get you some help. I've prescribed a dose of Prolixin that is safe for the baby . . . we will work through this."

"That's right, Drew. And I'm here. I'm not going anywhere," Adam said.

I wished I had died on the floor of my bedroom.

JUNE

Drew

"I can't believe I'm going to miss your pregnancy," Jolie says, standing over me. She's holding my hair back while I vomit, and I honestly don't think I'm going to get through this without her.

Since delivering our news, she's been at my side constantly—making sure I'm eating right and resting enough and that my hair stays vomit free.

Jolie is handing me a tissue when I hear the front door open. My pulse doesn't race like it does when I'm alone. I believe Jolie could protect me. The woman seems invincible.

And soon she's leaving.

"That's John. I asked him to bring over the baby stuff we had in the basement. I hope that's okay. Some of it's brand new, still in boxes."

He pokes his head in through the open bathroom door, and his expression of sympathy makes it hard for me to feel anything but appreciative. "That baby still giving you trouble, huh?"

"Better now than later, right?"

He laughs. "Great optimism."

"Should he bring the stuff into the spare room next to Michael's?" Jolie asks.

"Yes, that's great. Thank you, John."

"My pleasure. I'm happy to get my man cave back for a few months at least," he says with a wink.

My stomach completely empty, I stand and hug Jolie. "Thank you."

She sniffs and clears her throat. "Look, just because I'm in Seattle doesn't mean I can't be here for you. And I'm not leaving for another few months."

Unfortunately, I know that, unlike the rest of my life to this point, these next few months are going to fly by.

"Hey, Drew . . . while I'm here, I can set up this monitor for you," John calls from down the hall.

"Monitor?"

Jolie nods. "Yes, it's incredible. We had one for our kids, so I bought you one. Come on." She takes my hand and leads the way down to the nursery, where John is already taking a camera out of a box.

"I think the far corner, near the window, is the best place," he says.

"This is really thoughtful of you both, but I don't think we need anything this extravagant."

"You do," Jolie says. "It not only monitors the baby through an app on your phone or computer . . . it stores what it records in the cloud, so you can go back and watch videos as the child gets older. I wasn't sure I'd use that either, but I can't tell you how often I go back and watch videos of myself feeding the kids or playing with them, rocking them to sleep." She opens the box wider and takes out the manual. "Take a look," she says, handing it to me.

All I see is the C2 Technologies logo in the corner of the booklet, and it slips from my hand. A monitor from Adam's company. Like the one in the corner of Michael's nursery? The one that Adam used to keep an eye on me? I'd forgotten about that camera, but it saw so much . . . everything. Could it also have stored the past somewhere?

Jolie picks it up. "You okay? You look pale."

I swallow hard and hold on to the doorframe for support. "You had one of these?"

She nods. "Well, it was a previous model, but it's almost identical. You know how these tech companies like to make a tiny improvement just so they can charge more."

"How long ago? How long ago did you have one?"

She looks at John, but he's busy setting up the camera. "I don't think we had one for Ellie . . . but we had one for Jack. Are you okay?"

Nine years ago. "And how long are the videos stored?"

She shrugs. "Forever, I guess. The videos download to the cloud every twenty-four hours, freeing the memory card. Why don't you sit? You look really pale."

My heart is about to explode in my chest. Stored footage could be the answer to my darkest question about my past. What exactly happened that night I escaped?

I barely feel her guide me to the rocking chair. "How do you see them online?"

She opens the manual and holds it open to the instructions page. "Easy. See? You register the unit, and then it's just your home address and a password to log in."

I know Adam's home address. If I could figure out his password for the unit hanging in the nursery, I'd have my answers. I could go back and watch the footage from that night we escaped. Would he have erased it by now? Would it even still exist?

"Drew . . ." John's voice sounds far away. "Drew, are you feeling okay? Sit back."

"I'll get her a cold facecloth," Jolie says, leaving the room.

I sit back as he suggests, feeling overcome and more than a little dizzy.

This might finally be the key to unlocking the questions of my past, to moving forward, to knowing the truth about that night.

But it means that I'll have to watch myself murder the nanny.

The house looks deserted. No lights shine from inside, despite the late hour, but this time Dr. Collins's car is in the driveway.

I'd told Parker I needed to run to the grocery store. He'd argued that he'd go, but I'd insisted. Once Jolie and John had left, I'd had to pick Michael up from school, and then he was with me all afternoon. There'd been no time to sneak off to see Dr. Collins, and tomorrow is Saturday. I won't get this chance again for days.

I can't wait that long.

I need to tell him about David's murder and about the recorded video that I need his help accessing. That monitor saw a lot more than just a murder. There's proof of my abuse . . . proof of Adam's anger. Maybe there is something that could save Michael and me. Put an end to all of this.

I get out of the car and go to the front door; I ring the doorbell once, then knock when I don't hear the chime inside.

The sound of footsteps approaching provides relief that he hasn't once again tried to kill himself. I need him now more than ever. Figuring out Adam's password will be almost impossible on my own, but Dr. Collins's son was C2 Technologies' CIO, and he'd once before hacked into Adam's profile on the C2 Technologies systems. I'm reaching, but one thing's certain—Dr. Collins would know more than I would.

His eyes meet mine through the warped windowpane in the side of the door, and immediately he shakes his head and turns to walk back down the hall.

I bang on the door. This time, I'm not leaving until I get his help. "Dr. Collins, please open the door," I call out. "I need your help."

He turns, and an odd smile registers on his face as he moves closer to the window. He continues moving closer until his old face is pressed against the glass, his features distorted as they flatten out against it.

I take a step back. "Open the door. I have to talk to you," I yell, glancing at the neighboring houses.

Dr. Collins stares at me, his wide eyes and disturbing grimace making me shiver.

"Just open the door," I say. I don't love the idea of going inside this crazed man's house. His actions scream at me to leave, but I need information that only he might have.

He moves away from the window, and the door opens a crack but comes up short against a chain lock.

Bars on the windows. Chains on his door. He's gotten smarter. Who is he afraid of—Adam or me?

I move closer. "Dr. Collins, I have evidence of what happened the night of the murder. It's on a recorded video; I just need to access it."

"So you have nothing."

"Not without your help. Please. I need Adam's file. I need anything that will help me figure out the password to access the video footage."

"I can't help you. I don't know what you're talking about."

I shove against the door as he tries to close it. "You do. I know who you are, and you know who I am." I take a deep breath. "I know your son didn't commit suicide. I was there the day Adam killed David." It comes out fast, and the words seem to hit him harder than if he'd been hit by a train.

His face looks pained, and an odd, eerie-sounding moan escapes him as he pushes against the door.

I'm stronger and the door stays open. "I couldn't stop it. I'm sorry. But we can stop this from happening again. We can both finally get peace," I say.

"You're lying."

"I'm not. You know it's true." I take a breath. "David was involved in some insider trading . . . Adam found out . . ."

"My boy would never—"

"I'm sure he just wanted to get out from under Adam. I know he wasn't a bad person. Adam is the bad person. He killed David." Maybe if I say it enough, he'll believe me; he will stop resisting and do the right thing.

He stops pushing against the door, and a few seconds later I hear his footsteps shuffle down the hall. I wait. Have I gotten through to him?

My cell phone rings in my pocket—Parker. I've been gone far too long already. I don't care. Once I know the truth, maybe I'll finally be able to be honest with Parker . . . maybe we'll have some hope of a future.

Dr. Collins reappears. Through the crack in the door, I see him carrying a box. Adam's files. My heart races and I nod. "Good. Open the door. Let me in," I say, trying to reach inside to move the chain myself, but my arm gets stuck before I can get to it.

He places the box on the floor several feet away and kneels next to it. I see him take out a piece of paper and crinkle it. "What are you doing? Just let me in. I can help go through the files." My cell phone rings again. I don't have time for this. I'm not sure what I'm even looking for, but I know the answer is in that box.

A lighter appears in Dr. Collins's other hand, and my eyes widen. "No! Don't."

He lights the end of the paper in his hand, and it goes up in flames. He holds it until the burning yellow and orange reaches his fingertips; then he drops it into the box.

"No! Dr. Collins, don't. I need those files," I yell through the door, wedging my arm higher to try to reach the chain. It's no use.

The box continues to burn on the floor next to him, and he sits staring at it, a sickly grimace on his face. "I can help you prove your theories, just stop!" Evidence that Adam is a psychopath and notes about his therapy are burning in front of me. All the information I need is going up in flames.

Dr. Collins looks up at me. "You didn't try to save my son, and you can't bring him back; why should I help you save yours?"

His words are half-drowned by the sound of the smoke detector wailing above his head on the ceiling as smoke rises from the old box. By now it's crumbling, and everything inside would be unreadable.

The hallway carpet catches the flame, but he continues to sit there. His face, illuminated by flames, is eerily at peace.

"Dr. Collins, you need to get out of the house!" I yell.

He doesn't move. Just sits in his burning hallway, staring at me.

I can't stay. I have to go. He doesn't want saving.

I run to my car as lights come on in the neighboring house. I have to get away before the police or firefighters show up. Once again, I have no one to depend on, to help me out of this nightmare.

As I speed away from the house, a glance in the rearview mirror shows nothing but flames.

Drew

Six. The number of log-on attempts the C2 Technologies baby-monitoring device allows before locking the user out for twenty-four hours.

Damn.

I sit back in the library chair and stare at the log-on screen as the timer appears. Adam's password could be anything. I'd even been foolish enough to try my name and birthday.

Catherine hadn't worked either.

Without Dr. Collins, figuring this out rests completely on luck. The front-page news story that morning was about the fire at his home. The police and fire rescue crews hadn't arrived in time to control the blaze, and the house was nothing but ash.

Dr. Collins's body wasn't found. The police and the neighbors believe he wasn't home when the fire started but have been unable to locate him or contact him. I know he was home, and if he didn't die in the fire, he's still out there somewhere . . .

I hadn't slept the night before—tossing and turning, avoiding Parker's silent, questioning glances. Images of the old man's sadistic expression as he'd set the box of evidence to flames haunting me. His words taunting me.

You couldn't save my son . . .

Would I be able to save my own?

"Mom, can you help me now?" Michael asks from the table behind me.

I stand, push the chair in, and join him at a small table near the children's section of the library. "What do you need, sweetheart?"

"I have to finish my 'All about Me' report for school."

I swear this school is going to be the death of me. I can't wait for summer break in a few weeks. I've already had to download and print pictures of a strange baby for his photo-collage project a month ago, and now I'm going to have to make up lies about his life so far. Things that are so easy for other parents are going to be my downfall, and the truth is that none of this bullshit matters. Survival matters. But for now, my son needs to finish his assignment, and it's about the only thing I can control. "What have you written so far?"

"Not much." He taps the pencil against the desk. "Why don't we have any relatives?"

"My parents died," I say. "And I was an only child, so you don't have any aunts or uncles or cousins." A least most of that is true. My father is still alive . . . his position working for Adam holding him prisoner. I don't think about him. How he could have helped me. How he could have prevented all this.

Michael sighs. "At least I'll have a half brother or half sister soon."

"Where did you hear that word?"

"Amelia. She said you and Parker and the baby will be a real family . . ."

I turn his chair to face me. "We are all a real family. You are just as important to me as this new baby will be," I say. If only he knew how much I'd sacrifice for him. At one point, I'd been willing to sacrifice this unborn child. "And Parker loves you and Amelia very much."

He nods, still not looking entirely convinced. He hesitates. "How come we don't have any pictures of my real father?"

My jaw clenches. "Well, he died when you were just a baby . . ." Lying to him is torture, but I'd never burden him with the truth. "You know we move around a lot, and it's impossible to take a lot of memories with us."

He bites his lip. "Are we staying here this time?"

For now. I nod.

He at least looks relieved at that. "When's the baby coming anyway?"

"A few more months yet."

"Amelia says having a baby hurts."

I wish Amelia wouldn't share her knowledge about things with Michael. "It's painful, but it's worth it." My throat feels constricted.

"Did I hurt you?" he asks.

"No, sweetheart. You didn't hurt me at all," I lie, smoothing his dark hair away from his face.

The truth was, Michael must have known the hateful world awaiting him: twenty-six hours of labor, and he simply refused to come out. The pain of the contractions had stolen all my strength and had increasingly zapped my will to live.

Adam made regular appearances, sending me disgusted looks. "What the hell is wrong with you? Women do this every day. You are useless."

I barely heard the words.

I'd heard them over and over. I not only believed them when he said them but repeated them to myself.

He must have been right. Why else couldn't I deliver this baby?

Lying on a cot on the floor of the spare room in the basement, I silently pleaded for this baby to come out. Please, Michael, please . . .

I'd started calling the baby Michael weeks before. It was the name I wanted. I doubted I'd get a say. So, while I had some semblance of control, my baby boy's name was Michael.

The tightening of my abdomen made my heart race. Another contraction was mounting, and I wasn't sure I'd survive its peak. I clenched the bedsheet tightly in my hands and closed my eyes as it mounted and mounted . . . I wanted to cry out in agony, but Adam had had enough of that.

I panted through the pain at the coaching of the midwife Adam had hired, ensuring I wouldn't have to leave the house, and I searched for a sense of peace in her face. But, like everyone under Adam's control, she was emotionless, uncaring, going through the motions unwillingly. Adam wouldn't let her leave. I'd heard her tell him I should be at a hospital, but he'd refused to listen.

Two hours later, I was begging for death. Most women would be getting a C-section at that point, but the midwife and I continued to push through.

Adam entered the room again, and she stood and went to him. "It's time for a hospital. This baby doesn't want to come out. She's completely dilated, and she's been pushing for four hours straight. She has no strength left. She needs proper medical care."

Yes. Please. Doctors, nurses—no real safety from them, but at least they would have medication at the hospital. I'd readily have taken a needle to the spine.

Adam continued to refuse. "No. Do what you have to and get this baby out."

My heart was about to explode. My mind couldn't even focus on a solitary thought. I was exhausted and spent, and the pain in my legs, back, stomach, and chest were unbearable.

"Let me know when there's progress," Adam said, leaving the room again.

Tears were dried on my face. I wanted to cry, but I had nothing left. I wanted to scream, but my throat was hoarse, and barely a sound came out. The midwife lifted my upper body from the cot and sat behind me, supporting my weight against her hands, bending me in a *V* position that might have been uncomfortable if I could have felt anything other than sharp, shooting, indescribable pain. "You are going to die if you don't get this baby out soon," she said.

I didn't care. Death couldn't come fast enough. "I'm done."

"He's not going to let you be done."

She was right. Adam didn't care about me. His patience was running out. Any second now, he'd be back to take care of this himself. I still didn't give a shit.

"If you die, you leave this child with that monster," she said.

At the time, it wasn't so much leaving Michael with Adam that gave me the strength to continue to push and pray and struggle to get him out but the understanding from her that she knew the truth. She was the first person to acknowledge Adam for what he was. She didn't think I was crazy. She saw the cruelty in my husband and the inhumane way I was living, expected to bring a baby into the world.

She pushed against my back. "One more big push. You can do it, Drew," she said.

I didn't believe I could, but I pushed. As hard and as long as I could. The air expelled from my lungs as I felt the head crown. A new pain ran through me, but along with it was adrenaline from relief.

"That's it," she said, moving out from behind me; she propped my body up with pillows and blankets as she went to the foot of the cot. "Keep pushing. One more."

Adam reentered, and I shut my eyes, not wanting to see him watching me give birth. He stood at the foot of the cot, and I kept my eyes closed, knowing the sight of him would destroy any last remaining strength I had.

Three more pushes later, Michael was out.

As the midwife cut the umbilical cord, I collapsed back against the sheets, exhausted, near blacking out.

She took the baby to the bathroom down the hall, and my heart pounded in my chest as I waited.

When she returned a moment later, she was alone.

"Where's my baby?" I asked.

"Mr. Crenshaw took him."

I didn't even get to hold him. See him.

Outside the door, Adam walked past, and I called out.

He paused and entered the room, the baby in his arms. I took a deep breath as the tiny head full of dark hair that had caused me hours of pain appeared above the blue blanket. My heart swelled at the first sight of my baby boy. I reached out my arms, but Adam shook his head.

"This baby is mine. Useless," he spat one last time before leaving the room. Taking the baby away from me.

The midwife approached. Her unfeeling expression was back, and a breast pump was in her hand.

There would be no bonding with my baby. No first cuddles, holding him to my chest. He was gone with that monster, and I was forced to stay awake to pump milk so that someone else could feed my baby.

I thought I'd had no tears left to cry. I was wrong.

Michael

Everyone is asleep. Now's my chance.

I creep slowly out of bed and out of the room. If I wake Amelia, she'll tell on me. I tiptoe down the stairs and slowly turn the knob on the basement door.

I have to be brave now.

I hurry down the stairs and pull the cord for the light in the ceiling. Then, kneeling, I pick at the corner of the floorboard. I've seen Mom hide her stuff down here. I haven't told anyone about it, but I don't believe her when she says we don't have a picture of my dad.

I just want one for my project. That way, the other kids will see that I did have a normal family once.

I just want to see what he looks like.

Mom won't know. She doesn't take out the scrapbook now that Parker and Amelia live with us.

The board pops up, and I lift out her book. I know she will be so mad if she finds out. I'm not allowed to look at the things in here.

I open the cover and flip through the pages. All stories about the same guy. Adam. He must be my father.

I tear out one of the black-and-white-printed pictures and close the book, shoving it back where it was. Then I stare at the picture.

I think I look like him. He has dark-brown hair and brown eyes too. He's smiling and he looks nice. Why doesn't Mom like him? Why did she take me away from him? Why is she lying to me?

He looks nice, like Parker.

My dad's name is Adam.

Drew

With the scrapbook on my lap, I scan the years of articles for any hint of a password. Several mention the development of the monitoring system but say nothing of significance that can help me. Adam's password could be anything. It could take me a lifetime of trying.

I continue to flip through news articles, and my heart stops. A picture of Adam has been ripped off one of the pages.

Michael. That stupid class project.

I check the time: 9:48.

Please, God, don't let him have presented his "All about Me" assignment to his class yet.

I rehide the scrapbook, grab my purse, and hurry to the car. I fly through the quiet streets toward the elementary school.

I can't be too late. I need to stop Michael from showing that picture of Adam to his class.

I hit a red light and slam my fist against the steering wheel. How could I be so stupid to still have this book? I need to get rid of it.

I hope I haven't already fucked myself.

Deep breaths. In and out.

Would they believe that Michael was lying? That the picture of Adam was just some random stranger? Could I destroy my kid like that? Make him look like a liar in front of his class?

The light changes, and I speed into the parking lot.

There are no police cars waiting to arrest me.

I ring the intercom near the front door seconds later and wait.

"Hello?"

"Hi. This is Drew, Michael Baker's mom . . . he, uh . . . forgot his lunch this morning . . ." I'm not holding a lunch bag. My story is weak.

She buzzes me inside anyway.

I pull the door open, rush past the office without checking in, and head straight to Michael's classroom. He's standing in front of the class, and the other kids are seated on the carpet in front of him.

My heart races as I knock on the slightly open door and enter.

"Drew? What a nice surprise. Michael didn't mention you'd be stopping by to see his presentation today," Mrs. Harper says, a warm smile on her face.

I hadn't known it was an option. He obviously didn't want me there.

His eyes are wide now as he stares at me. Wide and knowing. Then embarrassed.

For the first time, I realize I didn't even change out of my pajamas. My faded yellow pants and oversize T-shirt are being eyed by the kids, and I hear several whispers. "Yes . . . well, I wasn't sure I'd be able to make it." I scan the poster behind him on the wall, and my heart rate slows. There's no picture of Adam. Just one of him with Parker and Amelia and two of him and me that Parker took a few days ago for the assignment. "Sorry to interrupt," I say.

"It's no problem. He was just starting. Have a seat," Mrs. Harper says.

I slowly lower myself into a chair along the back wall, relief and embarrassment fighting for top emotion. He's going to hate me for showing up like this, looking like this. I run a hand through my messy hair and slide my tongue over unbrushed teeth.

Protecting Michael, protecting our secret, is destroying any bond I could possibly still have with my son.

Michael restarts his presentation. He doesn't look at me again as he reads the lies I've told him out loud to his classmates.

I stay and watch, prepared to interrupt should that picture of Adam somehow appear.

It doesn't, and when I pick him up from school later that day, I don't ask him about it, and he doesn't say anything.

And because I'm not ready to confront my lies and confirm what he's already started to figure out, I tell him he did a great job that day.

LATE JUNE

Drew

My bladder is about to explode.

"I'm here!"

I can hear Parker's voice down the hall and release a sigh of relief. "What the hell took so long?" I'm not sure what's worse—my desire to pee or my growing anxiety over being here. Seeing the baby on the monitor will make all this so much more real.

"I got tied up. I'm sorry . . . I'm here."

He leans over me to kiss my forehead.

"Shall we get started then?" the technician asks, pulling up an extra seat for Parker.

She introduces herself, but my focus is only on holding in my pee. "Yes, please hurry." The minute we see the baby on the monitor, and she gets the required information from my uterus, I'm running to the nearest bathroom.

I'll appreciate this special moment later.

Parker sits and holds my hand in his.

"This is incredible." The love in his eyes looks so real, so genuine . . . but I'd once believed the same with Adam. Even if he is being honest, he would never love me this much if he knew the truth.

I force a breath. The more excited he is about all this, the worse I feel for not being so.

"Okay, this will feel a little cool . . . ," the technician says as she covers the wand with a clear jelly. She lifts the blue faded gown I'm wearing, and I tense slightly at the cold gel against my warm skin, and

Parker squeezes my hand as we wait. Eyes glued to the monitor, I hold my breath as she moves the wand around, trying to locate the best place to bring the image onto the screen.

"Is this your first child?" she asks.

"No," Parker answers, and my heart nearly stops.

He knows all the right things to say. All the right things that should put my mind and heart at ease. This experience with him is so different than it was with Adam; it's almost enough to make me forget how heartbreaking each of these pivotal moments were the first time.

But I won't be fooled.

"Ah . . . there we go," the tech says.

The blurry black-and-white image appears, and my escalating emotions refuse to commit to just one. Panic, happiness, fear, guilt, and longing all compete in my body.

My baby. Our baby.

Next to me, Parker swallows so loud I can hear it, and his death grip on my hand increases. "He or she is beautiful."

I'm jealous that he can enjoy this when I can't.

"A little pale perhaps," I say in an effort to make light of the moment and because everyone is expecting me to say something.

Parker turns to look at me. His expression steals my breath.

"Any baby of yours . . . ours . . . will be so beautiful," he says.

I suck my bottom lip in and turn back toward the screen.

"I'll give you three a minute," the tech says; she stands and leaves the room.

Parker moves closer once we are alone. The safety, comfort, and love he's offering is too good to be true. I long to erase all the hurt of my past, but it's deeply embedded, stealing my future joy.

I feel Parker's heart and his strength and his undying ability to love me despite it all.

But he doesn't know it all. Not even half of it.

"This baby will be so lucky to have you as a father," I say. It's true, and I want him to know it.

The surprise on his face by my words breaks my heart. I haven't been a fraction of the woman he deserves, and my softness in this moment isn't something I've displayed before.

"I love you, Drew. And I love Michael and Amelia, and I love this baby. And we are all lucky to have you."

I swallow burning remorse as I turn to once again look at the monitor.

"We are all in this life together," he whispers.

His words are meant to reassure and to offer a sense of family and peace, but a tightness grips my chest as they repeat in my mind.

We are all in this life together now, and what right do I have to condemn us all to it?

"You really need a home computer. This once-a-week Skype chat is hardly enough," Jolie says.

By the time I hear the words, her lips have stopped moving, and she's just smiling. The delay at the library on these dinosaur machines is at least twenty seconds.

"I know. I guess I could use Parker's," I say and wait.

"What's Parker's is yours now too," she says.

She could never understand that our lives—mine and Parker's—will never intersect in the ways most couples' lives do. No shared bank accounts. No buying a new car together. I don't want anything to do with his business. This baby is the only thing tying us together. It's already far too much.

Of course he's pushing for all the other things, but not too hard. He knows that too much too soon will make me retreat even more.

"How's the semester going?" I ask. Jolie left town three weeks ago, earlier than they'd originally planned, and it already feels like a lifetime.

"Great. I'm teaching six classes a week and making more than John ever made as a sheriff in Liberty. He's going batshit crazy just moping around, though. The Seattle PD have his application, but things are moving slowly."

Seattle Police Department. I'm not in a rush for John to start working. There's no reason for him to be suspicious of me, yet the idea of him having direct access to our missing person files has me on edge. If he saw the images of Michael and me, would he put the pieces together?

I need to get into those videos of my past. It's been weeks of trying to log on. Six attempts a day, five days a week . . . I don't get here on weekends. I've tried everything I can think of. I've studied the C2 Technologies website for any clues. I've researched everything I can find on Adam, going through my old scrapbook of news articles whenever I'm alone—I still haven't been able to get rid of it. And I've scoured my own memory for anything that could help.

Unfortunately, it's not the most reliable source, and I'm coming up with nothing.

Dr. Collins has yet to be found, and the calm and peace I'd slowly found in Liberty are once again threatened from having someone who knows my secret.

Michael is silently trying to put the pieces of the puzzle together.

I'm running out of time.

Jolie's talking, and I focus on the screen. "There's one course they have me teaching that's simply fascinating—it's a little out of my wheelhouse, though . . ."

I look at the timer on the screen. "What's the course?"

"Deviant Sexuality. It explores sexual obsessions that are considered abnormal by everyday standards."

Jolie's face lights up as she talks about the course. She's already made me uncomfortable with the word *abnormal*.

"All I can say is—do not hire a nanny," she says with a laugh.

My blood stills, an image of a dead one lying on the floor of the nursery immediately springing to mind. "Why not?"

"Part of the course talks about attachment disorders, and one is an obsession with a nanny. The bond the child is supposed to form with its mother is replaced by a connection to the caregiver instead, and in boys this can manifest into a lust-filled attraction in puberty. Unlike the Oedipus complex, where the boy knows a sexual relationship with the mother is wrong and therefore grows out of the attraction, with the nanny, he doesn't." She shakes her head. "Fascinating shit, but definitely unsettling."

My mouth is dry, and her face blurs slightly on the screen.

Adam's obsession with our nanny began with an obsession with his own.

He'd talked about her all the time. She'd raised him. He'd loved her. Been *in love* with her. My stomach flips. What was her name?

"Hey, you okay?"

I need to get off this chat. "Jolie, I just remembered: I have a doctor's appointment in ten minutes . . . baby brain." I force a laugh.

"Oh . . . no worries. Go. I'll call you tonight to see how it went."

"Thank you." For so much she'll never understand. Meeting Jolie has put my life back together in so many ways. The fact that I've never done anything for her doesn't escape my notice.

She blows a kiss to the screen as I disconnect the chat and immediately open a search engine. I type in *Adam Crenshaw's nanny* and wait. The image that appears causes a small gasp to escape me. For a second, I swear I'm looking at a picture of Catherine, but this woman is slightly older . . . and a teenage Adam is in the picture with her. But the dark hair and eyes, facial structure . . . she could be a relative.

The image blurs, competing with one of an identical woman lying on the floor, blood pooling around her.

This was why Adam was so obsessed with Catherine. She wasn't just any nanny; she was a mirror image of his own.

◆ ◆ ◆

I lie in bed, pretending to be asleep. Downstairs, I hear Parker making breakfast for Michael and Amelia. It's Saturday, and I have both kids all day while he works.

My time ran out on the library computer before I could try variations of Mariella Chavez's name, but my spine tingles with an awareness that I could be close to finally getting this right.

Parker enters the room, and I keep my eyes closed as he kisses me goodbye. I wait until I hear him saying goodbye to the kids and the sound of the truck leaving the driveway before I get out of bed.

I sit at the tiny desk and open his laptop.

Password protected. Fuck. Seriously?

"It's my mom's name and birthday."

The sound of Amelia's voice makes me turn quickly. "What?"

"The password to the laptop. It's 'Charlee 32281.' He wanted to use something I'd be able to remember so I could Skype call or email my mom whenever I wanted when she was overseas. Before she died."

Sadness in the little girl's voice tears at my heartstrings. Poor little thing has never really had her mother in her life, and then to lose her completely? I'd like to be there for Amelia in the ways she needs, but I'm starting to wonder if I haven't completely messed Michael up.

I need to do better with him and this new baby.

I turn back to the computer. "So, Charlee? C-H-A-R-L-E-E?" I'm fairly certain that's the way I've seen it spelled.

Amelia shakes her head, entering the room. "No, that's not a secure enough password. It's like this . . ." She turns the computer to face herself and types. "C-H-@-R-L-3-3. See, you replace certain letters with numbers and characters."

Kids were so much better with technology these days. "And is this something Parker taught you? Or is it something everyone does?"

"Well, maybe not everyone . . . but smart people."

Right. Like owners of a technology company.

Once Amelia and Michael finish breakfast, I send them out into the yard to play. Then, going back upstairs, I open Parker's laptop and log on to the C2 Technologies baby-monitoring system. It's already in his search history, as he'd set up our new one online a few days ago, so my logging on won't cause him any suspicion.

The log-on pops up, and my fingers tremble as I misspell our old address too many times. I take a breath and move the icon to the password section, praying this works.

M-@-R-

I pause. An *I* would be a *1*, I think.

1-3-L-L-@

I finish typing in the password and hold my breath. A spiraling timer appears on the screen, and my knees tremble beneath the desk.

It worked.

I sit on my hands to steady them.

When the image appears, the walls of my bedroom seem to drift farther away. I'm pulled in through the screen, back to the life I'd escaped. It's early morning in Seattle, and the room is illuminated by the sunlight coming in through the open curtains at the window. It looks exactly the way I'd left it. Dark-blue walls. Changing table and rocking chair still in place. Empty crib.

A dark stain across the floor.

Adam hasn't dealt with that yet? So unlike him. Has he not been able to bring himself to enter the nursery since that night? Or is he preserving a crime scene for when he finds us? There's no body. There was never one found.

Where is Catherine's body?

I click on "File" at the top of the page, praying the storage capacity has files from so long ago. Praying and dreading.

I enter the date into the fields in the search bar and wait.

Damn connection is so slow. My knees bounce under the desk, and I strain to listen for the sound of the kids still playing outside.

The file loads, starting with that morning so long ago. I tap the scroll bar along the bottom to advance the film. To nighttime. I watch and wait.

I've been desperate to see this, to know the truth about that night, but now I feel vomit rise in the back of my throat, and I have to force myself not to look away . . . not to black out as an eerie chill dances down my spine.

At 8:09, the door opens into the room, and my heart races so fast I fear going into cardiac arrest with my murder on the computer screen.

What if I can't handle what I'm about to see, and I black out?

It's a chance I'm willing to take for the truth.

On the monitor, the nanny enters, carrying Michael. She sits in the rocking chair—*my* chair—and props her feet up on the ottoman, gently rocking back and forth as she gives Michael his bottle. Of my pumped breast milk.

I can barely breathe as the pain returns in my chest. That was my baby. Seeing Catherine with him always broke my heart.

Ten minutes later, she sets the bottle aside and stands, hoisting Michael up onto her shoulder and pacing the room with him. I'm fearful of turning on the sound, but I know she's singing . . . always singing.

The door opens again, and I lean closer, seeing myself enter.

Jesus.

Suddenly, I'm not seeing the video. I'm seeing it all perfectly clear in my mind . . . all of it. Every last second of the day we escaped comes rushing back, as though that time hadn't been frozen in my memory for nine excruciating years.

Fragmented pieces and images fit together like a puzzle . . .

Moments before I'd entered the nursery, I'd watched through the dining room window as Adam and my father smoked their after-dinner cigars outside on the deck. Michael was asleep in Adam's arm, and the smoke from his cigar swirled around the baby's head.

Sitting at the table, I clutched my napkin. The urge to go out there and burn his eyeballs out with the lit end of the cigar so tempting. In my imagination I'd done it three times already. With the amount of Prolixin and other drugs Adam was forcing me to take from Dr. Bishop, it was a miracle I had any emotion at all. Nothing could suppress my hatred for Adam.

All through dinner, no one had said a word about the badly camouflaged black eye I was sporting. Why should they? I deserved the shots to the face I took for forgetting the baby in the bathtub hours before my parents' arrival.

Only I didn't forget Michael. Dylan. My son's name was Dylan; I had to remember that.

Adam's twisted sense of humor made me gag as my confused mind returned to hours before, when he wouldn't allow me into the bathroom, where Dylan was slowly sinking lower and lower into a tub of water.

"What are you going to do?" he'd taunted, blocking my access. "You can't save him. You're useless. Powerless."

"Adam, please . . . just let me get him," I'd begged, tears streaming down my face as I saw my baby boy's head dip below the water. "Adam!" I'd struggled against him, beating on his chest, kicking him as hard as I could, desperate to get inside the bathroom.

"You left him unattended," he'd said, slapping me.

Just for half a second to get a towel from the hall closet, a foot away. Or had it been longer? Sometimes time passed so fast. Other times excruciatingly slow. Either way, it was long enough for Adam to take advantage and use my mistake to torture me. He was right. I'd left the baby alone. I was a terrible mother, and I was desperate to get back into the bathroom to save him.

Instead, Adam rushed in just as the baby's face disappeared below the surface. He scooped him out of the water, wrapped a towel around him, and called out to the nanny.

"Can you take him away from her, please? Be sure she's never alone with him again," he told Catherine, kissing her cheek as she cradled my baby.

The affectionate way they'd looked at one another had me seeing red.

She avoided my desperate, frantic expression as she took the baby and headed down to the nursery.

Adam grabbed my arm and dragged me into our old room down the hall.

His room. *Their* room now.

He'd banished me to the spare room in the basement—far away from the nursery, from Michael. Dylan. Damn, I couldn't even remember my son's name.

"See? This is why you don't get to take care of Dylan. The baby could have drowned."

"You did that!" I was shaking from head to toe, and I didn't care what he did to me in that moment.

He slapped me hard across the cheek, and I didn't even feel the sting. I was immune to the pain he could inflict. Nothing got in anymore. I was dead inside for everything other than my child . . . and even that was slowly slipping away. I barely got to hold him, kiss him . . . I never got to put him to bed. I never got to bathe him. That day was a first. I was quickly realizing it had been a test. An opportunity for Adam to remind me I was stupid. Useless. To prove to me that I couldn't be a good mother.

But I could be. I knew I could be.

"You did that," I'd repeated, not sure why I continued to fight.

He gripped my wrists, forcing me to stare at the faint lines of scars. "You're crazy. You can't be trusted not to hurt the baby."

"You did these too!"

He punched me in the face. Once. Twice—harder the second time. I fell back against the bed. I slid to the floor, holding my throbbing eye.

He bent at the knees. "Stop your lies before I have you committed. You should be locked up. You are a danger to my baby."

His baby. It was all about possession for him. He didn't love him. He loved nothing and no one. "I'd never hurt my baby," I'd said. "You— I'd kill."

The third blow was lights out.

After waking up hours later, I cleaned myself up for dinner. I wiped the blood from my nose and face, and I covered the bruises as best I could. I'd learned some things from my mother after all.

And then I sat at the dinner table numb, completely dead on the inside. Hopeless, staring at my baby boy in the arms of a dangerous, unfeeling murderer, and I blamed myself for everything. Falling for Adam's charms, his lies, allowing myself to get this far into the worst nightmare.

And bringing a baby into it.

My mother was talking next to me, but I didn't hear anything she said. She had stared straight at my darkened eyes, and her unflinching expression had solidified the fact that I was completely alone.

I was fucked. There was no way out. I knew I could probably leave. I wouldn't get far. I knew too much, and all Adam cared about was his property. He'd kill me in a heartbeat, with no hesitation. I wasn't sure why he hadn't yet. Probably because he liked this power over me. He liked to watch me suffer.

His cell phone rang in his pocket, and he answered. I watched his face. A small, subtle change that no one else would notice flickered in his expression. "I have to go to the office," I heard him say.

"Should I come along?" my father asked.

Adam glanced my way as they entered the dining room and hesitated. "You'll stay with Drew?" he asked my mother.

"Of course," she answered, her words sounding slightly slurred. She was on her second bottle of wine, and it was nearly empty. "Would you like me to hold my grandson?" she asked.

"No. I'll bring him upstairs to Catherine," Adam said, and the two men left the room.

I sat staring at the wall, and I knew nothing until the sound of the car peeling out of the driveway had my mother immediately on her feet. She ran to the hallway, scanning for any of Adam's guard dogs he usually employed to keep me prisoner when he wasn't home, but no one was there that day. Then she approached, bending to look me in the eyes. "You have to leave."

Catherine

Isabella won't stop screaming. Her baby is due any day now. She should be happy, but all I hear are screams and crying in the room down the hall.

Adam spends the nights here with me now. He talks about the baby and how we will be a family soon. He says Isabella is as crazy as Drew was.

She didn't seem crazy. Not like Drew.

I was watching her. She seemed normal—gardening, swimming—up until a few weeks ago, when Adam came home. She'd asked him about this room . . . and the other rooms in this house that he keeps locked. They'd argued. I'd heard it all—sitting here, barely breathing, not daring to move an inch. Wondering if he'd tell her about me.

He did.

Now Isabella screams down the hall, and Adam says she's crazy.

I don't know anymore.

There were moments when Drew didn't seem so crazy either. My memories are better, clearer, lately. Not being pregnant anymore feels like a hazy fog has been lifted, but I don't like the things I'm recalling.

Drew didn't get to hold Dylan after he was born. I remember that now. I remember Adam bringing the baby to me—wrapped in a small blue blanket, his eyes barely open.

He said Drew didn't want the baby, and I remember thinking, "What mother doesn't want her own child?"

But Adam says Isabella doesn't want her baby either. Once the baby is born, Isabella will be gone.

I don't know what that means, but I struggle to believe no one wants these babies.

But I have to believe Adam. He's the one who's always protected me, kept me safe. He would never lie to me.

I have to stop imagining things, but lately, new flashes of memory of the night I was attacked are forcing me to remember everything differently.

I'm no longer sure that Drew is the one I should hate.

Drew

I blinked at my mother. Leave? Go where? What the hell was she talking about?

"Drew! Snap out of it!" She waved a hand in front of my face, and she sounded frighteningly sober.

"What?"

"You have to go. You and the baby have to get out of here."

"I can't."

"Yes, you can." She went to her purse and pulled out a tiny mailbox key. She forced it into my hand. "Take this. Post office on Lexi and Main. Box 56. Are you hearing me?"

I shook my head. She wasn't making any sense. Maybe she was drunk or high. Or just as crazy as I was.

"Drew! Listen to me. There's money. A lot of money. Cash. In this mailbox."

Was she serious? My heart raced, and I tried to focus on her words. "I don't understand . . ." The Prolixin and other medication Adam was drugging me with were making the world seem hazy . . . foggy . . . unclear.

"There's money," she repeated. "And a car key for a white Jetta parked on a deserted side street about ten blocks from there. The instructions are in the mailbox."

None of what she was saying made any sense. I must have been confused again. I got so confused all the time. "Mom . . . there's no money in a mailbox." This all sounded nuts. She was an alcoholic, and she was crazy. Like me.

She shook my shoulders until my teeth rattled in my brain. "Drew! Wake the fuck up!"

I couldn't remember the last time she'd cussed, and, oddly, that was what made me think she might actually be serious.

She touched my cheek, and I saw tears in her eyes. "I'm so sorry I couldn't do this sooner. Saved you from this sooner." Her voice was pure anguish, and I broke completely. She did understand. She did care. I grabbed her hand and squeezed tight.

"Mom," I whispered.

"I'm sorry about so, so much. I did what I had to do, Drew. I know you saw it as weakness, but if I'd left him . . . I'd have left you too. With my drinking, no one would have let me take you away from him . . . and then, over time, it was just normal. I accepted it."

I stared at her, not fully understanding.

She looked strong and determined again as she continued to speak. "But I was leaving. I was done." She paused and cleared her throat. "Listen to me. The mailbox is on Lexi and Main. Follow the instructions. Take the money. Get to the car."

Even if this miracle mailbox existed, this was crazy talk. Where the hell could I go? Adam would find me no matter where I went.

"Now, here's the most important part. In the glove compartment of the car, there's a business card with an address on it. Go there. They will help you with the rest."

The rest of what? Was she serious? "Who?" Part of me wondered if I was dreaming. I'd never seen my mother like this before. Determined. Strong. It couldn't be real.

I prayed all of it was just a bad dream.

She forced me to look at her. "Go to the address. Do what they tell you."

"Who?" I asked again.

"The only people in this world you can trust."

"But—"

"No buts. There's no more time. Adam will be back soon. It's now or never."

"What about Michael?"

She frowned.

"Dylan. I meant Dylan," I whispered. Adam hadn't let me name him Michael.

"The nanny is upstairs with him. We need to go get him."

I blinked again. The nanny? She wouldn't hand the baby over. I couldn't understand what was happening. I shook my head again.

"Drew. You have to do this for your child. Run, keep running, and never ever stop."

The harsh reality of her words finally rang true; the fog cleared. I stood, and we headed upstairs.

Classically trained soprano notes filled me with rage as we approached the nursery room door. It was open a crack, and the lighting from the night-light cast the reflection of the baby's mobile onto the hall floor.

My mother nodded silently toward it, and I noticed the knife in her hand.

What was she planning to do? Threaten Catherine?

My fear of the unknown wasn't enough to stop me. I pushed open the door and entered. My mother stayed hidden in the hallway. "Give me my baby," I said to the nanny.

Catherine clutched him tighter to her chest and shook her head. "Get out of this room, Drew."

"I said, give me my child." Behind her I saw my mother's shadow on the carpet in front of the door; then she appeared.

"Drew, if I tell Adam you were in here, he won't be happy."

"I don't give a fuck anymore. Give me my baby." My voice trembled, but I felt stronger than I'd ever felt before. Her protruding belly made my stomach twist. She was pregnant with her own child. Adam's child. They could have that child. I didn't care that Adam was moving on with her. I only cared about my baby boy. "Hand him to me. We will leave, and you'll have Adam all to yourself. You, him, the new baby . . ."

She shook her head. "You can leave—I won't stop you—but Dylan stays here. You know you can't take care of him," she said, almost gently, sympathy in her eyes. "Look what happened today."

"That was Adam. Not me."

"Drew, you should leave. Get yourself some help . . . but don't you want what's best for Dylan?"

"*I'm* what's best for him."

She shook her head. "I'm not letting you take this baby. I'm calling Adam." She reached behind her into her jeans pocket.

I watched my mother approach, stealthily as a cat, and, a second later, the nanny's expression was one of wide-eyed terror as the sharp edge of my mother's knife sliced across her throat. I dove forward to catch my baby as her arms went limp to her sides and her body crumbled to the nursery floor.

A gun lay at her side, not a cell phone. She'd been prepared to protect my baby from me at all costs. She'd believed I was the dangerous one.

My eyes met my mother's, and hers held no trace of remorse for what she'd just done. "Go. Now," she said.

I cradled the crying baby and grabbed her hands. "Come with us."

"No. I have to stay. Go to the mailbox. You and your baby run."

I swallowed the lump of terror in my throat. "He will kill you."

"He will kill you if you don't. You're my baby. A mother protects her child. I'm sorry I didn't do it sooner . . . years ago." She touched my swollen eye and brushed my hair from my face with her bloodstained hands.

And stared at me as though she would never see me again.

She wouldn't.

My mother's death the following week was labeled an accidental drowning. And no one bothered to question how a former Olympic gold medalist swimmer had drowned in her own pool.

Catherine

I glance at Adam. He's asleep. He doesn't move. He sleeps so soundly. I envy him that. I barely sleep at all anymore. I lie awake trying to figure out what's real and what isn't.

Not an easy task.

I still haven't shown him the picture of Mariella I have hidden, along with Isabella's sweater, in the back of my closet. Haven't wordlessly demanded an explanation.

I'm waiting. Waiting until I have more clarity of mind so I can figure out for myself whether or not what he tells me is lies. Until I can push aside my doubts and fears and challenge him.

I slide out of the bed and tiptoe across the room. My ninety-pound body makes less noise than a ghost. I reach into his pants pocket for his keys. He carries this key ring on him always. There's the key to my room, the key to Isabella's room, one to his office down the hall, and one to the nursery.

All the places only he has access to. All the places in this house that hide different secrets.

I open the bedroom door slowly and slip out into the hall. I see Isabella's light through the crack in the door and see the door vibrating under her brutal attacks. Her screams are louder out here, and I cover my ears.

I don't know why she hasn't stopped trying yet. Doesn't she realize she can't escape? No one can hear her except me.

Drew gave up a lot sooner.

I walk down the hall to the nursery and unlock the door, pushing it open. I hit the light switch, but nothing happens. It's burned out. Only the moon shining through the window lights up the space.

My own blood stains the floor at my feet, and I step around it to look inside the empty crib. I spin the baby mobile hanging above, and the shadows of animals dance across the wall. Silent tears wet my cheeks for all the lost babies.

I wipe my eyes and shut them tight, trying to remember. I need to remember. I need to know for sure that Adam is telling me the truth. I need to know who tried to kill me, because if it wasn't Drew . . .

I stand in the room, facing the door, my arms cradled like I'm holding Dylan. I would have been singing to him.

All the lovely pieces fall to the floor . . .

A song from my childhood. One that always made me feel safe. Now I shudder at the lyrics.

I watch the parade of animal shadows on the wall, and, in my mind, I see Drew enter.

I don't remember what she said, but I remember holding Dylan tighter. I wanted to keep him safe from her. Protect him. I moved to stand in front of the open door.

I do that now . . .

Then what?

I need to remember this part.

I shut my eyes tight. Drew wasn't holding a knife. I'm certain of that. And she was standing inside the room, facing me . . . we were alone.

She was threatening to take Dylan. I reached for the gun Adam had given me for protection. I never would have used it. I never would have hurt Drew . . .

My eyes fly open, and I catch my reflection in the window.

Another reflection appears. A woman. Drew's mother.

A knife in her hand.

My breath catches in my throat, the truth a sucker punch to my gut.

Drew's mother tried to kill me. To help Drew. To save her. To save Dylan.

I shake my head. No. That's not right. Drew was the dangerous one. Everyone knew she was crazy. Why would her mother help her escape with a baby when she knew she shouldn't be trusted with a child?

Adam lied.

No! I grip my head between my hands. No! Adam is good. Adam is the one I trust.

I hear the sound of the bedsprings creaking under his weight, down the hall. Quickly I lock the nursery and rush back to my room, shutting the door quietly.

Adam is still asleep.

I stare at him, questioning too much. I hate myself for not believing him, but I remember now.

Adam says Drew tried to kill me. But that's a lie.

What else is Adam lying about?

Drew

I was terrified. Taking my mother's car and driving away from the house . . . trusting in her. If her words, her plan, turned out to be the crazy ramblings of a drunk, I'd be far worse off than before. I would have to go back. And I'd pay deeply for the attempt to escape.

My hands gripped the steering wheel as I followed the directions in the mailbox to a house fourteen miles outside town. So far, the money had been there where she'd said it would be. I had to believe the house would be too.

The place looked abandoned. No lights were on. No other cars were around. The next house I could see had to be eight blocks away. A deserted acreage hidden among tall, overgrown grass. Weeds swayed like ghosts in the darkness as I stared at the house: 456 Heathrow Lane—the address on the card inside the post office box. Though I couldn't be sure, as the 6 hung on a nail, turning it into a 9.

Unfortunately, my gut told me this was the place. There wasn't a 456 somewhere else with the lights on and a welcome mat in front of the door.

But I hadn't expected this place to look completely deserted. Silence echoed inside the car and all around it, the baby sleeping in the back.

My hands clenched the wheel tighter, and regret twisted my insides into a knot. What if my mother wasn't only a drunk but a crazy person with delusions? What if this escape existed only in her mind? My fears were being confirmed the longer I sat there, fighting the anxiety attack threatening to take hold. The bag of money from the post office box sat on the passenger seat next to me. I hadn't counted it, but it was heavy.

A bag of money and this address.

Where no one seemed to be.

A knock on the passenger window sent me jumping so high that I hit my head on the roof of the car. A young woman stood outside with a flashlight pointed on an angle, downward, so as not to blind me. She nodded once and then headed back toward the house, her figure blending with the shadows until she was almost no longer visible.

I strained in the darkness to keep her in my sights, the dim stream of light the only thing convincing me she was actually there and not fabricated from my desperate hope for salvation.

I hesitated, not moving, not breathing. Watching. She didn't go into the house but instead opened a small tornado-cellar door in the yard, barely visible from all the overgrown weeds. Another source of light escaped the tunnel, and I could make out her jeans and sweatshirt, her long hair covering most of her face. She was so still as she waited. She didn't wave or smile or encourage me to get out of the car. She just waited.

Could I trust this strange woman? Could I trust my mother? None of it made sense to me yet. I'd been moving on autopilot in a cloudy haze since leaving the house. My fate had been sealed the moment I left the security gates. There'd been no turning back.

What if my mother was helping Adam? What if this was all a ploy? What if death awaited me in that cellar instead of the freedom promised?

My pulse was out of control, and my heart echoed against the windows of the car.

The young woman was still waiting for me. I had to make a decision. I could go back, but that was certain death. Whatever awaited me there was the only future I had. Wheels had been set in motion, the die cast.

Funny how the brain resorts to clichéd thoughts in moments of uncertainty, a dullness of consciousness reverting to the only comforts in the familiar, the mundane, the meaningless.

This was our way out. The only way out.

I opened the car door and grabbed the bag of money, clutching it tight to my chest, as I took Michael from the floor in the back of the car. He was awake, but he made no sound. His big dark eyes looking as frightened as I felt.

I somehow made my way to the open cellar door. The woman saw me approach and disappeared inside. She waited at the top of a set of stairs.

I hesitated.

"You're both safe here," she said, and for the first time I believed it.

I don't know what happened to the car. Within minutes of our arrival, it was driven away. I didn't ask many questions. It wasn't the process.

Three women were my saviors that night—besides my mother. I didn't know their names or who they were. They called me number 317 and handed me a folder with a new birth certificate for Dylan—his new name was Michael. My name for him. It felt like a small victory in a sea of unknowns. According to the certificate, he was already a year old, and I prayed for the strength to take a year of life away from my baby boy.

I had new identification as well: driver's license and passport. They let me keep my first name, but my last name was changed to Baker. It didn't matter, I guess. I'd never be the real me again.

The most important thing they gave me was a certificate of death for "Michael's father"—a William Baker. Just a man who didn't exist.

All to help erase one life and create an opportunity for another.

I was warned to keep a low profile, not to use the fake documents unless absolutely necessary. They talked well into the night about where to go, how long to stay, when to move on. I listened, unsure if I was taking it all in, not knowing if I could pull this off. I had so little strength and will to live left when I arrived there that night, but somehow they brought me back to life—just enough.

They took turns lying with us while I cried in fear of what was to come, in relief of the nightmare coming to an end, and in apprehension of the next day.

At the time, I could focus only on our survival and what this all meant. I would need a clear head and strong will to live if I were to last a day on the run. I didn't think about the fact that I'd never see my friends or family again, that I'd never be safe in one place for too long, that I could never tell anyone the truth about who I was, or that I could never be that person again.

Had I let any of those thoughts in, I might have hesitated to do what needed to be done. Had I thought about the consequences should I fail, I might have given up right then and there. But I focused only on the sleeping baby in my arms and successfully forgot about the dead woman in the nursery.

Catherine

Adam wakes, looking startled to see me standing in the room, watching him sleep.

I've been staring at him for hours, thinking about the past and all the things he's said, all the things he's done. He may have lied, but maybe that was to protect me too. Maybe he knew the truth would be confusing to me. He's done so much for me.

He saved me.

But what kind of life do I have? Will I ever have a real life again if I continue to trust Adam?

"Darling, come to bed." He pulls back the sheets on my side, but I shake my head. I sit on the ottoman at the foot of the bed instead, exhausted and weak.

He gets up and sits next to me. "What's wrong?"

Everything.

With a shaky hand, I pick up my tablet and write: *I want to leave this room.*

I need to leave. I need to get real help.

Adam shakes his head. "No. The outside world is unsafe for you. You need to stay here where I can protect you."

I struggle to stand and cross the room to the closet. I reach into the pocket of Isabella's sweater and retrieve the picture of Mariella. I hand it to him, and he looks at it. "You left the room?"

I simply stare at him. I need answers if I'm going to keep trusting him, believing him. Is he ever going to give me my life back?

"This was Mariella. I told you about her. She was my nanny. She was everything," he says quietly, staring at me. His hand extends to touch my hollowed cheek. "So beautiful, so caring, so nurturing . . ."

I can tell he's not talking about me. He's not even seeing me anymore. He sees her.

Had he always seen her whenever he looked at me?

"I need you." He clutches my hands in his, desperation on his face. "Don't leave the room again. Don't leave me again. Don't leave me all alone."

This pleading, weak man is not one I've seen before. He's not reassuring. He's not strong. He looks slightly crazed as his dark eyes continue to stare, unseeing, at my face. Seeing only someone else's face. Mariella's.

He can't fix me. He doesn't want to fix me. He doesn't want me to leave this room. Ever.

I struggle to remove my hands from his grip, then move toward the bedroom door.

"Where are you going?" he asks.

I keep walking, feeling my legs wobble beneath me. I fall and claw my way up the wall to get back on my feet. My fingernails scraping against the paint like a cat.

Adam doesn't help. He sits there. Silent.

I reach the door, and everything feels far away. It's as though I've died and left my body, and I'm watching myself from somewhere above . . . I turn the handle and the door opens.

"Darling, stay," Adam says.

Torturous pain in his voice is almost enough to stop me, but the truth has hit me, coming back in pieces over the last few months. Clarity in its distortion, telling me that all this is wrong.

Drew didn't try to kill me.

Maybe she wasn't crazy either.

Maybe she did want her baby as desperately as I wanted mine. Maybe Dylan is somewhere safe with her.

He wouldn't be safe here, just like I'm not safe here.

I leave the room and make my way down the hall. I pause outside Isabella's door and try the handle, but I know it's useless—I forgot to take the keys with me. She's a prisoner. Her crying, her screams . . . she's been locked up in there. The way Drew was.

My door was only ever locked from the inside. Why am I free? Why have I always been free?

Because whenever Adam looks at me, he sees Mariella. He knows I wouldn't leave him.

I have to get help. For me. For Isabella. I couldn't save Drew . . . but maybe I can help Isabella and her baby.

I stumble toward the stairs, and my vision is blurry, my breathing is shallow . . . I hold the wall for support, my strength disappearing.

I take the first step down, but my legs are finished. I fall and I tumble, the impact of the stairs breaking my bones . . . pain shoots through my body first, followed by numbness.

At the base of the stairs, I look up and see Adam standing there. Darkness closes in, and I take one last breath, knowing it's my last and that I couldn't save anyone.

Michael

I can't find Mr. Floppy. I know I left him under my bed, but he's not there now. Amelia was teasing me about still sleeping with a stuffed toy, so I hid him.

I know it's silly, but I need to find him. He's the only toy that Mom's let me keep since I was a baby, and I've been having bad dreams without him.

He's not under the rollaway cot Amelia sleeps on or under her bedsheets. I looked in the closet, but I can't find him anywhere.

If she's done something to him . . .

I search the rest of the house for Mr. Floppy and finally find him in the new baby's room. In the new crib Parker put together for Mom. The baby gets new everything. New crib, new dresser . . . I'm stuck with the old stuff that was here when we moved in. There're even new toys and clothes in the room already, and the baby's not even here yet.

I grab Mr. Floppy from the crib and hug him.

The baby has so much stuff already. He's not getting my things.

Aw . . . look at the baby still needing his stuffie.

Amelia doesn't know anything. I wipe angry tears from my eyes. She'll see. When the baby gets here, Parker will forget all about her too. The baby will get everything, and we will get nothing.

Drew

I'm innocent. I didn't kill the nanny.

It's been a week since I learned the truth, yet relief is slow to sink in. All the years convinced I was a murderer have me reluctant to believe otherwise. I didn't kill anyone. I'm not a bad person. I have proof now.

I've resisted every urge to log on to the monitor again. I don't want to keep looking back. I want to move on with my life. Forget the past completely and hope for a peaceful future.

I'm innocent, and that's all that matters.

My stomach jumps, and I sigh. This baby moves a lot more than Michael did. He or she hiccups a lot, and the bouncing makes me feel nauseated. Jolie says I must be having a girl. She says boys don't cause their mommas trouble the way girls do.

I need to finish painting the nursery, so I gather my painting supplies and head in to the baby's room. A legless giraffe still waits to be given his majestic height, and an elephant's trunk is only partially completed. Otherwise, it's done. Trees and big green jungle leaves, butterflies, and birds cover one entire wall.

All I feel is guilt when I look at the mural. Duplicating the design I'd wanted in Michael's nursery for this new baby feels wrong. I'd thought it would help me let go of the hurt and pain from the first experience, but it's only made me feel worse for not being able to give all of this to Michael.

There's something in the crib, and as I move closer, I see Mr. Floppy, partially hidden beneath a baby blanket.

Michael gave his favorite toy to the baby?

My heart breaks a little at his kindness and the fact that my little boy is growing up. The first part of his life was so challenging; I vow to make the rest of it better. Once Parker builds a new room for Amelia, I'll design new murals for both of them.

Try to make a real home for all of us. Once this baby is born and I have more energy, I'm determined to start rebuilding my life as much as I can. Be a better mother. Be better for Parker too.

I pick up Mr. Floppy, and my pulse quickens. Stuffing falls out of the holes in him, and the eyeless expression staring back at me makes me drop him.

Who did this?

Not Michael. He'd never do this. He cherished that thing.

The sound of a vehicle running outside has me turning to look out the bedroom window.

Parked in front of the house next door is a large SUV with blacked-out windows. Dented side panels and a busted front light. It's dirty and the engine is loud. I've never seen it before, and I'm sure it doesn't belong to the neighbors. I can't see the driver's face, but I feel their eyes on me through the window. My hand fumbles for the string to pull the blinds, but the vehicle tears away from the curb and disappears before I can close them.

My heart pounds as I stare at Mr. Floppy on the floor. Someone is watching us. Someone was in my house.

Mr. Floppy is a warning.

Michael

I watch the clock on the classroom wall. I'm not listening to the teacher.

I'm running away. I can't trust anyone. No one cares about me anymore. All they care about is the baby.

My pencil snaps in two in my hands, and I jump.

I just want to get out. I can't wait for the bell. Mom will be there then. I took some of the money from the bag downstairs, and I'm heading to Seattle . . .

I raise my hand. "Can I go to the bathroom, please?"

"Um . . . sure. Just hurry back."

I take my backpack from under the desk and hurry out. She doesn't notice.

I run down the empty hall and peek into the principal's office. The receptionist is away from her desk, and Principal Bradley is on her phone. I look behind me. No one's there.

A bathroom door opens down the hall, but it's just a kindergarten kid. I walk past him and head for the front door.

No one is around to stop me. I'm going to Seattle, and I'm going to tell John and Jolie everything . . .

I push through the front door and start to run across the parking lot.

Big hands grab me from behind, and I think it must be Mom, but it's a man.

Not Parker.

What's going on? Who is this man? My heart starts to beat really fast.

I struggle. Kick my legs hard, but I can't get away.

"Let me go," I say before a hand is clasped over my mouth and I'm thrown into the back of a vehicle.

I blink and try to make a run at the open door, but it shuts fast.

I bang against dark windows, but no one hears me. "Help!"

No one comes. No one knew I was leaving, and now no one comes looking for me.

An old man gets into the front seat. A stranger. "We're just going to take a little drive," he says.

I continue to bang against the window, and I scream for Mom. But she doesn't come.

"Just relax back there. You'll see your mom soon enough."

I lunge at him, and the vehicle swerves.

"Stop that!" He holds me back, but I fight against him. I have to get out of here. I don't know where he's taking me, but I know I'm not safe.

He reaches into the glove compartment and takes out a gun. "I said sit back and relax," he says, pointing it at me. I see his hand tremble, but I move away from him.

Tears make it hard to see as the old man drives farther away from the school. He turns the corner near the playground, and I know if I stay in this vehicle, I'm going to get hurt.

I have to save myself. I take a big brave breath and reach for the door.

Drew

The school's number lights up the call display, and instinctively I know something is wrong. "Hello?"

"Drew? This is Principal Bradley. Is Michael with you?"

I'm shaking my head. My sight is blurry. The sight of Mr. Floppy in pieces has the room waving beneath my feet. "He's at school." It's barely more than a whisper, and I'm not sure she heard me. "He's there, isn't he?"

"He went to the bathroom about half an hour ago and hasn't returned."

The phone slips from my hand.

Michael's gone.

I have to find my son. I run out of the nursery and down the stairs, colliding with Parker as he steps out of the living room.

In his hands is my scrapbook. Behind him, in the living room, is my bag of money.

My chest is about to explode, and I hurry toward him. "Michael's in trouble."

"You are Drew Crenshaw."

"Where did you get this?" Someone being in our house, going through our things, has my body trembling.

"I tripped over a loose floorboard in the basement." His voice is cold. His expression is one I've never seen before. Angers burns in his eyes.

"Parker, I'll explain everything. But right now, Michael is missing . . ."

"He has been for nine years."

I'm going to be sick. I try to sidestep him to get out, but he blocks my exit through the front door.

Once again, I'm a prisoner. "I'm not a murderer or crazy or anything else those articles say I am. I'll explain, but first I have to get to Michael." I push against him, but he stands firm.

"You're not leaving. I have to call the police."

Maybe that's the right thing to do. But if we call the police, I'll be taken in. No one will believe me when I tell them I'm innocent. Just like before.

It's too much of a risk. I need to try to find Michael on my own. Maybe he just left school on his own . . . maybe he's okay . . .

"Look, Parker, Adam is a monster . . . he was abusive and dangerous . . ."

"A multibillionaire philanthropist. Michael's father."

He sounds hurt, and I'm desperate to turn his brief sign of weakness to my advantage. "He was dangerous. I left to protect Michael. To keep him safe . . ."

"By the sound of these articles, the only person Michael was in danger of is you."

Kick to the gut delivered. "This is why I didn't tell you the truth."

"Do you even know what's true anymore, Drew?"

"Parker, I have to go." He's not going to believe me. No one ever has. But I need to get out of here and find Michael. Time is wasting.

He looks unsure. Hesitant. His mind and heart in obvious conflict. "If Adam is what you say he is, why didn't you tell me? Why didn't you tell anyone the truth? Instead of running . . . abducting a child!" His gaze is on my pregnant stomach, and I know what he is thinking.

"I wanted to tell you. And I will, but first I have to go find Michael. Please help me." I've never asked him for help, and all I can do is pray that Parker is the man I think he is. Hope to God he is . . .

He's wrecked as he says, "I have to call the police, Drew." He steps into the living room and reaches for his cell phone.

There's nothing I can say to stop him. He's made up his mind. And I need to get out of here. Fast. Sensing my only opportunity, I grab the lamp from the table and swing.

The ceramic shatters as it makes contact with Parker's head. He looks stunned as his eyes meet mine, a red gash starting to bleed on his forehead.

"I'm sorry, Parker," I say as I swing again with the remaining base, this time knocking him to the floor. Unconscious. Sheets of news articles from my scrapbook scattered all around him.

I step over him, unlock the front door, grab my car keys, and run from the house. There's no time to think about what I've just done. No time for remorse.

A caged animal will always find a way out.

I go to the school. Maybe he hasn't gone too far. Maybe they've found him. But the police squad cars parked in front of the entrance and the group of teachers and parents gathered on the front lawn have me throwing the car in reverse and backing up the street.

Instead, I drive . . . looking for any sign of him. My eyes scan the streets and peer through the frantic wipers swishing back and forth on the windshield. A sharp pain in my side makes me wince, and I press against it.

Please, God, no baby today.

I turn onto the first side street and drive past the playground, slowing just enough to see his backpack hung on a tree branch. The tree he'd hidden behind that first day at the playground, the day I met Jolie . . . I pull over and get out, running as fast as I can toward it.

I pick up his backpack and walk farther into the woodsy area. His coat is hanging on another branch . . . and one shoe lies on the ground beneath it.

"Michael!" I yell his name as I move deeper along the park trail. Over and over. My voice echoes against the big tree trunks and bounces back at me. "Michael! Where are you, sweetheart? Come out! I won't be mad." A crack of thunder makes me jump, and a second later, a flash of lightning illuminates the sky on the path in front of me.

Heavy rain falls between the overhang of the branches, and it's as dark as early evening. "Michael!" I turn in circles, scanning between the openings. "Michael!"

The sound of sirens in the distance has my heart forcing its way through the skin of my chest. He's not here. I can't be here. I didn't go to the school, and I'm standing here holding evidence of my son's disappearance.

The only person Michael was in danger of was you.

Parker's voice has successfully replaced Adam's now, for better and for worse.

I run back to the car, oblivious to the pounding raindrops drenching my clothes, the wetness seeping into my shoes from the puddles on the concrete. My hair hangs in wet, limp locks against my forehead, blocking my view.

The hand gripping my arm as I reach for the car-door handle is clammy and rough. I swing around and try to pull away but stop moving when I see Dr. Collins. He survived the fire, and I know he has my son. "Where's Michael?"

"Dylan, you mean?"

Another sharp pain in my right side steals my breath. I resist the urge to throw up as another viselike grip wraps around my stomach.

He chuckles. "He's a fighter, that one. Jumped out of the moving vehicle. I had to chase him through the park."

The coat . . . the shoe . . .

My little boy must be so terrified. He jumped out of a moving vehicle. "Is he hurt?"

He ignores the question. "David was like that . . . as a kid."

"What do you want with Michael?" Why is he doing this? What could he possibly have to gain? How long had he been planning this? "Is this why you were watching us before?" Was he the one who broke into our house? He was looking for Michael?

He reaches for the handle of the door and opens it. "Get in."

"Did you break into my home?"

"Get in the car!"

"I will kill you if you've hurt my son," I say. I have no idea how, but I know I will. I wish he'd died in that fire.

His laugh is full of pain and despair as he pushes me into the back seat. "I was ready to die months ago, remember?" He climbs in with me.

Where are the sirens now? Though, help will only make things worse. More disbelievers who I can't trust will only prevent me from finding my son. "Just tell me where Michael is."

"He's okay. For now." He grips both of my wrists. I struggle, but he's much stronger than I would have thought. I try to kick at him, but he's too close, and my stomach prohibits my movements. He tightens his hold as he ties my wrists together, fastening them to the garment hook in the back seat. I wiggle my arms, but the knots are too tight. "I learned my lesson the hard way with your son. He can run fast. Sit tight," he says, climbing out and then going back behind the driver's seat of my car.

I rub my face against my shoulder, brushing the matted hair, sweat, and rain away from my eyes. I scan our surroundings as we move farther and farther out of town. Where the hell is he taking me? Maybe I'm not going to Michael. Maybe I'm going to my death. Maybe Michael . . .

No, I refuse to believe the doctor is capable of that.

Thunder cracks outside and inside my chest. Flashes of lightning continue to be the only light in the increasingly dark sky. "Where are you taking me?"

He ignores me, lighting a cigarette.

He's never smoked before, and I see his hand trembling. He's not confident in his actions.

"Just tell me where we are going." I'm watching the road signs pass one by one, but I have no idea where we're heading.

"Please, just tell me if Michael is really okay."

"Shut up. Just stop talking."

"Dr. Collins, please, I just want to know where my son is. Please just give me that. I saved your life."

"A life I don't want," he says, rolling down the window and blowing out a puff of smoke. The rain comes in through the opening, hitting me in the face. The cold little drops feel like BB gun pellets against my cheek.

Questioning him is useless, so I watch the scenery passing. An abandoned warehouse . . . a gas station . . . an old mill. If I get an opportunity to get out of this car, I won't be wasting it. "I have money. I'll pay anything to get Michael back. We can all move on . . ." Can I use the doctor's poor financial situation to get out of this?

He raises an eyebrow and looks ready to ignore me, but then he tosses the half cigarette out the window and glances at me through the rearview mirror. "This isn't about money."

"It's always about money."

He shakes his head. "Revenge is sweeter."

"Revenge?"

"An eye for an eye. Crenshaw killed my son, and now I'm going to kill his. He took everything from me . . ."

Sweat drips into my mouth from my upper lip. The salty taste is sickening, and my arms are losing feeling from their overhead position. "Don't you think you're to blame for bringing your son into all of this?

Adam talked about you—said you were a quack who couldn't help fix him. If you had, maybe your son would still be alive."

His glare threatens to burn a hole through my forehead. "You. You should know more than anyone there's no escaping Adam. No one gets out . . . not alive anyway. But at least I can make him suffer too."

"You think he cares about his son? He doesn't. He'd want the world to believe he does, but Adam is incapable of caring. He's inhuman. You know that. Let me go and I'll help you."

"Like you helped my son?"

Pain, not anger, in his voice gives me the slightest hope. He's hurting. Adam has hurt him too. We share that in common.

Is that enough?

"I'm sorry, Dr. Collins." I soften my tone. "I was pregnant and terrified, and there was no way . . . just give me my son back, and together we can go to the police . . ."

He glances at me through the rearview mirror, and for a brief second I think he might reconsider all of this.

"Adam will pay for what he's done. You can finally have peace."

He hesitates, then shakes his head. "No. Adam's money is more valuable than the word of two crazy, damaged people."

Being lumped into that category with him might actually be the most accurate assessment he's made of me yet, and I have no other choice but to wait for my opportunity to fight.

We drive, passing nothing of interest . . . and the farther I get from Liberty, the more my body shakes. No one knows where we are. They couldn't help us if they did.

A beeping sounds above the rain pelting against the roof of the car, and I strain to see the dash. The gas light. We're almost out. This piece of shit doesn't warn until it's on empty—I learned that the hard way. I've never before been grateful for this hunk of junk.

"Damn it!" Dr. Collins hits the steering wheel as the car chugs along on fumes.

Another mile or two at best. Then what?

There's nothing around. We will have to get out of the car. I force several breaths and try to ease my shoulders to relieve the tense pressure along my neck and upper body. The jabs coursing through my stomach are coming faster and harder. If this baby survives this, it will be a miracle.

If any of us survive it.

Parker.

I hope someone finds him before it's too late.

The car slows to a stop, and the doctor swears under his breath as he climbs out into the storm. He yanks open the back door and grabs me, pulling me out.

"What now?" I ask. "We hitchhike?"

"Shut up," he says, scanning the deserted road.

"You really don't think you're going to get away with this, right? The police are looking for Michael." Anger is my only option, since trying to identify with him didn't work.

"Adam will find him first. He will find all of us, but it will be too late . . ."

"Adam? You called Adam?" Terror runs through me at his words.

He will find all of us, but it will be too late.

Murder-suicide?

I look around, desperate for a car to drive by; even the police would be a welcome sight now. But no one's coming.

Then I see something glistening in the pocket of this ugly flower-patterned maternity top.

A piece of the broken lamp.

My chest fills with air, apprehension mixing with relief as I carefully reach my hands into the pocket to grab it.

Clenching it tight, I'm careful not to cut myself as I hide it next to my thigh. I just need him to come closer. I don't want to hurt him, but he's giving me little choice. I need to save Michael. I can't let Dr. Collins kill us all. Adam will kill me when he gets here, but at least Michael will be unharmed . . .

I swallow the emotions choking me. "Your son begged for his life."

He spins around to face me. "Stop. Just stop talking. I'm trying to think." He paces, running a trembling hand over his gray, disheveled hair.

"You said he was a fighter, but I don't believe that. He was a coward." I hate the words coming out of my mouth, but they are working.

"I'm warning you . . ." He shoves me forward on the road. My time is running out. He wants to make Adam pay by killing Michael; I'm just an added bonus.

A fatality whom no one on this earth will care about.

"David was cheating the company. He was a liar . . ." I never knew the young man, but anger seeps from Dr. Collins as he stalks toward me.

That's it. Just a little closer.

"Don't you dare say those things about my son. David was kind and compassionate. I never wanted him working for Adam . . ." He grips my shoulders, and, seeing my opportunity, I plunge my hands upward as fast and hard as I can.

I'm sorry, Dr. Collins. So, so sorry . . . that I couldn't save David or you.

The lamp shard jabs him in the throat below his chin, and blood spurts out around it.

His wide-eyed expression as he backs away from me is full of terror. I watch him gurgle and choke and fall to his knees. I watch him struggle to pull out the sliver and see him collapse to his side in a puddle on the side of the deserted road.

I watch him die.

Drew

I fight to catch my breath and wipe the blood from my hands onto my jeans. I twist and rotate them until they are free of the rope; then I take the doctor's cell phone out of his pocket and use his lifeless thumb to unlock the phone. I drop his hand and stand, searching for a signal. The open road on either side of me and the lack of cell towers in the area make finding one near impossible.

"Fucking come on!" I shake it, desperate for a miracle. Finally I get a single bar in the corner.

I stare at it, knowing my lifeline is completely useless without someone to call.

There's never been anyone I could trust in this world.

Even Parker, the one man who promised to love me and who had never wavered from his commitment, is my enemy now. If he is alive, he has probably already called the police, thinking I've run off with Michael and this new baby. His baby. I can't blame him. Abducting children was my thing, right? The constant instability of a crazy woman . . .

I kick at the mud and fall to my knees on the side of the road. The service bar flickers, telling me I'm on borrowed time. If I'm going to make a call, it has to be now.

With trembling hands stained by the doctor's blood, I dial the Seattle cell phone number I've never forgotten. My entire body is hot, my internal hell competing with the Missouri rainstorm to form a condensation film on my skin. My stomach is in knots, and I ignore every voice in my mind begging me to hang up before it's too late.

I don't.

He must know where the doctor has taken Michael.

Adam's voice on the fourth ring has me wanting to vomit. "Hello, Dr. Collins."

I swallow all hesitation. He is the only one who can help me right now. "It's Drew."

"Drew."

"Where were you meeting Dr. Collins?"

His laugh is cruel and long, and for a second I think he might hang up. He could go get Michael, and there would be nothing I could do about it. I've killed the only other person who knew where Michael is. But then he says, "Where are you?"

"A side of a road . . . I have no idea exactly where I am . . ." No part of my brain is comprehending what I'm doing right now, but my gut tells me it's the only way I'll see my son again.

"I'm downloading your GPS coordinates from this number. I'll pick you up, and we can go see our son together."

My stomach heaves at his words.

He hangs up, and I can't do anything else but wait.

I pull the doctor's body away from the street, leaving a trail of blood as I roll him into the ditch, hidden from the occasional car passing by. I sit far away, covered in his blood, staring at the corpse, hoping he's not really dead. That he will wake up and tell me where Michael is.

I'm covered in dirt and dried blood, my clothes soaked into my skin. My mouth is parched, and I'm licking the sweat from my lip as a black Jeep approaches an excruciatingly long time later. The slightly tinted windows are not dark enough to shield the sight of Adam behind the wheel. An odd fluttering in my stomach is the last thing I expect to feel. It sickens me, and I take solace in hatred and fear.

What the hell am I doing? Getting in the car willingly with a man I've been running from for so long makes no sense. But Adam is the only one who knows where Michael is, and he certainly won't tell me.

Michael's been missing for hours, and the thought of him alone and afraid has driven me to the brink of insanity. I pray Dr. Collins hasn't already hurt him.

No sirens have flown past. No one has found me.

Or Dr. Collins's body.

As my gaze locks with Adam's through the windshield, I realize I'm prepared to kill again. I grip the fragment of ceramic—my only weapon—at my ankle, wedge it into my shoe, and stand as the vehicle stops a few feet away.

I walk toward it, though I should be running in the opposite direction. My legs don't want to move, but I propel them forward—one, then the other. I need to save Michael, and this is the only way. I need him safe before Adam kills me.

I open the car door with no idea of the fate awaiting me inside.

"You look like shit."

I ignore him and climb inside. I stare straight ahead, my right hand on the seat, ready to grab the shard if necessary, but Adam makes no move to reach for a weapon. He simply puts the vehicle in drive and pulls out onto the deserted road. The air-conditioning inside would be a welcome relief if my blood wasn't already frozen in my veins.

"I assume that's Dr. Collins's blood all over you?"

I don't answer. My fingers creep lower on the seat, and the piece of ceramic is so tempting. A quick jab through his neck—the same as Dr. Collins—and all this would be over. But I'd never find Michael. I'd never hold my son again or have the chance to tell him I love him.

I have no delusions that I'm going to survive this. Adam won't take a chance at keeping me alive, even if he would love to see me rot in a jail cell, suffering.

"I'm glad the old man called. I'll be happy to reunite with my son again. I think he's ready to learn the family business," he says.

"Never."

"You won't have a say. You'll be dead."

If only there were any way to win against Adam. But my shard of ceramic is no match for the gun I know he must be carrying.

"Dylan will take over the company someday. Hell, he'll probably acquire it the same way I did." He laughs.

My jaw clenches tight. "Michael's nothing like you."

"Really? I think you've sufficiently fucked him up . . ."

Blackness surrounds me.

He doesn't know Michael at all. My son is nothing like him. I focus straight ahead.

Adam glances at a device in his left hand. A GPS. "How did you kill Dr. Collins?"

I ignore him, but my grip tightens on the seat, and I move as far away from him as possible. "Where are we going?"

I could jump out and run. Search for Michael myself. I'd never rest until I found him.

"Silent Meadows."

The insane asylum. "Why would he take Michael there?"

Adam laughs. "Crazy old man used to bring his patients to the psychiatric wards. Threatened that if we didn't listen to him—let him fix us—we'd end up there. I told you before: his methods of treatment weren't always conventional."

Jesus.

"He left me with a paranoid schizophrenic once. Thought I'd learn to take his treatments seriously. I was the more fucked-up one in that room."

I swallow hard.

"I'm glad you called too, Drew. I am. You made the right choice. No one else could help. Everyone believes you're insane."

Everyone believes I'm insane. There really is no way out of this for me. I feel my pulse throbbing. I gag, and I swallow the vomit rising in my throat.

"I assume you told the good old doctor what really happened to his son?"

I don't answer.

"You never could just keep your mouth shut. Dylan is in this position now because of you."

I hate the truth of his words.

"You could have kept running and hiding forever. I'd given up searching a long time ago. The idea of you running scared was enough for me."

Could I have? I should have. I should never have gone in search of answers. The need to know the truth—my selfish plight to have a future, a life of my own—has made things worse.

He pulls the vehicle off the road at the next exit.

Michael was this close? I could have walked to him and stabbed everyone in my way to get him back to safety. I still will. Adrenaline is pumping through me so hard that my body shakes like I've consumed a case of energy drinks.

He turns the Jeep onto an overgrown lane, heading toward the abandoned building. I stare at it as we drive closer.

Silent Meadows Insane Asylum.

I want to shut my eyes. Wake up and find that this has all just been another nightmare. Boarded windows and the decrepit exterior bricks look hauntingly uninviting. My baby boy has been in there for hours—scared and alone.

When Adam stops the car, I go to open the door, but he hits the lock button, yanking my shoulder to turn me back to face him. My hand is inches from my weapon, but my body remains motionless, frozen.

His menacing stare is one I've seen a thousand times. The real Adam. The casual chitchat air about him has vanished.

"Just so we are clear—you are going to die in there. Then Dylan and I are going back to Seattle."

I clench my jaw, knowing that he's right about my death awaiting me. The idea of Michael alone inside, my little boy about to witness horrendous things, is something I have to push out of my mind. He is strong. He is brave. He will be okay. But not if Adam lives.

The piece of glass is so close. I could kill him now . . .

As I reach for it, he's faster, leaning toward me and yanking my weapon free of my shoe. The blade tears into my flesh, and I wince, feeling the hot blood trickle down my leg. "Do you honestly think this would be enough to kill me?" His laugh is maniacal as he grips my hair and pulls my face closer to his. Cologne I'd grown to despise fills my nose, and I hold my breath. The tip of the fragment presses against the flesh at my neck, under my chin.

"I should slit your throat right here, right now. The way you did to the nanny."

I refuse to look away. I refuse to beg. I refuse to give Adam any power.

"You are a useless cunt. You are nothing. You always were, and you'll die being a nothing. Not even strong enough to save your son."

The sharp sliver presses deeper, cutting my neck, but I won't flinch. With every ounce of strength, I pull my body backward, away from him, and reach for the door handle before he can grab me again.

Adam unlocks the doors. "Fine. If you want Dylan to see you die, that's fine with me. First, you're going to tell him the truth about how you kidnapped him."

Next, I'm running toward the building, ignoring Adam's words. I need to believe in the bond Michael and I share. He'll never believe Adam. And he will know I did the right thing . . . the only thing.

I yank open the wooden door and stumble inside the dark building. A faint light comes through the cracks in the wood, and I squint until my eyes adjust and I see movement in the far corner. "Michael!" I yell, rushing toward him.

"Mom!" The sound of his voice has my knees weakening. He's alive.

"Are you okay, sweetheart?" I call out as I approach. He is sitting on the floor against the wall. His arms are tied and connected to a rope around his feet, but, as far as I can tell, he's unharmed. I glance behind me and see Adam approach.

"Are you hurt?" Michael asks, staring at the blood on my hands and clothes.

"I'm fine. Michael, everything is going to be fine, sweetheart . . ."

"Your mom's good at lying, isn't she?" Adam moves closer, and I huddle next to Michael. I see the gun in his hand, but for the first time I feel a desperate source of strength, a need to fight.

"Who are you?" Michael asks. He is staring at Adam in awe, as though he already knows. As though a ghost from his imagination has finally materialized.

"I'm your dad. I've been looking for you." Adam bends at the knees and opens his arms, holding the gun out to the side. He unbuttons his dark charcoal suit jacket, letting the flaps open as he waits for Michael to run into his arms.

I hug Michael tight. "Stay here, sweetheart."

He turns to look at me, his dark eyes glaring. "I knew he wasn't dead. I knew you were lying. This is the guy in all those pictures."

"Michael . . ."

"She says a lot of things that aren't true," Adam says. "Did you know that you are only nine years old . . . not ten?"

Michael stares at me.

"It's true," I say. I'm done with lies. What's the point? My life will be over any second. These could be my last words to my son. "We ran away when you were a baby. You've always known our life was a little different than other people's." I smooth his hair out of his eyes, hoping to find forgiveness there.

"But why? Why did you take me away?"

"Adam is a very dangerous man, sweetheart. I was protecting you." I untie the rope at his feet and hands . . . maybe if he could run for help . . .

He glances at the gun in Adam's hand. He believes me.

"Come to me, and I'll take you home," Adam says.

Home. A prison. A dungeon. "No, Michael. He's dangerous. Just stay right here." I look around to the various exits in the old building. Everything is too far . . . Adam's bullet would kill me before I could take the first step.

Would he shoot Michael?

I can only hope there's someone, somewhere, looking for us. Looking for Dr. Collins. Someone who could save us.

Michael looks between us. The expression on his face is not confused, but knowing. Intrigue reflects in his eyes when he turns to Adam, but then only anger remains in them when he swings around to face me. "You lied to me before . . . How do I know you're telling the truth now?"

Fuck, no. Even Michael is believing Adam. Choosing Adam.

He struggles to his feet, and I grab at him as he takes a step forward. "No . . . please, Michael. Trust me . . . I should have told you the truth before. I'm sorry, but you were so young, and I didn't know how—"

"You took me away," he says. Accusation in his eyes, coldness in his voice.

"I did what I had to do to protect you," I tell him. I reach for his arm, but he pulls away.

"There was no danger for you, Dylan," Adam says.

Michael whips around to look at him.

"That's right—that's your real name. There's so much you don't know," Adam says as he stands. "So much I want to tell you." The gun is resting by his side, but I know a quick snap of a wrist and I'm dead.

"You're going to have a brother soon. Any day now. Not the one your mother is carrying—that one will have to die with her. But you'll have a new family with me. And I'll hire you a new nanny. She will take care of you. You'll love her."

Jesus. No.

Michael's eyes widen. "You're going to kill my mom?"

Adam nods. "She's not a good person. She took you away; she lied to you and everyone you care about. She's forced you to live this horrible life."

Michael stares at him.

"Back in Seattle, I have a big house, with a pool and a bedroom for you full of toys."

What can I say? It's true. But Michael doesn't know the cost of that lifestyle . . . what it will mean.

"There're toys for me?" he asks Adam.

Adam smiles. "All the toys in the world. But more importantly, you'll be safe with me and have a better life. No moving, no running or hiding. No more lying."

Michael looks at me. "I don't want to run and hide anymore. I want to live in a nice, safe house . . ."

"I know, sweetheart . . ." My heart breaks. I haven't been able to give him a good, stable life, the childhood he deserves. "But please believe me. I did what I thought was best for you. I love you."

Tears fall onto his cheeks as confusion clouds his expression.

"I'm so, so sorry, Michael."

Michael takes a few steps closer to Adam and turns to glance back at me hesitatingly. He's unsure for the briefest of moments, but truth is written on my face. He knows it. Adam's telling the truth. My reasons don't matter. I've done exactly everything Adam is accusing me of.

Michael steps closer and stands next to Adam.

I fall to my knees in front of him. "Michael . . ." Maybe this is it. Maybe this is the way it has to be. If he refuses Adam, he will be a corpse in this insane asylum, too, within moments. Adam will no doubt make our deaths appear to be the actions of a crazy pregnant woman.

"I win, Drew. Dylan has chosen me. Michael doesn't exist anymore. He never existed, except in your dark and twisted, fucked-up mind. I'm the bad one, right? What about you? You held him hostage for years. Do you really believe that's love? That you are a good mother?"

No, I don't. I've failed as a parent. I stare pleadingly at Michael, silently begging for his forgiveness.

Adam raises the gun and points it at my forehead.

I stare up at him, unflinching. I knew this would happen. I deserve to die. I've failed to protect Michael.

I glance at him and whisper that everything will be okay.

One last lie before I die. There is no one here to save me. I'm going to die, and my unborn child will die along with me. Parker's child. And Michael will suffer the worst fate of all.

"It's okay, baby."

This is the end of my nightmare but only the beginning of Michael's.

He moves closer unexpectedly and wraps his arms around my neck. "I'm sorry, Mom."

I hug my son so tight, and he clings to me just as hard.

"Move away, son," Adam says. "Come stand by me." The command in his tone is one Michael will need to get used to.

He pulls away slowly and turns to Adam. "Can I do it?"

I blink as the building swirls around me. I won't feel the bullet piercing my skin. I'll be passed out. Darkness closes in as Michael's words register in my mind.

Adam laughs. "You think you're ready, big man?"

Michael nods. "You're right. She isn't a good person. She lied to me, took me away . . ."

"That's right. Bad people need to be punished."

Michael nods.

I reach out around me for something to grab hold of, to steady my trembling body.

Adam hands Michael the gun, bending next to him to teach him how to hold it.

I stare at my son . . . my baby . . . as he points the gun toward me. My child is holding a gun. I shake violently, knowing everything I've done has been in vain. I've created a child who wants to hold a gun, who wants to kill his own mother.

Another Adam . . .

"Whenever you're ready," Adam says. Pride. There's actually pride in the man's voice as he cocks the hammer. I watch the cylinder revolve to align the next bullet.

I close my eyes, and, an indeterminable amount of time later, a gunshot reverberates against the hollow building.

I gasp, expecting it to be my last breath, but I feel no pain. I'm not bleeding. I force a breath and open my eyes.

Michael is now pointing the gun at Adam, his hands shaking violently. His gaze locked on Adam's body on the floor in front of him.

A pool of dark liquid forms beneath him. His eyes are open, but they have rolled back into his head, and his limbs hang limply around him.

Michael shot Adam. Not me.

Relief steals my breath, and I rush toward Michael, forcing the gun out of his hand as I hug him tight. Tears stream down my face. We are alive. We are safe. Adam is dead. "It's okay, sweetheart. It's all okay now, sweetheart."

A hand grips my ankle, and I push Michael aside as Adam struggles to pull himself up. I hide my son behind me as I pick up Adam's gun and point it at his head. I don't allow evil another chance to win. I pull the trigger, and Adam collapses against the floor.

This time, he's not getting back up.

DAYS LATER . . .

Drew

I sit across from a man who bears an uncanny resemblance to Adam, and my pulse threatens to explode through my wrists.

My lawyer. The one Jolie and Parker hired with my money in the duffel bag. Mike Bennett is supposed to be the best criminal defense attorney in Seattle, but right now I'm wondering why my only allies in the outside world thought it would be a good idea to hire a man who looks like he could be the twin brother of the man I just murdered.

The thin gray pinstripes on the dark charcoal suit start to wave, and I blink several times and focus on my breathing. The last few days have been a whirlwind of activity that my mind is struggling to catalog.

Turning myself in to the police . . . my arrest and the flight back to Seattle, where my trial will be held . . . and the brief conversation with Parker, in which he promised to take care of everything.

Like he had before?

"Let's get started," Mike Bennett says. He opens his briefcase and takes out a yellow legal pad and pen. "The good news is you turned yourself in."

"Did I have another choice?" I'd assaulted Parker, murdered a doctor on the side of the road, and shot Adam in an abandoned insane asylum. I regret none of those things, but there'd been only one thing left to do.

"You could have kept running," he says.

"I had nothing left to run from. Adam's dead."

He studies me, and I know that my future—my sentencing—depends on this man's ability to defend my actions, which subconsciously at least depends on whether he believes my story.

"The bad news is your bail has been denied because of the nature of the crime."

I'm a flight risk, and I'm good at hiding.

He sets his cell phone on the table between us.

"I'm going to record this so that I don't miss anything."

I nod.

"Whenever you're ready, just start at the beginning."

A memory of Adam's smiling face outside the Sea-Tac arrivals gate that day ten years ago steals my breath for just a second, but, knowing that's not the beginning Mike Bennett means, I say, "Three months into our marriage, Adam became abusive . . ."

I tell my story, and an hour later, he stops recording.

He sits back in his chair and continues to stare at me. Uncertainty, disbelief, and several other equally disheartening looks flash in his expression. The most terrifying one—sympathy. Because I know it's not for what I've endured but rather for what's about to happen next.

"I'm going to jail."

His chest fills with so much air that I expect his shirt buttons to fly off. Leaning forward, he clasps his hands on the table between us. "Your case won't be an easy one to win. While it's evident that you acted in self-defense of you and your son, you murdered two people and essentially abducted your child. You were in possession of fraudulent documents and produced them as real to various authorities."

"All to keep Michael safe."

"The judge may not be convinced that Michael was in any danger."

"But Adam . . ."

"Was abusive toward you . . . toward Isabella Barnet—whom we've already collected a statement from—and toward Catherine, but the parent relationship between Michael and Adam may never have gotten violent. The judge may feel that you had other options—"

"Adam is a murderer."

He stares at me.

So am I. For real this time.

"Can you help?" I'm at the mercy of this guy and his capabilities as a lawyer.

"I can . . . but I can't promise you'll simply walk away from this. We will be pleading not guilty on all counts based on self-defense . . . but . . ."

"What?"

"My gut tells me that they will want to make an example out of you."

"How so?"

"They can't acquit you of all charges without every woman in an abusive relationship thinking it's okay to flee with their children . . . or kill their spouse . . ."

"Isn't it?"

He shifts on the chair, but if he's looking for a remorseful client, he won't find that here.

"I've spoken with the DA the state has appointed . . ." He clears his throat. "They want the information about the organization that helped you escape."

"My mother helped me escape."

"She had help. You had help . . ."

I shake my head. "I don't know what you're talking about." My bones will creak and my hair will turn gray in a maximum security prison cell before I will give up the only people in the world who believed me. The ones who saved me and, despite potential doubt, saved Michael.

"Are you sure?"

"Yes."

He stands and gathers his things. "Okay. Well, I'll prepare your official statement, and I'll be in touch soon. You doing okay in here?"

I nod. I'm numb. Lucky for me, I've had a lot of experience blocking out pain, hurt, terror . . .

"Can I see Michael?"

"I'll make sure they approve a visit. It will be a short one."

If this guy can't help me, short visits with my son might be all I will ever get.

◆ ◆ ◆

"When's my real birthday?"

It's the first question Michael asks as he and Parker sit across from me in the visitation room. I just want to hug him so tight, but we're not allowed contact, so I sit on my hands and swallow the lump in my throat.

Parker speaks before I can answer. "Michael, maybe we can talk about all of that after . . . when your mom comes home."

Michael's staring at me. If he's even heard Parker, he makes no indication.

"It's okay," I tell Parker, quickly assessing the damage I caused to his head. The gash and bruise extend along his forehead and down the side of his face. He's forgiven me, and I search for the guilt I should feel and come up with nothing. I had no other choice. I tried to tell him. I asked him to believe me . . . to help me. He didn't.

They've been staying here in Seattle with John and Jolie and the kids, and they plan to stay for however long this takes. I'm glad Michael is nearby, but being away from him is torture.

I turn to Michael. "Your real birthday is September third."

He nods. "Are my grandparents really dead?"

"Yes. That was true." Someday, I'll tell him everything. That's enough for now. "How are you?" I'm devastated over what Michael witnessed. Is he having nightmares? Is he afraid?

He shrugs. "I'm okay." He points to the vending machine in the corner. "Can I get a snack?"

Parker reaches into his pocket for change. "Sure, buddy."

When Michael's out of earshot, I say, "Really, how is he?"

"Honestly, I don't know. He says he doesn't want to talk about what happened. I've tried. Jolie has tried . . . he seems okay during the day, but he's not sleeping at night."

I bite my lip as I watch Michael select a candy bar. I need to get out of here. I need to be there for him during all this. Help him get through . . . maybe I need to reconsider the plea deal Mike Bennett offered . . . but the truth is, I don't even know who my saviors were, and I've had to live with so much regret already . . .

"Jolie has a colleague . . . she's offered to talk to him."

"No."

"She might be able to help."

"No therapists."

Parker doesn't argue. "Okay."

The guard in the corner announces our time, and my heart beats fast. I don't know when I'll see them again, and I don't want them to go.

Parker stands and reaches across to squeeze my shoulder. The guard looks away. "It's going to be okay."

Is it?

Michael comes back with the chocolate bar, and I don't give a shit about rules. I fall to my knees and hug him. So tight. He doesn't hug me back, but he doesn't even wince despite the fact that I'm probably suffocating him. "I love you. Be brave, okay? We will get through this."

When I'm forced to let go, he simply stares at me. "I'm okay, Mom. Jolie and John's house has a pool and lots of toys."

My blood runs cold in my veins, and I shiver at his familiar choice of words.

My little boy regrets not choosing Adam.

AUGUST

Drew

"All rise. Court is now in session, the Honorable Judge Kulipis presiding."

I stand, my hands in cuffs in front of my protruding belly in the orange oversize suit. My wardrobe as the days leading up to my trial have dragged on. My only thought as they'd handed me the clothes was at least they're not beige.

Standing behind me is my family. Parker and Michael and Amelia. Jolie and John sit a few rows back, and, having them there, feeling their full support, I'm not afraid of whatever happens next.

No one thinks I'm crazy anymore.

At the back of the room is Isabella Barnet and her new baby. My gaze meets hers, and her silent thank-you resonates in my chest.

My actions saved her too. Her testimony against Adam could help me, along with the journals they found in Adam's home—Catherine's diaries of years in captivity.

"Mrs. Crenshaw, please step forward," the judge says.

Hearing my married name, I cringe, but then joy replaces the dread. I truly am a widow now. Free of the shackles of my disastrous marriage. Adam is dead. That thought gives me hope, above all else.

"Based on the evidence provided to the court on this matter, the court finds you not guilty on the counts of murder for Dr. Henry Collins and Adam Crenshaw. It is evident to the court that you were acting in self-defense of you and your son."

Murder was a life sentence. I'd already been acquitted for the murder of the nanny, based on the video footage I'd miraculously found and Catherine's journals.

"On the count of kidnapping, you are found not guilty. It is evident to the court that you were acting in the best interest of the child."

I breathe a sigh of relief. Kidnapping was the next-longest sentence. I hear Parker release his own breath, and my throat constricts.

"On the charges of fraud—guilty," the judge continues. "I'm sentencing you to three years in prison for fraud, including but not limited to the obtaining of fake documents, assuming fake identities, and misleading public organizations, along with your failure to cooperate with the authorities in naming the organization that facilitated your exit from your situation."

Three years. I'm going to jail.

My lawyer leans closer. "It won't be that long. You'll be up for parole in less than a year," he says.

Three years is still a whole hell of a lot shorter than the life sentence of fear I'd been previously facing.

The judge wraps it up, but I'm lost in my own thoughts, mentally preparing for what's next. What happens to Michael while I'm in there? Adam's dead. He has no other living blood relative. My father was found hanging in his bathroom a few weeks before, when the media announced that we'd returned. Obviously death looked better than jail time to him.

"What happens to Michael?" I ask my lawyer. Parker's not a legal guardian. The courts won't recognize him as a caregiver without him filing proper applications.

"Worst-case scenario is foster care temporarily, but don't worry: I'll meet with Parker, and we'll file the required paperwork for temporary custody right away."

I hate that it might be the only option.

Everyone rises. I struggle to stand, and I watch the judge leave the courtroom. Mike Bennett leads the way out into the hall moments later.

News reporters swarm us, shouting questions, snapping photos. A group of women protesters call for my release. I blink, blinded by the flashes, as a bailiff escorts me down the hall.

Next, he will take me to jail. Real jail. Not the holding cell I've been living in but real prison, with steel bars and no escape. It doesn't scare me.

It's where I'll stay for about a year. Where my baby will be born. Where I'll spend Christmas and my thirtieth birthday.

"You have five minutes," the bailiff says as Michael and Parker join me in the hall.

I nod.

The most important person in my life hurries forward to hug me. His little arms squeeze tight, and I struggle to find a breath. I have to leave him for now, and the thought nearly shatters me.

Parker embraces me next.

"My lawyer says six months to a year," I whisper.

"That's nothing. A blink," Parker says. His words are meant to reassure, but I hear the worry in his voice.

"Do you have to go back, Mom?" Michael asks.

"Only for a little while longer." I brush his long hair away from his eyes and force a smile. I stare at his face. He will be older when I see him again. He's older now already. This experience has aged him. I hope the love and peace he will now have with Parker will ease some of his fears. I hate that I can't be there for him to help him through this.

But Parker will be.

I hug Michael tight; then I stand. "I have to go." I can't break. Not yet.

Parker nods, kissing my forehead, holding me a second longer, unwilling to let go. "We'll see you soon. I love you."

The fact that he does, after all this, amazes me. But it's easier for him now. Knowing I did what I had to do. Knowing I'm not crazy, just damaged.

He's a good man. This baby I carry is his. So, I can make a life with him when all this is over.

"Ready?" the bailiff asks.

"Yes."

He leads me away, and I glance over my shoulder a final time.

I board the van, and the minutes and the scenery pass in slow motion until I'm led to a six-by-six cell with a bed and a toilet and a small window high above. Sun shines in through it, and, as the cell door locks behind me, I fall to my knees in liberation.

It's all over. My son is safe.

Michael

Standing next to Parker, I watch my mom walk down the hall in handcuffs.

He wraps an arm around me. "It's going to be okay, buddy."

I don't say anything. I don't know if he's telling the truth. If things will be okay or not. I have no idea what will happen to me.

But I'm not afraid. I know what I'm capable of now.

The newspapers said it was Mom who killed Adam, but I was the one who shot him first. It's okay, though; I still kept the articles. Hidden away from Parker.

He threw out Mom's scrapbook.

I'll start a new one for her.

ACKNOWLEDGMENTS

Thank you to my agent, Jill Marsal, for her many reiterations of this manuscript. Your dedication to making this book the strongest submission it could be, and pushing me to be a better writer, are something I'm so grateful for. A big thank-you to my editor, Jessica Tribble, for seeing what this story could be and making it even better with your amazing notes and guidance. A huge thank-you to Charlotte Herscher for your wonderful editorial notes and, more importantly, your patience with my last-minute major changes. And lots of love to my husband, Reagan, and my son, Jacob, for putting up with me during deadlines, supporting me through countless hours of self-doubt, and celebrating the wins with me—you both are everything!

ABOUT THE AUTHOR

Photo © 2018 PhotoJunkies

J. M. Winchester is the dark alter ego of an author who usually writes happily ever afters. Her fascination with the workings of an evil mind compelled her to start writing psychological thrillers, and *All the Lovely Pieces* is her debut novel in this genre. Originally from the east coast of Canada, she now lives in Alberta with her husband and son. She is a member of Romance Writers of America, International Thriller Writers, and Film and Video Arts Society of Alberta. More information can be found on her website at www.authorjmwinchester.com.